ABOUT THE AUTHOR

Phil Clinker lives by the sea in Bognor Regis, West Sussex.

After a life in the print industry, on retirement he decided to take up painting, which he now does with more enthusiasm than talent. However, he also went back to his first love of writing, and to his great surprise he actually managed to finish a novel. This was *Bakerton*, the first outing for Sheriff John Withers, which was published in 2019.

This book, *Thurlow Junction*, is the next adventure for the unorthodox sheriff.

For more information about the author, as well as his blog, go to www.philclinkerwrites.com

ALSO BY PHIL CLINKER

Bakerton

THURLOW JUNCTION

A SHERIFF JOHN WITHERS NOVEL

Published by Phil Clinker 2020
Copyright © Phil Clinker 2020

ISBN 978-1-911-412-97-7

*To my wonderful daughters
Louise and Helen*

The contiguous towns of Copper Ridge, Thurlow Junction and Bakerton form what the locals refer to as 'The Triangle'. Copper Ridge came first, of course, created out of the lumber sites set up in the late 1860s, when the abundant copper birch trees were felled to make canoes and roof trusses for buildings. Twenty years later, the railway authorities built a junction in the valley immediately below the Ridge, believing that the great age of the copper birch was still to come. They were wrong. Although the tiny hamlet of Thurlow grew up around the junction, the timber trade fell away sharply by the turn of the twentieth century and the junction itself became obsolete, forming now a mere backdrop to the increasingly cosmopolitan little town of Thurlow Junction.

In 1920, Hiram Baker bought a huge tract of land to the west of Thurlow from the rail company. Baker had been almost physically destroyed by the Great War, and it was his intention to develop a new town where like people could recover and live in peace. The fact that he was a multi-millionaire through inheritance meant that the people he attracted were also well-heeled, so Bakerton began life as a playboy's haven. Firstly, Baker constructed the Western Lake, the largest mass of blue most people had ever seen, and built his mansion beside it, as far away from Thurlow Junction as he could get. His friends did likewise, and by the 1930s the little town was ticking over very nicely, thank you.

However, life does not go on, and Hiram Baker died in 1953, leaving the town – and the vast tract of unused no-man's-land to the east – to his sons, both of whom were business graduates with an eye to the bottom line. It took them less than two years to start selling off small chunks of the land for development, and within a short time the town of Bakerton was firmly on the map as *the* place to be for middle-class families looking for peace and tranquillity and a 'rural' outlook.

Although Thurlow Junction was clearly the poor relation, its residents aspired to greater things. Most of them kept within the letter of the law, but evil can enter the most tight-knit communities – and can even come back, threatening more destruction than ever before...

Prologue

It is almost dark, and he is running. *Scared.* Scared of what has happened, and scared of what could happen. He is running away, every painful step releasing a tiny grain of hope that he could escape from this nightmare and perhaps get back to a normal life. But who is he kidding?

He stops to get his bearings. He knows Thurlow pretty well, having been brought up here, and he recognises the corner of Silver and Cherbury Streets, the latter leading to the old, long-forgotten railway sidings. This is the first time he has been able to catch his breath, and he hears the wheeze of his chest and sees the puffs in the cold air as he exhales sharply. He is sweating, but feels cold. He rubs his hand over his brow, sensing the dampness. His ears are pricked, like an animal expecting predators. He feels a wry smile curl round his lips, realising that, after all, he is indeed prey for a larger beast.

Silence, save the muted sounds of cars over on the highway, some leaving Thurlow headed for Bakerton, others aiming the other way to the city of Altona, the place where his nightmare began. He throws his arms around himself, suddenly feeling the chill of the night air.

He heads down Cherbury, now at a steady trot, his

breathing easier after the few seconds' rest he has allowed his body. It is getting much darker now, the houses beginning to take on their black, more sinister appearance, as if they are about to crowd round him and squeeze the life out of him. Some of them wink at him, their little lights going on and off as their people move from room to room. He craves the normality of it all, and still he trots.

He reaches the familiar creek where they used to go tadpoling as boys, and he takes the opportunity to stop again, still listening, but relaxing just that little bit more. A car approaches, so he crouches, nerves jangling and body shivering, with both cold and fear. He slides down the bank and ducks his head under a clump of roots, willing the car to go on its merry way. It slows to negotiate the slight bend leading to the new housing estate, and for a few moments its headlight beam picks him out. How can the driver not see him? He shrinks back, gripping a root to avoid sliding into the shallow water just below. He looks down, and then he sees it… the blood, now congealing on his hand and around his fingers. A tear fills his eye, because he knows it is not his blood.

Thankfully, the car moves on, and the darkness once more envelops him, this time welcoming, as if protecting him from the pains of the world. He sighs deeply, his chest hurting with the exertion of it all. He loses his grip and slides down into the cold water, only a few inches deep, but enough to chill him to the bone. Now he cannot hold back, and he silently cries, his body jerking, the water lapping around him as if in sympathy.

He doesn't know how long he sits here, but understands that he must move on. He scrambles to his feet, standing uneasily in the water, his trainers slipping on the mud beneath the surface. Again he draws his hand across his brow, but this time he does it quickly, aware of that blood on his hands.

Forcing his legs to move, he clambers out of the creek and looks around, listening, before continuing his journey into oblivion.

He heads for the disused sidings…

Chapter One

They were all there. Sheriff John Withers, standing in some discomfort, the wound in his body still tender, despite the three weeks that had elapsed. A tall man, at just over six feet, recently turned forty (with deep regret), a sharp jaw sprinkled with a greying medium-stubble beard, black hair a little longer than regulation and with a pronounced silver-grey tinge in some places, he had always had problems with his vision. How he had passed the medical to become a policeman, let alone rise to the rank of sheriff, he never could understand. He thought it might have been due to the new fad in diversity, where half-blind men were able to walk around with guns and arrest thugs young enough to be their own children. No matter, he got the job, perhaps because he wore thick bifocal glasses which made his sparkling hazy-green eyes more pronounced. Or he might possibly have got the job because he was bloody good at it.

Judith Wiseman was beside him, clasping his hand, acting as his crutch, both physically and emotionally. She was perhaps two or three years younger than the sheriff, and stood almost as tall, a statuesque woman with a shock of auburn hair framing a remarkably beautiful face, her crystal-clear, light brown eyes dimmed just a fraction as her heart felt for her man.

Deputy Dawg Janowski, the limp not so pronounced now, gripped the hand of his wife Kitty, both with a tear in their eyes. Special Agent Pat Rafferty, as was his custom, stood a pace back, his hands locked in front of him, deep in thought about another man. By a quirk of fate, Rafferty shared physical shortcomings with both lawmen. Like Dawg, he walked with a pronounced limp; although Dawg would soon be free of his, Rafferty's was a permanent reminder of an arrest which had gone badly wrong, the bullet still lodged somewhere in his leg. He was also forced to wear sunglasses outside due to something he was born with – a defect in both eyes which reacted badly to any kind of natural light. He was thin, with a pock-marked face and a bulbous nose, so perhaps it was no wonder that the Irishman appeared a little introverted. Withers, though, had eventually warmed to him – not least because Rafferty had saved his life – and their relationship had become one of equality and friendship.

Behind them were twenty or so other people. They were all in black.

At the rear was a policeman, in full uniform, his medals glistening on his chest, his peaked cap in his hand, a look of anguish on his face. Beyond him was a small group in police uniform, their faces as grave as his.

The vicar began to chant, but Withers wasn't listening. He just watched as the coffin was gently taken out of the hearse and hoisted aloft by six fellow members of his force, and they all began a sombre procession into the little church.

Withers had never been in this church before. Set in a

leafy, pastoral churchyard on the outskirts of Thurlow Junction, it dated from the late eighteenth century, according to the blurb he had read in the leaflet while he was waiting for the others to arrive. He had also taken a thought-provoking stroll around the churchyard, reading the tombstones and shuddering to a halt when he saw the gaping hole and the mound of earth which would signify the last resting place of Deputy Phil Lenier.

The memory was painful, but his mind forced him to relive it. Phil, brave Phil, facing the monster who called himself the General, the man who had killed his own father and several other innocents, the man who had kidnapped a young woman – the man who went berserk with a machine-gun and killed the deputy, while also wounding Dawg Janowski and Withers himself. Only three weeks ago.

Withers had stared blindly at that mound of earth, before sighing heavily and moving on, hoping that his life would do the same thing. The General was dead, but the story wasn't quite complete. There was still Ty Cobden…

Judith had called him then, and hurried to his side, enclosing his big hand in both of hers. She had kissed him gently on the cheek and fortified him for what was to come.

Together, they had moved to the head of the cortege, behind Phil's parents, to enter the church. Laura Lenier, Phil's mother, paid no attention to him.

Inside, the church appeared expansive, its ceiling high, its thick, solid walls whitewashed and welcoming. Withers looked up at the beautiful stained-glass window, depicting who he thought might have been John the Baptist. Salome slipped into his mind, but not the biblical one. This one was altogether more earthly, but she disappeared as quickly as she had come, and his eyes fell upon the rows of pews, now empty, but about to be occupied by living, breathing people – while the wooden box they were placing on the trestles held no such thing. Withers almost stumbled. He had not realised how close he had been to Phil Lenier. They weren't just work colleagues, him the boss and Phil the subordinate. No, it was more than that…

"Are you okay, John?" Judith whispered, full of concern.

He nodded, and took his seat in the second row, behind Jim Lenier. Now there's a man who must have been feeling the pain. His face was drawn, pale, lines imprinted on his forehead like the tracks from the old railway line barely a mile away from here. Laura, his wife, looked worse, far worse. She had been sedated when she heard the news, and it looked now as if some kind doctor had boosted her dosage especially for this day, the day they buried her only son…

The vicar waited patiently for the congregation to settle. There were older residents here, Phil's aunts and uncles, a granny-figure holding tightly to a zimmer frame, two younger men fussing around her, making sure she was comfortable, perhaps vying for top spot in her will. Withers dispelled that last thought, knowing that his cynicism was out of place here. They were all there to remember and honour a fine man.

"I thank you all for coming today," began the vicar, his voice strong and reverberating, "not to mourn the passing of Philip, but to celebrate the time he spent with us."

Withers looked behind and caught Dawg's eye. How many people had called him Philip, they both seemed to say without opening their mouths? Perhaps his mother, but to everyone else the dear departed was Phil, good old Phil…

*   *   *   *

"It was a lovely service," said one lady, as they approached the car park after the interment. Withers couldn't be sure how old she was, but the jacket and skirt looked to be last century. Her face was pinched, weather-beaten almost, but her eyes sparkled, and he could see Phil in her. "Maureen Pelham," she introduced herself, "Phil's aunt, his mother's sister."

Withers took her hand, a delicate little thing, bony and cold like china. He dare not squeeze too tightly. "John Withers," he replied.

"Oh," she gasped, "we all know who you are, sheriff. We are just surprised that you didn't wear your uniform, like your colleagues."

He nodded. "I wanted to be here as Phil's friend, not as a policeman. Hence the ill-fitting suit," he added with a weak smile.

Maureen tweaked his arm. "You look very smart, sheriff. And this is?"

Ah, the point of her approach! Gossip. "This is my… friend, Judith."

"My dear!" exclaimed Maureen, scooping Judith up in her arms and planting a kiss on her cheek. "How very sweet!"

Judith eased out of the grip and smiled warmly. "Mrs Pelham."

"Maureen, *please*!" she said, putting her arm through Judith's and guiding her towards the line of cars. "Will you be attending the wake?"

"Of course," confirmed Withers, desperate for a drink and the chance, eventually, to loosen his tie.

"Oh, good," Maureen said, her eyes twinkling even more. "There is someone I want you to meet… if that is agreeable with you?"

"Of course," he replied, intrigued. He was beginning to like her. She was nothing like Phil's mother, who was a little overweight and seemed to carry the woes of the world on her shoulders, even before the tragic event that had befallen her and her husband. She was a bit of a cold fish, he thought, not allowing people to get through to her. He knew she was basically shy, and her husband was the spokesperson for the family, but at times Withers had wanted to shake the woman into life. Maureen, her sister, appeared to be the total opposite: a thin, almost skeletal woman, but with a burning desire which seemed to explode from her eyes and the stunning smile she offered to everyone.

They stopped at Withers's car. "My!" Maureen said, rubbing an admiring hand along the bonnet of his beloved MX5. "You have a sports car, sheriff."

"I do," he said.

"Two seats," she pointed out in disappointment.

Judith picked up on it. "We're sorry, Maureen, but we can't offer you a lift."

"Oh, that's all right, dear," she replied, although it clearly wasn't. She wanted to stay with this young couple. "I'll go back to the house with Eric. He brought me."

Withers spotted Dawg about to get into his car. "I'm sure my deputy can give you a lift."

Maureen's face lit up like a Christmas tree. "A police car!" she exclaimed.

"Well, not exactly, but he is a policeman," said Withers, enjoying the excitement on her face and in her voice.

"That would be wonderful, sheriff. How exciting!"

Dawg hobbled over at Withers's call, and the introductions were made.

"I would be honoured, Mrs Pelham," said Dawg, navigating her across the car park to his vehicle.

"No, no," Withers and Judith heard Maureen say, as she happily followed the deputy, "the pleasure is all mine, young man. How exciting! How very exciting!"

Withers and Judith touched hands and smiled at the retreating figures, before climbing into his twelve-year-old car and roaring away, their laughter almost tangible in the chill air of the afternoon, a happy release from the funereal cloud that had hung over them.

There was a subdued atmosphere as Withers and Judith entered the house. It had been Phil's home all his life, and yet Withers had never visited. Now he could see why his deputy had not wanted to leave. It was a stunning thatched cottage set apart from the other properties simply due to its extensive grounds, which had been beautifully manicured, presumably by Jim, and most probably with a great deal of help from his son. Somehow, Withers could not visualise his mother taking an interest. The woes which appeared to press down on her shoulders simply would not have permitted her to find the art of gardening at all fascinating. He wondered how anything would have created a spark within her.

Now, as Withers and Judith walked in, gentle conversations filled the air, and when someone laughed, silence followed, as if the whole world felt embarrassed. Then, slowly, the soft murmurings would start up again, growing very slightly louder, more confident, as each memory of the dear departed was related. Withers thought that Phil might very well be turning in his new-found grave.

Jim Lenier stood at the door, a one-man welcoming party, his shoulders stooped, all life gone from his face. He limply took Withers's hand. "Thanks for coming, John," he said without feeling. "Sorry Laura's not here. She's having a lie-down. You know how it is…"

Withers felt a chill as he remembered Heather… "I understand, Jim. Give her my best."

Jim levelled his eyes at the sheriff. "I'm not sure she'd accept that," he said sadly. "She still blames you for…"

He didn't need to finish the sentence. Withers knew. Laura had gone for him twice after the killings. Once in the police station, and once in the morgue, when she had accompanied her husband to look at the body of her slain son. She blamed the sheriff, and the pain and venom in her eyes as she tried to punch him was just too pitiful; so much so that Withers had been forced to look away, even as Jim and a deputy held Laura back. But it was okay for her to blame him, because, in some measure, he blamed himself, if only because he had been the one to survive.

Judith leant forward and took Jim's hand. She had nothing to say, but her look was enough for Jim to offer her a weak smile, and she and Withers swiftly moved on, allowing other people to offer their condolences.

Thank God that's over, Withers thought, moving to the table and picking up a glass of sherry. He downed it in one go, but felt no better.

Judith came in close to him, her hand seeking out his. "She'll get over it," she whispered, but Withers wasn't listening.

Eric Marsland sidled up to them, a little worse for drink, his long nose arriving seconds before his long, skinny body. "Sheriff," he slurred, "what have you done with my Maureen?"

Withers felt like pushing him away, but thought better of it. "Ah," he said, "you must be Eric…"

Marsland looked delighted. "She mentioned me?" He swayed slightly. "I saw you talking with her. Is she here?"

"We had no room in the boot," said Withers, not expecting Marsland to understand, but enjoying the joke himself. "She is coming with my deputy."

"Very good," pronounced Marsland, peeling away to grab another glass from the table. "Very good."

Suddenly, a uniform appeared in Withers's vision, and he stretched upright, almost ready to salute. "Sir!" he said with emphasis.

"Relax, John," the commander said gently, his medals tinkling just slightly. "How are you feeling?"

Withers eased his body back to normal. "I'm fine, sir. Ready for duty."

The commander begged to differ. "I think not. You will take the full six weeks. That is an order."

Judith answered for him. "Of course he will, commander. I will see to it."

The commander smiled at her. "I'm sure you will, my dear," he said with humour in his eyes. Then, more seriously,

"It was a terrible thing, losing Phil, but we will grow strong again. In time." And he was gone, mixing with the family, recounting anecdotes from the young deputy's career and offering support where he could. Withers watched him go, wondering how he managed to cope with it all.

Just then, Maureen entered, grabbed Jim Lenier in a womanly clinch, kissed him on both cheeks and offered him words of comfort. Phil had been the son she could never have, and Jim knew it. He was grateful for her presence, even if her sister, his wife, refused to come down. Maureen spotted Withers and walked over, deftly lifting a glass of sherry without breaking her step. "Ah," she breathed, "I need this." And it was gone in one movement, the empty glass settling back on the table before Withers could respond. "You know, sheriff," she said softly, "Phil was very special to me. I shall miss him so much." The darkness in her eyes reflected the sorrow in her heart.

"So will we all," replied Withers, his voice catching slightly. He hated funerals.

Judith leaned in between them to say something, but she was stopped by the re-arrival of Eric Marsland, a replenished glass in hand, and swaying perhaps a little more than before.

"Maureen, my love!" he blurted, just a little too loudly. Others in the room stopped to look at him.

Maureen was mortified. "I am *not* your love!" she spat angrily. "And you've been drinking too much again!"

"Just waiting for you, my sweet," he said by way of explanation, although that cut no ice with the object of his desires.

"Kindly remove yourself from this house, Eric!" she demanded. "You are an embarrassment."

His face buckled at the onslaught, and Withers thought he might dissolve into tears. Instead, he rallied just enough to fight on. "Come with me, Maureen. Out into the wide, wide world… together!" Then, his legs almost gave way – reminding Withers of a new-born foal attempting to stand – and he put his hand on the table to steady himself. Several glasses went flying, their contents covering a lady standing nearby. "Oops, sorry," he mumbled, regaining some control of his legs, just in time for Jim Lenier and another man to escort him out, their hands gripping his arms tighter than was perhaps necessary, both with scowls on their faces. Maureen felt total humiliation.

Before someone could say anything else, Judith led Maureen out of the back door and into the garden. The sun was weaker now, the wind getting up, and both women felt the chill as they stood there, speechless.

Finally, Judith said, "So, Maureen, who exactly is Eric Marsland?"

Maureen sneered. "A loser, my dear. One of life's perpetual morons."

"He seems to be fond of you."

"And the bottle," Maureen added scornfully, but Judith felt something in her voice. There were feelings, she was sure: sadness, regret, *affection*?

It didn't take long for Maureen to recover. "Come, my dear," she said brightly, "we must find your sheriff!"

Judith liked the thought of that: *your sheriff*. Yes, he is, isn't he? He *is* mine!

Arm in arm, they went back into the house, ignoring the silence that greeted them, intent on only one thing. Withers was standing with Dawg and Kitty, a glass of orange juice in his hand. He turned as they approached. "Everything okay?" he asked, concern in his voice and on his face.

Maureen touched his arm and smiled. "Everything is fine, sheriff, thank you for asking," she said, before adding, "Please, do you have a moment?"

"Of course."

She looked around the room until her eyes fell on a woman who appeared to be lurking in the shadows. Maureen beckoned her over, and Withers saw a black Caribbean face beneath a mound of carbon-black hair held in place by a grey scarf, in keeping with the occasion. She wore a black shift dress which bore a large silver brooch in the shape of a football player wearing a claret and blue shirt. It was a statement piece, and seemed at odds with the grim face of the woman. Even her large blue eyes looked cloudy.

"Sheriff, this is my friend Nona," said Maureen. "She needs your help."

"Okay," Withers said slowly, intrigued.

Nona hesitated. "I'm pleased to meet you, sir," she said. "My name is Nona Carmichael."

They shook hands, and he felt the tension in her grip. "Mrs Carmichael. I'll certainly help if I can."

Nona looked relieved. "Thank you, sir. It's…"

Before Nona could continue, there was a loud scream of horror and all eyes turned to the door, where Laura Lenier stood, arms gripping the doorframe, hair dishevelled, make-up running through her tears, and her eyes blazing with hate. "Get him out!" she demanded, her voice breaking. "Get the bastard out of my house. NOW!"

Jim raced to her side, attempting to placate his distraught wife, but he had no chance. She glared at Withers. "You killed my son! Get the hell out!"

Withers had already made a move, but he knew he wouldn't be able to get past the heart-broken mother. He offered up both hands in a sign of deference and resignation, then went out the back door into the garden, hoping there was an escape to his car that way. Judith and Maureen followed, both shaking with emotion.

Outside, Withers tried to pace his breathing until it was back to normal. Judith saw the pain and tears in his eyes and reached out for him, but he had already found the gate leading out to the street, and was soon running to his car, to the sanctuary of silence and solitude. His heart was breaking: for Phil Lenier, for Phil's mother… and for Heather. Death does that to people.

Chapter Two

Heather had been Mrs Withers for eight wonderful years – our extended honeymoon, he had often said to her; and now in his mind's eye he could see her smile back at him, her hand reaching out and softly caressing his cheek. He looked through the car windscreen, down the road, his vision clouded, just like his memories. Heather, sweet Heather had been murdered by a burglar in their flat, taken from him in the swish of a blade, her life extinguished, leaving so much unfulfilled. Withers hurt desperately, then and now.

The words of Smokey Robinson had played in his mind for weeks after:

> *So take a good look at my face,*
> *You'll see my smile looks out of place,*
> *If you look closer it's easy to trace*
> *The tracks of my tears.*

Yes, he had smiled, but that was a lie: he had nothing to smile about. While, in the song, Smokey had been with other girls, that had not been possible for Withers. He had turned into a shell.

He didn't notice the car door opening, or the gentle words as Judith put her hand on his knee and squeezed it oh so gently, a gesture of total love. He turned towards her and gave her a watery smile. "Sorry," he said.

Judith muzzled up to him, her head on his shoulder. "For what? Having feelings? I wouldn't expect anything less from you, John Withers. I've always known you have a heart."

He wiped away a strand of her hair which had fallen across her face and kissed her forehead. "Guilty as charged."

She looked up at him. "I know you were thinking of Heather. It's okay."

He didn't answer her. He didn't need to. He could see in her eyes that it really was okay – she understood, and he loved her so much more because of it.

They sat for some time, neither of them moving or speaking, just breathing together, holding hands. It was Judith who first noticed a concerned Maureen standing at the gate. She had obviously been there since Withers had stormed out, and Judith felt so guilty. She wound down the window.

"Are you both all right?" said Maureen, full of concern.

"We're fine, Maureen. Sorry, we didn't realise you were still there."

"I had to make sure the sheriff wasn't too distressed. It's been a bad day."

Judith sighed. "Yes, yes, it has."

Withers leaned over to the open window. "I'm fine," he said, perhaps not really feeling it. "Look, I'll come round and see your friend tomorrow morning, if that's okay?"

Maureen grinned at him. "Wonderful, sheriff! I'll give your deputy the address."

* * * * *

Following the funeral service, Agent Pat Rafferty returned to the police station in Bakerton. He was not one for mixing, and, even though he had been invited back for the wake, he had politely declined. After all, he had said, he was an outsider, and the post-funeral gathering should be a family-and-friends-only affair. He had offered more condolences and had embraced his friend John Withers with a shared feeling of loss, before withdrawing to the sanctuary of his car and his own thoughts. He had sat in the car for some time, going over the events of that fateful day. Could it only be three weeks ago? It didn't seem possible. Already parts of the case were beginning to drift into the dark recesses of his mind, clouding over and tainting the very memory he needed to keep alive. Young Abrahams, one of his newest agents and certainly the most gifted, had been killed just before Deputy Lenier. Rafferty had read the eulogy at his funeral only four days ago, tears misting his eyes as he talked of a man who offered so much, but who was cut down in his prime by an assassin's bullet. And all because of the General…

"There's been another sighting, sir," Deputy Keene broke into his reverie.

Rafferty was now sitting at Sheriff Withers's desk, a pile of untouched paperwork and a cold cup of coffee in front of him. He was still wondering how this had come to pass. When Withers had been wounded and sent on sick leave, along with Deputy Janowski, there was an urgent need for their places to be filled. Deputy Keene had been drafted in from Altona city's force, but that still left the one vacancy…

Rafferty shifted in his seat. He wasn't sure who had nominated him to take over as sheriff for the interim, but it sure as hell wasn't his idea! He just wanted to get back to the smoke and continue what he was good at: tracking narcotics, illegal arms, and very bad men. No chance! Here he was, stuck in the middle of nowhere, filling the boots of a very large man, in more ways than one. He sighed heavily.

"Where was it this time?" he asked, dubious.

"Up on Copper Ridge, sir."

Rafferty scoffed, "We've had more sightings of this guy than Bigfoot and the bloody yeti put together. How many is it now?"

Keene hesitated. "Er, sixteen, I think, sir."

"Right. Now, tell me, Deputy Keene, if you were wanted for murder in Bakerton, would you hang around for a few weeks up on Copper Ridge? No matter how scenic it might be."

Keene thought about that one. "No, sir, probably not."

Rafferty chewed over those two words. "*Probably not.* Hm, I suggest you don't carry out murder, deputy, because, if you did, we'd soon catch you. The one thing you should do after committing a murder is…?"

Keene shuffled his feet nervously. Life had been so simple in the city. "Er, run, sir?"

"Good!" Rafferty suddenly realised he sounded just like Sheriff Withers, and it worried him. "So that is probably what Ty Cobden did, don't you think?"

Keene stood his ground. "The sightings have been pretty clear, sir. One witness said the suspect now has a beard growing, but he looks just like the poster we put out."

"Okay, deputy, file them all under 'Almost convincing',

and we'll take a look later. Who knows, we may even find Jack the Ripper while we're at it…"

*   *   *   *   *

For Ty Cobden, it had all begun four years ago, when the six of them flew into the island of Lanscarges in his friend Leroy's private jet. It had all seemed so simple: get in, pick up the goods, and get out. What could possibly go wrong?

The answer, of course, was Billy Rhodes, although Ty didn't know his name at the time. He just knew him as the General. A two-timing bastard of the highest degree.

Only Leroy had known that the cargo was to be drugs, but once the General found out, he had hijacked the whole operation, and it had been down to Ty to recover the cache and teach the General a lesson. Ty thought he had killed him, but just weeks ago, the General had wreaked his terrible revenge by taking out Leroy and the others who had been on that trip. In the final showdown, Ty had narrowly escaped death, but the General – this time – had not been so lucky. He was blasted to hell by the police. Good riddance.

Ty had made a rapid escape with Hector, the man who helped the General in both the seizure of the drugs and the killing of Leroy, and that weighed heavily on Ty's mind. However, Hector had also played a part in saving Ty's life at the last shoot-out, so Ty's appraisal of Hector was, to say the least, conflicted.

They had managed to bypass the blanket roadblocks laid on by the authorities, sometimes by the skin of their teeth, and had lain low in some woods close to Bakerton.

They had hidden out there for three weeks, scurrying from place to place, finding shelter where they could, always alert to any danger. His military experience had certainly been a help in keeping one step ahead of the agents sent out to hunt them down.

Much to Hector's dismay, Ty had insisted on staying close to the town, but would not explain his reasoning. Hector had been baffled, but he liked this madman, even though Ty often suffered nightmares and cried out in his sleep. Ty had tried to dismiss the subject, but Hector had worked out that it had something to do with Ty's life in the military. Hector therefore felt that he needed to protect his friend, and so had tagged along willingly, despite the potential hazards they had inevitably encountered.

They were up on Copper Ridge now. It always offered spectacular views, no matter what time of day or season; and, as the sun began to set and the autumn evening closed in, Ty sat cradling a tin mug of coffee, looking out over Thurlow Junction and the wide expanse of countryside beyond. It was breathtaking, and he savoured the experience, wondering how much longer he would enjoy it before having to move on again, or before the law finally caught up with him.

Ty was tall, at six-four he towered over Hector – who was no shorty himself – and had deep blue eyes and the physique that clearly marked him out as an ex-soldier, his back straight and his body lithe and supple, despite his advancing years: he was over forty now, he brooded with some sadness. He had been proud of his macho-man stubble, but now he had a blossoming beard, which could be a suitable disguise, he mused, and he stroked it thoughtfully. But he was here for a purpose, and he had to get results soon, or everything would be gone.

Hector plonked his body next to Ty, grunting as he did so, and spilling some of his own coffee. "*Mierda*!" he swore. "I hate this life, *señor* Ty."

Ty looked at his companion. "You are free to go, Ector," he said, as always pronouncing the other man's name in his pidgin-Spanish which dropped the initial letter.

Hector was used to it, and actually felt strangely honoured by it. They had been through a lot together, almost being killed by that crazy General, but managing to escape both him and the federal agents sent to find him. They did well, but Hector also knew that they had been extremely lucky, and he wasn't sure how long that luck would hold. He gazed out at the horizon. "Tell me, Ty, why are we here? What is holding you so?"

There was silence for a moment as Ty took a swig of his coffee. He felt that now was not the time to explain. Hector wouldn't understand. Besides, he might get greedy. He patted Hector's shoulder and smiled. "My friend, you saved my life back then. The General was going to kill us both, but you reacted quickly enough to save us. For that I will be eternally grateful."

Hector grinned. "It was nothing, *mi amigo*; I would have done it for any madman!"

Ty laughed. "Yes, I suppose I am a bit of a madman. But it takes one to know one!"

They both chuckled, clinked their mugs in salutation, and drank silently.

Finally, Ty said, "Leroy Figgis was my friend. When we

went to your island…"

"Ah, Lanscarges," sighed Hector sarcastically, "the island of dreams!" He spat out a mouthful of coffee to show his disgust.

"We assumed it would be easy. Pick up the goods, fly back out and pocket a fistful of dollars."

Hector became moody. "Life is never easy, *mi amigo*. I am sorry for what I did to you… and your friends."

Ty nursed his coffee thoughtfully. "There is something I have to do… for Leroy, for his memory."

Hector looked at him. "But you cannot tell me."

"Not yet, no." Ty said, knowing full well that he would never tell Hector the whole truth. He wasn't that much of a friend.

They drank on in silence, each man going back to Lanscarges in their minds, and trying to make sense of it all.

* * * * *

Death comes in many guises. Phil Lenier went in the blink of an eye, despatched from this earth in a matter of milliseconds, blasted by a crazed gunman. Heather, on the other hand, had suffered for more than three hours, lying in the darkened hallway of their flat, her hands over a gaping wound as the blood and life spilled from her; holding on, as if desperate to say goodbye to her darling husband. What thoughts had gone through her head in those lonely hours, as she finally realised that she was not going to survive? What desolation must she have felt?

Withers took a long shot of his whisky, swirling the remainder around the glass as he sat in the garden. Churchill called these moments his Black Dog, and Withers, had he given it any kind of thought, would have certainly agreed. Instead, he just sat there, in the gathering gloom of the night sky and the overpowering misery of his memories.

Thank God he had at least got to Heather before… He had phoned for an ambulance, of course, and then cradled her head, while holding a towel to the wound, the sight of her blood gagging him and the tears running down his face and into his mouth. Then, suddenly, it was all over. Her struggle had ended, but he was sure she had a smile on her face as her glazed eyes looked up at him. Neither of them had spoken, but the love had been transmitted. The bond would never be broken.

Withers took another swig. He suddenly needed some-one to talk to, someone to be near. He wished Judith was here, but she had returned to her flat in Altona. After all, she did have a job to do. As the *Altona Oracle*'s best reporter (her words!), she had a duty to her readers. Withers had to smile at that thought.

He felt better. Judith always seemed to do that for him. He had known her little more than a month, and yet she was everything to him. He just couldn't understand it! What was it about her? When she had first entered his office, he had felt like a naughty schoolboy having a crush on his unattainable teacher. He had even blushed when she sat down, crossed and uncrossed her legs in that Sharon Stone way, and sucked provocatively on her pencil. God, he had been smitten! She had toyed with him, twisting him not only round her little finger, but into all shapes, like one of those metal puzzles you used to get in a Christmas cracker. The weirdest thing of all, though, was that he did exactly the same to her! She, too, had fallen, as if from a great height. They were like love-struck teenagers aged forty (at least in his case!), and it made him feel *wonderful.*

He made up his mind. Why should he wallow? That was for sad old men with no future – and that wasn't him. He couldn't have Judith tonight, so he would have the next best thing. He put down his glass and took his phone from his pocket, dialling his closest friend. He said, "Hi, do you mind if I come over?"

"Got the entrance fee?"

"Sure."

"Fine," said the voice. "It'll be great to see you."

The drive took fifteen minutes, the roads clear at this time of the evening. The rain had held off, but there was a chill in the air, and Withers had picked up his windcheater, as well as his 'entrance fee', a bottle of wine he knew his host would enjoy.

Brad Moody was on the stoep, reclining in his wicker chair, two glasses placed on the chess table in front of him. The beautifully carved Staunton set was in place, ready to do battle. Brad was caressing a black knight when a giggling Millie ushered Withers in.

Both men embraced warmly, as befitted their deep friendship. Millie took the bottle offered by Withers and went into the house in search of a corkscrew.

"She's looking good, Brad," said Withers.

"Yes, John. I think she's over the worst."

They said no more about it, although both recalled the horrific moment when Brad's daughter had been kidnapped by the General and came close to death. It was something neither of them would ever forget.

"I've given you White," said Brad with a snide smile, indicating that Withers should sit opposite him. "You need all the help you can get!"

"Thanks, pal," Withers grinned, as he sat, his eyes looking out over the large garden and the fields beyond. "I never get tired of this view."

"Yes, it is pretty special," Brad agreed, just as Millie returned with the open bottle. She poured the wine into their glasses.

"Are you joining us, Millie?" asked Withers.

"At chess? *Boring*!" she replied, emphasising and elongating the word. "I'm off to see a film about cement-mixing – much more interesting!"

As she disappeared back into the house, Withers looked enquiringly at Brad, who explained, "She's pulling your leg, John. She's actually off to have a long-distance love affair with Danny Parsons's boy."

"You mean Shaun?"

"Yeah, the good-looking one in that family."

Both men laughed. Then Withers had a thought. "You said long-distance. But the Parsons place is only a couple of streets away."

"Right. But this is a modern romance – they'll be texting the night away."

"*Boring*!" Withers imitated Millie perfectly.

They placed their glasses on the coasters on the table

and studied the board. Withers moved a pawn, and Brad whistled through his teeth, a note of mock ridicule. Withers did likewise when Brad made his first move.

The evening soon turned into night as they sat there, discussing the merits of Lasker and Capablanca, the weakness of Withers's openings and the disastrous antics of the Opposition in the wake of some dodgy dealings by the Government. It was all so *natural*.

As he drove home, Withers sighed contentedly. After a harrowing day, he was human again.

Chapter Three

The cottage was difficult to find, hidden as it was behind a sea of bushes and shrubs, flowers and pot plants, all haphazardly laid out, as if some giant hand had lifted them all up and dropped them, to fall where they would. It had its own kind of quaintness, but it would never win Garden of the Year.

As Dawg stopped his car, he saw Maureen Pelham and waved. She responded with a two-handed version, her excitement mounting once again, now that she was going to be in the orbit of the police. Praise be!

Withers emerged from the passenger side and greeted her by trying to shake her hand; but she was having none of that, and she scooped him up, as best she could with such a broad-shouldered man, and proceeded to hug the life out of him. "Sheriff!" she beamed. "Thank you so much for this."

He smiled weakly. "I'm not sure we will be much help, Mrs Pelham."

She tutted. "Nonsense! You will solve this mystery. Mark my words!" And, with that, she opened the garden gate and ushered him onwards, urging him through the now-open front door and into the sitting-room, both of them passing a pensive Nona Carmichael.

Dawg closed the door behind him and followed the others, sitting on a chair in the corner, as dictated by Nona.

Maureen sat beside Withers at the table, her hands shaking and restless. Dawg noticed that she was on the edge of her seat, excitedly fidgeting and desperate for the meeting to begin.

Nona offered them tea, which they declined, so she took the chair at the table opposite the sheriff.

Withers waited a second, before leaning forward. "How can we help, Mrs Carmichael?"

"Oh, call her Nona," burst in Maureen. "Everyone else does!"

Nona gave her an old-fashioned look. "It's my son," she said slowly. "He's missing."

"Missing?" said Withers, already wondering how this was going to unfold.

"Start at the beginning, Nona," prompted Maureen. "Tell the sheriff everything!"

Nona gave her another look.

Withers was more sympathetic. "Tell me about your son, Mrs Carmichael."

After a few seconds of reflection, Nona said, "Learie is a professional footballer. He…"

Before she could go any further, Dawg had a light-bulb moment. Awestruck, he blabbered, "Wait! Are you talking about Jet Carmichael?"

Withers was none the wiser, but Nona gave Dawg a warm smile. "Yes, he is my son, although I don't like his nickname. We give our children their names; everyone should respect that. Don't you agree, sheriff?"

Withers squirmed just a little, knowing that Dawg was glaring at him. The sheriff had always called him Dawg, even though his name was Doug. "Deputy Dawg," Withers had said on their first meeting, and Doug Janowski *still* didn't understand it.

Dawg returned quickly to the present. "I never put two and two together," he said. "Well, you don't, do you? I mean, you never expect a famous person to be living so close…"

"They've got to come from somewhere," responded Withers flippantly.

"Go on, Nona!" urged Maureen, trying to get back on track. "Tell them!"

The two men fell silent, waiting. Nona continued, "Learie always telephones me, every day, without fail. Until five days ago. Then, nothing…"

"You say he plays football?" said Withers. Nona nodded sadly, so he asked, "Have you been in contact with his club?"

"Of course she has!" Maureen burst in. "What, you think she's stupid or something!"

Nona put her hand on Maureen's, a tender but warning touch. "It's okay, Maureen. The sheriff needs to have all the facts." She turned to Withers. "They haven't seen him, either. I spoke with the chairman, Barry Mason, yesterday. He said that Learie was taking a few days' break."

"Perhaps he is," ventured Withers.

"Not without telling me, sheriff. He is a good boy."

"Look, I'm not a private detective, Mrs Carmichael, but I'll do my best. It just so happens that I have a little time before I go back to work," said Withers. Absent-mindedly, he rubbed the scar on his side, still feeling the discomfort. It seemed to mirror the pain on the face of the mother sitting opposite him.

*   *   *   *   *

Ty had been getting restless, so he had made the decision to go down into Bakerton and think things through. He realised that it was a bloody stupid thing to do, and Hector had tried to talk him out of it.

"But the law, *señor*," he had pleaded.

"As Charles Dickens once pointed out, Ector, 'the law, sir, is a ass'," the quote coming out in what Ty hoped was a suitable Mr Bumble voice. "They must think we're long gone. Anyone with an ounce of sense would be hundreds of miles away."

"Ah, yes, an ounce of sense. I have heard this saying. It is something we do not have, eh?"

"Never have had, Ector, my friend. Never have had."

Ty climbed into the VW Golf that Hector had 'acquired' the day before. The Spaniard had a proven track record when it came to purloining anything he needed. In the case of a car, it would take him two days to carry out the operation. On the evening of the first day, he would remove the number plates from his chosen target, then spend an hour or so chiselling out the letters and numerals and adding dirt so they looked realistically worn and almost unreadable. On the second day, he would take a suitable saloon car which would not attract too much interest, and swap the plates. It was a pretty near fool-proof system which Hector had carried out twice now since they had encamped on the Ridge.

Ty drove into Bakerton, parking as far from the police station as he could get. Now he was walking the streets, oblivious to the risk he was taking, and savouring every moment. If only he could live like this forever, not constantly looking over his shoulder, but melting into the background without a care in the world. Sweet dream!

He knew that Sheriff Withers frequented Scotty's Diner, so he made his way to Chicken Shack, ordered a coffee and skinny fries, and sat at a table in the corner, far away from the window. There was no point in tempting fate too much.

He waited for his order to arrive, before pulling out his mobile and checking through his contacts. He deliberately hadn't used his phone since the day Leroy was murdered, and now his mind went back to that dark time, when Ty himself had also become a murderer. He still wasn't sure exactly why he had shot Ralph Baxter, but at the time it seemed like a case of self-preservation. A bit like now, he thought, as he continued to evade capture by the authorities.

He coughed nervously, before pressing the keys, and waited for a response.

"Grace Templeman," a voice answered.

Ty froze.

"Hello, who is this?" she asked, confused. "Hello?"

"Grace," Ty whispered, "it's Lucas."

It was Grace's turn to freeze.

"I'm sorry…," he began.

"Lucas, where are you?"

He hesitated. "I can't tell you that, Grace."

"Of course you can't! It was a stupid question." She paused. "What do you want, Lucas?" When she knew him, he had been Lucas Black, hired heavy for billionaire Leroy Figgis the Fourth, the man she acted as PA for at the Mercurial Bank. Lucas might have been a heavy, she had thought bitterly at the time, but he couldn't save Mr Figgis from a maniac.

"I want to put some things right," he said simply, as if she would understand.

"What things? The killing of Ralph Baxter?" she asked, her voice venomous and accusing.

He recoiled. "I can't put that right, Grace."

"No, no, you can't. Unless you go to the police."

He had thought of that many times in the last few weeks, but what good would that really do? It sure as hell wouldn't bring Ralphie back to life! He felt like hanging up, but the next time Grace spoke, her voice was soothing, motherly.

"Listen to me, Lucas. I know you. You're a good man. Tell me where you are and I'll come and get you. We'll go to the police together."

"I might just do that, Grace," he said in all honesty, "but not yet. Like I said, I've got something to do first."

"And you need my help."

"Yes… please."

Grace waited. She knew she should talk to Sheriff Withers straight away, but she also knew that she wasn't going to. There was something in this man's voice which reached out to her, a desperation to perform one last act of goodness before evil destroyed him completely. "What do you want me to do?"

* * * * *

Kitty Janowski's fish pie was a marvel to behold. Withers had enjoyed it on several previous occasions, but tonight there was a buzz around the table. Kitty and Judith ate sedately, enjoying the flavours of the three-fish meal with its glazed sweet potato topping and three veg. Dawg, on the other hand, was all movement and eagerness, relishing not just the meal but also the chance to play at detectives. He looked eagerly at Withers.

"So, boss, what's the first move?" he asked.

Withers had already checked MisPers and spent the day going through reports of possible sightings, without success, and now he needed some background information. He grinned at his deputy's enthusiasm. "First of all, you tell me all about Altona City Football Club."

After the meal, the girls cleared the table and washed-up. Dawg normally shared the chore with his wife, but she could see how excited he was, so she insisted he and the sheriff should retire to the lounge, where Dawg had previously laid out all the relevant paperwork, ready for the education of his boss.

He brought over two bottles of beer, and they sat on the floor, surrounded by documents and photographs that Dawg either owned or had downloaded. He offered up a black-and-white picture of a Caribbean player heading the ball towards goal. "Jet Carmichael," he said by way of introduction. "Judith kindly sent it to me from the *Oracle* archives." Judith's help would prove invaluable. "Taken last year," he added, "when he was playing for Melrose Nomads."

"Melrose?" queried Withers. "That's miles away. So he was transferred."

"That's the first puzzle I don't understand," said Dawg. He drank from his bottle and put it on the coffee table, careful not to spill any. Kitty would notice. "Melrose is a top-five club. Nobody leaves until their career is on the way down, or they've seriously upset management. Neither is the case with Jet. He's only twenty-seven, and at the top of his game. Any club would welcome him with open arms."

"And he didn't rub somebody up the wrong way?"

"No chance," Dawg said. "He's a model player in all respects." He picked up another picture, this one showing a smiling Jet shaking hands with a man dressed in a three-quarter-length sheepskin coat and trilby.

"My God!" exclaimed Withers. "Talk about a caricature! Who's the guy with Jet?"

"Barry Mason, chairman of Altona City. Taken three weeks ago, when Jet signed on the dotted line. The biggest shock in football."

"Why?" asked Withers, oblivious to the machinations of the game.

"Like I said, Melrose are top-five, crowds of fifty thousand-plus. Altona, near-bottom, crowds of ten thousand – on a good day."

"Okay," said Withers. "So why did Jet transfer?"

"Beats me," said Dawg, rifling through the papers. He drew out a newspaper cutting. "League positions last week. Melrose are actually third; Altona nineteenth out of twenty. Relegation position. Last time the teams met, Melrose won 4-1. Easy."

"So, he didn't move for the prestige – and probably not for the money, either."

Dawg whistled through his teeth. "Took a massive pay cut to come back to Altona, I hear."

"Back?"

"Yes. He began his career at Anstey Lane – that's Altona's home ground."

"I know that!" snapped Withers, although he probably wouldn't have been able to recall the fact if asked. He didn't like being educated by his deputy. "You know, Dawg, it is a recognised fact that only two games have ever been invented for intelligent people."

Dawg waited.

"Chess and cricket. Nothing else. In fact, I would hazard a guess that your friend Learie 'Jet' Carmichael was given his birth name to commemorate the legendary West Indian cricketer, the great Sir Learie Constantine."

"Really?" queried Dawg, having never heard of the gentleman in question. "He didn't play football, then?"

Withers gave his deputy a frown, and tutted loudly. Rather than offer one of his caustic comments, bearing in mind he was in his deputy's house, he picked up one of the photos. "Nice looking lad," he said.

Dawg nodded. "A real ladies' man." He shuffled through the papers on the floor and came up with another photo. "Jet with Brandy Summers."

Withers looked at the picture. "Stunning."

Judith was suddenly framed in the doorway. "I assume that comment was not directed at me?" A sexy smile played round her lips, causing Dawg to blush. Withers grinned.

"The same applies, but I *was* referring to her," he said, showing Judith the photograph.

"Oh," she said, "is that your footballer? So he knows Brandy Summers, does he?" She registered the distant look in Withers's eyes. "You've never heard of her, have you?"

"Well…," he began, defeat already etched on his face. "No."

"You really ought to get out more, John," she scolded lightly. "Or stay in more. She's a reality TV star. On twice a week, flaunting her… er, ample body in a tiny bikini most of the time."

"I never miss it," mumbled Dawg, and immediately regretted it. Kitty stood behind Judith and giggled softly.

"So, are they an item?" Withers wanted to know.

Judith sat on the sofa. "The publicity machine would have you believe it."

"But you're not convinced."

Judith scoffed. "Ha! Two beautiful young things, thrown together. What do you think?"

"I think," said Withers, studying his deputy, "we should go and see Miss Summers."

Dawg's blush grew in intensity, and Kitty picked up a cushion and threw it at him. "Down, tiger," she teased. "You're mine!"

Chapter Four

He wasn't Japanese. And he wasn't a wrestler. But Mr Sumo *was* a very large man. And a very strong one. Born Richard Towers, his mum used to call him Dickie, which he hated; while his dad gave him the name Bruiser, which seemed to sum the little boy up. At the age of twelve, he was the leader of a gang of young thugs, mostly older than himself, who terrorised the neighbourhood; but the cops could never touch him. He dealt in the simple things of life, like extortion and thievery. On one occasion, he even tried pimping, when he offered the sister of one of his friends to a passing motorist for a packet of fags and a tenner. When the client got upset because the girl wouldn't play ball, Mr Sumo punched them both and ran off with the money. He kindly left the cigarettes for them to fight over.

It was about that time that he was introduced to his forever friend: steroid. As he filled out and lost his puppy fat, he gained muscle and the bulk of an athlete. One year, he even took part in the Iron Man event, but lost his temper and eventually his place in the contest after beating up a fellow competitor he had accused of cheating.

Now, he was just a huge hunk of brawn encased in made-to-measure suits and silk shirts, courtesy of his boss, who always looked after his best employees. And Mr Sumo *was* the best.

Mo Sanders, at the age of fifty-three, was a little man, in both stature and outlook. He thought the world was too good for him, and any self-doubt he had was enhanced ten-fold whenever he looked at somebody else. With mousy-coloured hair and a thin, pinched face, he could have passed for any waif or stray on the street, and the fact that he had become a respected sports agent had shocked him far more than it had surprised his acquaintances. He may not have been full of self-esteem, but he was full of talent.

He had just been for a run. He preferred evening jogs, because it meant he didn't have to see or talk to anyone. He was a solitary man. He had showered, thrown on some old tracksuit bottoms he wore only indoors, together with a frayed Arsenal t-shirt, and was relaxing on the sofa with the *Sports Record* and a healthy green smoothie he had made earlier, when the doorbell rang.

Rising slowly, annoyed at being disturbed at this time of the evening, he made his way down the hall and opened the door. Normally, his porch was awash with brightness from the outside light, but this time the whole view was taken up by a man-mountain in a suit, blocking out everything else. All he could see was a wide, grisly face perched on a massive body. There was no sign of a neck, and Mo suddenly had the stupid thought that he was being confronted by a wild caricature of SpongeBob Square Pants. He stifled a giggle.

"Maurice Sanders?" enquired the mountain, its voice so high and squeaky that Mo had to hide another snigger.

"Yes," he said tentatively, his mind racing as to what this man might want. Oh, perhaps he's a weightlifter looking for representation. Mo relaxed just a little, but instantly he was being bundled into the house, the breath taken out of his body by the sudden push, and he stumbled along the hall. He tried to speak, but the mountain had already slammed the door and was marching forward, his face a mask of terror, his eyes bulging. He grabbed Mo and lifted him off the ground as if he was a puppet, arms flailing, head rocking.

When they got into the lounge, the mountain threw Mo heavily onto the sofa and hovered over him. "We need to talk, Mr Sanders," it said, and Mo no longer felt the urge to giggle at the strange voice. He gulped heavily instead.

"Who are you?" he managed to say, although he didn't recognise his own voice.

"You can call me Mr Sumo."

Mo sat up, rubbing his chest where the mountain had gripped him. It hurt like hell. "What do… do you want?"

Mr Sumo smiled then, but it wasn't a pretty sight. "I just want some information… that's all."

* * * * *

Judith snuggled up to Withers on the sofa and sighed contentedly. "You know, John, I could get used to this."

He brushed her hair tenderly, his fingers entwined. "What, crashing out on the sofa? Yeah, I like it, too."

"No," she said. "I mean being here, with you." She looked at him. "Here," she repeated, her voice suddenly laden with sexual tension, which he wasn't slow to pick up.

"Then stay," he whispered.

She sat up then, her eyes moist, her heart racing. "Are you serious?"

"Why wouldn't I be?" It was at that moment that Heather filled his head, and he understood Judith's reticence. But he knew it was the right moment. "It's all right, sweetheart. I want you."

She chose not to say anything, just in case it was the wrong thing. Instead, she leant down and kissed him on the lips, her tongue searching for his, her hands wrapping around him, pulling him in, melting him with the heat of her love.

She couldn't believe this moment had finally arrived. They had never been able to consummate their relationship, firstly because of his work tracking down the General, and then due to the wound he had suffered and the convalescence ordered by the doctors. She slid her hand under his shirt and gently ran it over the plaster covering the scar on his side. "Are you sure?"

He put his hand on hers. "I'm sure. Anyway, it only hurts when I laugh, not when I…"

"John!" she blurted. "Language!"

"I never said…"

"I know what you were thinking."

He grinned wolfishly. "I bet you don't! Not exactly, anyway." He eased her off his body and stood, pulling her to her feet in the same movement. "It's been too long, Judith. I can't wait any more."

She kissed him. "No, nor can I."

They moved as one towards the stairs, Withers switching off the light, their breathing heavy with expectation.

Chapter Five

The following morning, Dawg tried desperately to hide his disappointment. He had been expecting a two-hour drive up the ME13 to Newburn, home city of the dazzling Brandy Summers.

Instead, he found himself entering the near-archaic portal of Altona City Football Club, walking stride for stride beside his sheriff, both in civilian clothes.

"No uniform for this, Dawg," Withers had instructed over the phone first thing. "This is unofficial. We're just helping out a friend of a friend."

"Yes, boss," Dawg had replied, and immediately went to find his best shirt and trousers, as well as his leather jacket. A cool dude.

Now it had all been wasted. He vaguely flashed his warrant card at the security guard and walked on, looking up at the floodlights and down over the club's shabby buildings – the shop, the reception office, the narrow path leading to the dressing rooms, and beyond them the pitch, its Astroturf surface looking welcoming, whatever the weather. It was a place he had visited many times over the years. His father had guided him through the rusty turnstiles almost from the day he could walk, and they had stood proudly on the terraces, shoulder to shoulder with men of like mind, hearing the chanting and banter between the fans and the players. It had taken several years before he understood why so many of the referees had no parents, and he thought of that now as he looked over the pitch to the grandstand on the far side and could see himself, in short trousers and waving the claret-and-blue scarf his mother had knitted. A lump filled his throat.

They went through a door with its paint peeling and were greeted by a gruff voice. "Can I help you?"

Withers didn't think it sounded remotely like someone wishing to help, but he smiled anyway. "We're looking for Mr Mason's office."

"Well, you won't find it in here!"

Dawg stepped forward. "And you are?"

"Who wants to know?"

Withers sighed. He had met many people like this before. This one had quite a bit of a paunch on him, his claret and blue-striped tie was askew and his belt was far too wide for his trousers, so he wore a set of blue braces as a secondary support. He was clean-shaven, but a shadow fell across his face, as if he was standing in a permanent half-eclipse. His shirt sleeves were rolled up to the elbows, revealing some unsightly tattoos. Not a pretty sight, decided Withers.

"We have an appointment with Mr Mason. I am Sheriff John Withers from Bakerton, and this is my deputy, Doug Janowski. Now, sir, you are?"

"Oscar Castle."

"Well, Mr Castle, perhaps you can direct us to Mr Mason's office."

"Sure. Back through that door you came in, left down the corridor and look for the office that says 'Chairman'."

There was a heavy hint of sarcasm in his voice, but Withers did not pursue it. Instead, he thanked Castle and the two officers retraced their steps through the door and walked down the corridor, Dawg gaping at the large framed portraits of Altona's great and good hanging on the walls both sides.

"Jamie Kinross!" he exclaimed. "Greatest striker ever. That was thirty years ago."

"Before your time, Dawg," said Withers.

"Yes, boss, but not before yours!"

"Careful, deputy," chided Withers, but with a thin smile on his face, which Dawg couldn't see.

Dawg was awe-struck. "Graeme Peacock! Now there was a goalkeeper. Sublime! Trev Robbins. Brilliant!"

They reached the chairman's office just in time, as far as Withers was concerned, before his deputy blew a football-fan gasket. All this exposure to his boyhood heroes was threatening to overwhelm him. Withers waited for Dawg to calm down, then tapped on the door.

"Come in."

Withers and Dawg entered. Barry Mason sat at a small desk, containing just a telephone and a very large ink blotter, on which were scribbled dates and names, as well as numbers which may have represented huge sums of money – all scrawled, presumably, while Mason carried out contract negotiations with football agents over the phone. He was, Withers estimated, in his early sixties, but still slim and agile-looking. His eyes were wide, inquiring, and they were surrounded by a small network of wrinkles that gave the impression of two oases in a sun-baked desert. His cheeks were slightly flushed, and this was echoed in the blush of colour across the top of his forehead where his hair was rapidly receding. His smile was welcoming.

Pictures of him with various dignitaries, both national and international, adorned the walls. Pride of place was given over to a team photo taken on the day the club won the title, almost thirty years ago. The last time Altona got a whiff of any kind of silverware. The ubiquitous sheepskin coat hung on a stand in the corner of the office. Mason rose and smiled, offering a hand. "Sheriff Withers."

Withers took his hand and shook it. "Mr Mason, thank you for seeing us."

"Not a problem at all. Please, take a seat. Perhaps your colleague, er…?"

"Deputy Janowski," said Dawg.

"Right, okay, pull up the chair in the corner, deputy."

They sat and sized each other up for a few seconds. Withers liked what he saw. Mason was clearly a no-nonsense kind of guy, a professional and rich man who felt comfortable in himself, a man who exuded wealth in a positive way. "So, you found me okay," he said. "Shut away in my little hovel." His smile was infectious.

"Yes," said Withers. "Mr Castle directed us."

"Ah, good old Oscar. He's been around the place since forever."

"What does he do?"

"He's director of the youth academy…"

"He trains them?" asked Withers, incredulous, remembering the size of the man.

"Good God, no!" replied Mason with a laugh. "He's purely administration is our Oscar. You wouldn't catch him on a training pitch."

"Not what you would call the friendliest of people," Withers pointed out.

"I have to agree, sheriff. He's a rough one, but he's close to the kids."

Withers leant forward. "We're here about Learie Carmichael."

"Of course. I understand his mother is concerned, as she phoned me a day or so ago, but we see no problem."

"Where is he?"

"He asked if he could take a few days away. We have no game this week, so I agreed, due to the pressure he has been under lately."

"Pressure?"

"The transfer. From Nomads."

"Ah, yes, the transfer." Withers paused. "Why did he come back to Altona City, Mr Mason?"

"I believe that it was personal and most definitely confidential, sheriff. But he certainly didn't confide in me. Suffice to say that he was pretty desperate to get back home, and had refused to play again for the Nomads. They tried to enforce his contract, but he wouldn't budge. He's a tough cookie, sheriff; won't take any nonsense. In the end, Melrose gave up on him and I agreed to take him off their hands for a nominal fee. We're not a rich club, you understand."

"I appreciate that, but Carmichael's return must have been a bit of a coup for you," said Withers.

Mason nodded. "Absolutely. It added bums to seats

and was a publicity dream. He's a great player. But it still all came down to the money. Jet took a fifty percent pay cut to come back to us…"

"So he *was* desperate."

"I would imagine so, yes."

Dawg said, "Is he close to any of your players? Would they know where he is?"

Mason thought for a moment. "He gets on well with everyone. He's a lovely lad. But, to answer your question, he's pretty close to Bryn…"

"Bryn Owen, your defender?" asked Dawg.

"Yes. They were in the boys' team together for three years before Jet left us. Until Jet's transfer to Nomads, they were destined to be our golden couple… in the footballing sense, of course. It was all before my time, of course, but I can imagine how excited the club must have been about both of them. Now they share a flat in Thurlow."

"So why did you sell him in the first place?" asked Withers.

"Well, sheriff, I'm told that Jet had been adamant. He was still only a boy, really – around fifteen, I would say – but he had such potential. The law is strict on the employment of minors, and the club had no choice in agreeing to a deal. Melrose was his chosen club, and he accepted all the terms of the transfer without quibble. Because of his age, he hadn't even secured an agent, so the previous chairman oversaw the negotiations. Done and dusted in five minutes, almost. That sort of thing is pretty unusual. Fortunately, Altona had the insight to insert a clause where we would make a financial gain once Jet had played twenty-five games for the Nomads' first team."

"What about when he came back?"

"To be honest, it was more of the same. Jet didn't make any demands. He was just desperate to get back down here. It's the best deal I'll ever make, that's for sure."

"Mm," Withers mused, nursing a thought. "Thank you, Mr Mason. You said he shares with Bryn Owen."

"Yes."

"Perhaps you could let us have their address."

"Certainly, sheriff. I'll arrange it with our secretary for you to pick up on the way out." He rose and shook Withers's hand warmly. "I'm confident Jet is okay. He's a resourceful young man."

"I'm sure he is," said Withers, walking out of the office. Dawg was slow to follow, his gaze resting on the team photograph and the caption beneath it.

"That was a great season, Mr Mason," he said.

Mason grinned like a true fan. "And some! We haven't reached the stars much since then, I'm afraid, but I'll keep trying." He shook Dawg's hand. "Now Jet's back, perhaps our luck will change."

* * * * *

Ty arrived first. He parked the car under a spreading chestnut tree and walked towards the lake. It was a beautiful sight, the sun dappled on the blue water, a man-made marvel which still had the capacity to excite. One or two joggers were negotiating the perimeter, their white legs flashing through the trees as they meandered round, their minds on nothing much but timings and personal bests. A pair of magpies swooped down and scuttled through the fallen leaves, intent on whatever meal they could find.

Ty watched, mesmerised, as he sat on the same bench he had shared with Sheriff Withers just three weeks ago. He re-read the love messages scratched into the wood, and recalled how he had jokingly called it their 'love seat', although there had never been any feelings between them other than perhaps animosity and, at a push, a grudging respect. Actually, he now remembered Withers with something close to fondness, sharing with him their pleasure in this place and their determination to bring down the General. Ty had made an early escape when the time came, but he had read all the papers about the events leading up to the madman's death, and was pleased to learn that the sheriff had survived. Enough people had suffered, and it was time to make amends in some small way.

He had been thoughtful enough to bring some bread, and he threw it out to the handful of ducks which had paddled by, their quacks disturbing the magpies and forcing them to flight. Two of the ducks waddled out of the water and approached this man with food, their beaks working noisily as they demanded personal attention. Ty threw the remainder of the bread and sat back, watching the pitched battle as the ducks vied for a place at the table.

"Such innocence, Lucas."

Ty swivelled, expecting her, but still surprised at the suddenness of her arrival.

"Grace," he said, rising. "Thank you for coming." He indicated the bench, but she chose to remain standing, the distance between them both physical and monumental.

"According to the papers, I should call you Ty," she said.

He smiled. "Lucas is fine. Either is okay. Please, sit with me, Grace. I have to explain."

"To clear your conscience?"

"No," he said sadly. "I can never do that. But I do want you to understand."

Grace Templeman, a woman in her late sixties, had the air of authority. Her back was straight, her head held high, her button nose raised just a notch above horizontal. Her grey eyes peered resolutely through spectacles that were on a chain, and her mouth appeared to have just the slightest upturn at the corners. She was dressed in a single-breasted city coat over a jumper and black trousers, the epitome of class. She studied him closely. She had known him for such a short time, but there had been much to admire. He had shown such respect for Leroy Figgis, her boss at the bank, and he must have been shattered when Leroy was brutally murdered. But was that an excuse for what he did? "I can't get past the fact that you killed poor Mr Baxter," she said. "In cold blood."

Ty winced, the truth hurting more than he could handle. "Yes," he agreed slowly. "That was unforgiveable. But his days were numbered, Grace. The General would have come back for him eventually, and that could have led him to me."

"Do you think that's a good reason?" Grace demanded, her control leaving her momentarily. She gathered herself. "That's just an excuse, Lucas."

"Yes. I know."

She sat beside him, studying him. "Will you hand yourself in?"

He thought about that, weighing up his options. "I will, Grace. I promise. But, like I said, there is something I have to do."

She hesitated, her mind in turmoil. She saw in his eyes a determination, and something else. He was silently pleading with her. "Go on," she said with a heavy sigh.

When he started, it all came out so quickly that he hardly paused for breath. "We went to Lanscarges to pick up drugs. No, don't say anything. It's not what you think. Leroy was buying the stuff so he could burn it! As you've always said, Grace, he was one of the good guys. But that is one of the reasons why people died. In the eyes of the General, we had crossed him. Never mind that he had betrayed Leroy. It's a long, complicated story, but you know how it ended. Anyway, the crux of this story is that I was in charge of Leroy's laptop. He trusted me enough to carry it and operate it, even down to the secret codes he had installed on it. I used it to transfer huge sums of money from Leroy's account to other people's – just like that. I had magic in my fingers, Grace."

"Why are you telling me this, Lucas?"

"We need to find the laptop."

"Why? How?" She was confused.

Ty put his hand on hers, which were resting in her lap. She looked down, but did not move away. He said, "The why is easy, Grace. Because there are millions stashed away in Leroy's secret accounts. Nobody knows anything about them but me…"

"And you want it," stated Grace, her face ashen.

"No, no! Well, yes, but not for me, Grace. I swear. You have to believe me. That money can do so much good in the world. It would be Leroy's secret legacy." He waited for her to lift her head and looked at her. "Grace, I want you to dispose of it how you think fit. You were closer to Leroy than anybody I know. Think what you can do with it."

"Is it stolen?" she asked, not wanting to know.

"No, definitely not. Grace, you know Leroy would never do something like that. He had so much money that he could siphon it away without the accountants getting a sniff at it. I don't know how, but he managed it. I tell you, Grace, there are millions."

"So," she sneered, "what would be your cut out of this?"

Ty was stunned. He stood up and walked down to the lake shore, scuffing a twig and some stones into the water and watching the ripples. Slowly, he turned and retraced his steps, standing above her. "I'll make you a deal, Grace. You help me find this laptop and I'll give you all the codes. I don't even need to see the computer. After that, I'll turn myself in. What do you say?"

Grace was silent for a long time, her mind playing through what she had just heard. "You wouldn't need to see the laptop?"

"Not if you don't trust me, Grace. Please, I'm doing this for Leroy's memory."

"You'll go to the police afterwards?"

He smiled. "You can take me to Sheriff Withers personally if that would help."

After a pause, she said, "Sit down, Lucas. We need to talk some more."

* * * * *

The pile on the desk was getting larger, and Rafferty threw up his hands in exasperation. "What the…? Keene!" he bellowed, and the deputy gingerly popped his head round the door.

"Sir?"

"How am I going to get all this done?"

"Don't know, sir."

"Paperwork! Bah! I wasn't put on this God-forsaken earth to rummage through paperwork, Keene!"

"No, sir."

Rafferty looked hard at his deputy. "That file."

"File, sir?"

"The one I told you to… er… file."

"Sir?"

"Ty Cobden, man! The sightings."

"Ah, yes, sir." Pause. "What about it, sir?"

"Get it, Keene!"

"Yes, sir."

The deputy was back in a flash, handing the file to his boss. Rafferty took his time as he studied the various sightings. He knew damn well it was a fool's errand, but what the hell. He was fed up with this office life, and couldn't wait for Withers to come back through that door and regain his kingdom. Perhaps a short trip out might blow away the cobwebs and make him a little less cranky. He stretched his shoulders and looked up at the neatly-uniformed young officer, who had been desperately trying to impress him.

"Tell me, Keene, in your estimation, which of these is more likely to be a real sighting?" He fanned the documents across his desk, and Keene looked at each, before pointing a shaking finger at one.

"This one?" said Rafferty, enjoying the other man's discomfort.

"Yes, sir." Keene's voice was as shaky as his finger.

Rafferty picked up the sheet and read it. "It says here that the suspected Cobden was seen with another man."

"Yes, sir."

"Any description?"

"No, sir."

"What, was he invisible?" Rafferty's voice was rising.

"I don't believe so, sir. No. I'm sure he wasn't. They wouldn't have been able to see him if that was the case… sir."

"Are you taking the piss, Keene?"

"No, sir."

"Good. Get the car. We're going up to Copper Ridge. I need the fresh air."

"Yes, sir."

* * * * *

Dawg was driving a little faster than perhaps he should have. He was excited. Studying the road, he was pleased to finally see the name Newburn on a sign.

"Left here," said Withers in a flat voice, like a satnav.

"Yes, boss," replied Dawg, steering effortlessly into the left-hand lane and filtering off the ME13 and onto the local road leading into the city.

At last he was going to meet Brandy Summers!

He had queried their destination at first. "Are we not going to see Bryn Owen?"

"I need some more background," Withers had said.

"While Miss Summers lives in Newburn, she spent a lot of time in Melrose with Jet. She can tell us about his life up here."

Dawg couldn't argue with that. Actually, he wouldn't have dreamt of it! He was desperate to meet a real-life reality star, and he almost salivated at the prospect.

Withers navigated the car through the city, encouraging Dawg to slow down on occasion, until the car came to a stop on yellow lines in front of a very high-class high-rise block of flats. Withers placed his police notice on the dashboard and stepped out of the vehicle, stretching his legs after a long and at times frantic journey. He looked up. "Penthouse, I assume?"

"No, boss. Second floor," said Dawg, disappointment in his voice.

"Never mind, Dawg, I'm sure it will be spectacular."

Dawg followed him into the building. "Just not the penthouse," he mumbled sadly.

They located the flat and Withers rang the bell. He noticed from the corner of his eye that Dawg was combing his hair and then straightening his tie. He wondered when Dawg had put on the tie, because he certainly didn't have it in Altona. He smiled to himself.

The door opened on a chain, and a woman's voice asked who they were.

Withers waved his warrant card. "Sheriff John Withers…"

"And Deputy Doug Janowski," Dawg added quickly, in case his boss forgot he was there.

The door closed, the chain rattled and the door opened again, revealing the lovely Brandy Summers… dressed in torn jeans, oversize jumper, no make-up and hair dishevelled. Dawg looked at her almost in horror, although he had to admit that her natural beauty did shine through.

"Come in," she said, her tone smooth, cultured and welcoming, not at all like her television voice. Dawg thought it sounded like a fluffy blanket, wrapping itself warmly around him. But, then again, he might have been a little biased.

"Thank you for seeing us, Miss Summers," said Withers.

"No problem, sheriff."

She led them through a short hallway and turned right into a large living room. It was beautifully decorated, as expected, but Withers was impressed with the accessories the young woman had put into the room. There were prints of a Jack Vettriano, a Hockney and a Lucien Freud, as well as small ornaments of delicate flowers and ballet dancers. All very chic, Withers had to concede.

"Please, gentlemen, take a seat," she said, and, after they had both sunk into the plush sofa, she offered them a drink.

"Coffee would be nice," said Withers.

"Nothing for me," Dawg tried to say, but his tongue appeared to be unusually tied, as if a Boy Scout had been experimenting on it. In the end, he just waved his answer.

Brandy soon came back with a cafetiere and two coffee cups in saucers, together with a matching milk jug and sugar bowl. "Milk, sugar?"

"One sugar, please. I prefer mine black," said Withers, still surveying the room. Yes, it was a place that both he and Judith would be happy in. Perhaps this woman wasn't as shallow as he had presumed.

Brandy sat opposite them, her eyes not straying. "So, sheriff, you want to talk about Jet?"

Withers was in the process of taking a sip, so he had to replace his cup before he replied. "Yes. He was a particular friend of yours, I believe?"

She gave him a quick smile. "I'm not sure what you mean by *particular*..."

"Forgive me, Miss Summers, I didn't mean to imply..."

"I understand, sheriff. But, firstly, can we dispense with the formalities? Please, call me Rachel."

Dawg sat up. "Rachel?"

"My real name." She looked hard at Dawg. "Do you know anybody who's really called Brandy?"

He squirmed. "Well, no, but..."

"My name is Rachel Winters. Get it? Just like Cilla Black, I reversed things."

Withers nodded. "Her real name was Priscilla White."

"Exactly."

Dawg also nodded, although he wasn't convinced. "So, why not *Rachel* Summers?" he asked.

"My parents had a dog called Brandy."

Withers waited for that fact to sink into Dawg's befuddled brain before continuing. "Now, about Learie Carmichael – Jet, to you – when did you first meet him?"

Brandy placed her cup and saucer on a coffee table and reached for the shelf under it, pulling out a photograph album. "I dug this out after you phoned. I thought it might be of interest."

"Thank you." Withers took the album and began looking through it. "It says here, 14th February 2014."

"Yes, we met on Valentine's Day. At a party in Melrose. I had been invited by a friend, and Jet was there with some of his teammates. He'd only just got into Melrose's first team, so he was still finding his feet."

"Were you introduced by anyone?"

Brandy thought about it. "Not really, no. We just sort of… gravitated. We had a few things in common, so we chatted for quite a while. It ended up more of a two-person debate than a party!" She smiled at the memory. "Neither of us are party animals, sheriff, despite what you might read in the press."

"What sort of things did you discuss?"

"You name it… He is an extremely well-read young man – for a footballer!"

Withers wanted to say that she was extremely erudite for a reality star – but that would just be rude. However, he really was impressed with her, and vowed to watch her programme at the first opportunity. Dawg just sat there, mouth almost agape.

"Can you shed any light on why he wanted to leave Melrose?" Withers asked.

"No," she replied, "not really. He did become very morose just before the move, but he wouldn't talk about it. It was so sudden. I thought that perhaps he had received some bad news…"

"Bad news?" repeated Withers. "What makes you say that?"

"Well," said Brandy, thinking back, "it was like a tap being turned on. One day he was fine, the next he was agitated, troubled. It was quite frightening, to be honest. I didn't know what to make of it. I tried to push it once, and he did mention an Altona player, but then he closed up. I couldn't get anything out of him after that."

Withers pondered. "Would that be Bryn Owen?"

"Yes," said Brandy, "that's the name. I couldn't remember, but, yes, that's him. I don't follow football myself," she ended by way of explanation.

"Me neither," said Withers. "I'm more of a chess man."

"Really!" beamed Brandy. "My father loves the game. He tried to teach me once, but I was hopeless. I kept mixing up my prawns…"

"Pawns," Withers corrected her.

Brandy gave him a wry smile. "Just slipping into my reality TV persona, sheriff. I really do know what they are called."

Withers returned the smile. "I'm sure you do, Brandy… Rachel." He closed the album. "Do you mind if we take this with us? We will guard it with our lives, won't we, Dawg?"

Dawg reached out and took the book, clutching it to his breast. "I will!"

Withers and Brandy smiled at each other, then Withers asked, "Finally, when was the last time you saw Jet?"

"Two weeks ago. He invited me down to Thurlow Junction, his home."

"Yes, we know it," said Withers. "How was he then?"

"Still troubled, I'm afraid. I stayed overnight in the second bedroom. I believe his friend was out for the night. Jet was restless, on edge all the time. It was an uncomfortable visit." She sighed for her friend.

"You have been very helpful," said Withers, feeling that he had upset her enough. "Thank you."

Brandy reached out and put her hand on the sheriff's arm. "Is he all right? I mean, what can you tell me?" The concern on her face was clear to see.

"You are very fond of him, aren't you?" said Withers.

"Not like that, sheriff!" she said. "He's like a brother to me. I love him, yes, but in a…"

Withers put his hand on hers and lifted it from his arm. "I understand, Miss Summers." He stood, indicating that Dawg should follow suit. "If we hear anything, we will let you know."

* * * *

The car edged into the disused timber yard and rolled to a halt, dust kicking up from its tyres. Rafferty and Keene stepped out, the latter putting on his regulation police hat and taking an inordinate amount of time in ensuring it was at the correct angle. He stood to attention as a man approached.

"Mr Logan?" enquired Rafferty.

"Aye, that's me," the man acknowledged.

Rafferty squinted at him through his shades. He looked a bit rough-and-ready, unshaven, a battered leather coat thrown over a chequered cowboy shirt, complete with a bandana tucked into the collar, stone-dried blue jeans and cowboy boots. No spurs, Rafferty thought sadly, but the look would have been okay on a twenty-something – Logan was clearly a seventy-something. "So, Mr Logan, what business do you have up here?" Rafferty asked, suspecting the man's intentions were nefarious.

"Oh, you know, this and that," he said, hoping there would be no more questions.

Rafferty wasn't in the mood to pursue his line of questioning. The sun was shining, and he just wanted to wallow in it. "Okay, sir, what can you show us?"

"I'll take you there, sheriff."

Rafferty couldn't bring himself to explain his correct rank, so he just said, "Fine."

They followed Logan into the wood, leaving the small track and stepping into the undergrowth. Keene was almost marching, his arms moving in rhythm. Rafferty tried not to stumble, conscious of the strain this was putting on his bad leg. It didn't usually play up, but today he just needed any excuse to be cantankerous. Eventually, their guide stopped at what had obviously been a makeshift campsite.

"There," he said, "I told you I'd seen them."

"Yes, Mr Logan, but who exactly did you see?"

"I told your deputy there," he said, pointing an arthritic finger at Keene. "I told him it was your fugitive. I saw them."

"When was this?" Rafferty asked.

"Three days ago it was. I reported it then," Logan said accusingly. Bloody police never did take him seriously.

Rafferty had given the file a cursory inspection, like all the others, and had dismissed all of the sightings as fantasy. A fool's errand, he repeated to himself, nothing more. But then again, why shouldn't he have a bit of fun? Keene was gullible, and the old cowboy would certainly be impressed by some police sleuthing.

He made a show of examining the site, reaching down and pushing aside tufts of grass, turning over fallen branches to inspect the undergrowth, all the time careful not to disturb too much – just in case. Keene and Logan watched with admiration, not daring to interrupt the law enforcer's concentration. Suddenly, Rafferty rose up, apparently triumphant. "Keene!"

"Sir?"

"Evidence bag, if you would. And tread carefully, for God's sake!" Rafferty added, a delicious smile on his lips, knowing that his back was turned towards the others. He was enjoying this fiasco.

Keene approached with caution and opened the bag for his superior to deposit what looked like a sweet wrapper.

"Now, deputy, we might actually find out if this did belong to our wanted man," said Rafferty, sounding more like *Columbo* than Peter Falk ever did.

The deputy was none the wiser. "Yes, sir," he said, almost saluting in admiration.

* * * *

Bob Travers had been trying to get hold of his mate for a couple of hours, without success. He had phoned, of course, but it had just gone to voicemail on all three occasions. Now, he was banging on the door, and still no response. Mo's car was out front, so he had to be in. Travers lifted the letterbox and peered through the slit. Nothing. He put his mouth to the opening.

"Mo, where are you?"

No reply, so he tried to phone again. He could hear Mo's mobile ringing inside. "Silly bugger!" he said to himself, annoyed that he was wasting a good day. Mo didn't socialise much, so Travers had been surprised when he'd agreed to a round of golf this afternoon. Neither of them were any good: Travers played off a handicap of twenty-four, while Mo said his handicap had always been his clubs. It was a painfully old joke, but Travers had grinned. It was the way Mo told it.

Travers began to feel uneasy. This was not like Mo Sanders. Perhaps he was ill, sick in bed? Or worse – lying in the bathroom after a heart attack. Now Travers's mind was racing. What to do? He looked through the letterbox again and wiped the sweat from his hands.

"Mo, I'm calling the police!" he shouted, as if his friend could hear him. "Hang in there, buddy!"

* * * * *

"Well, what did you make of Miss Brandy, then?" asked Withers, sitting beside his awe-struck deputy as they made their way back to town.

"Beautiful."

"For once, Dawg, I agree."

Dawg whistled. "She wasn't what I imagined."

"You mean, she was intelligent."

"Well… yes. I mean, she wasn't at all like she is on the TV."

"She's an actress," Withers said simply. "She acts."

They had just got back onto the ME13 motorway, and Withers was trying to digest everything. Jet and Brandy weren't an item, but just good friends. Not only that, but Bryn Owen was coming into the mix. He took out his phone and dialled. No answer.

"If he's not answering his phone, there's not much point

in going round his place," reasoned Dawg.

Withers agreed. "Okay, I'll try something else." He dialled another number.

"Altona City Football Club."

"Hello," said Withers. "I wonder, could you put me through to Mr Mason, please?"

"Certainly, sir. Please hold."

Moments later, Mason came on the line. "Hello?"

"Mr Mason, it's Withers here."

"Oh, hello again, sheriff. Is there some news?"

"Not that quick, I'm afraid, sir. I can't track down Bryn Owen."

"Leave it with me," said Mason, and hung up.

Withers put away his phone and gazed out of the window. Now that Dawg wasn't heading towards the delightful Miss Summers, his driving wasn't so erratic, and this was turning into a very pleasant ride. He half-closed his eyes and relaxed. Dawg was just about to put on the radio when Withers's phone rang.

"Mr Mason?" Withers said.

"Yes, sheriff. Sorry, but no one seems to know where Bryn might be. Obviously out enjoying himself somewhere."

"Obviously," Withers agreed, disappointed. He knew nothing about football, but he understood the system, and there was one person, apart from their mother, that a sportsperson cherished… "Tell me, Mr Mason, who is Jet's agent?"

"Both Jet and Bryn have the same agent… His name is Mo, Mo Sanders."

* * * * *

Mr Sumo was having a restful day. Last night he had obtained the information he needed, but there was no hurry now, so he had enjoyed a leisurely breakfast with a double helping of bacon, sausage and eggs, washed down with a mug of steaming tea laced with six sugars. The paperboy had delivered, so Mr Sumo had read through the *Oracle*, taking in the sport and also that good-looking Judith Wiseman's column. Her picture always topped the article, and he never failed to give her a good look. Boy, would he like to meet her!

Now he sat at the kitchen table in his favourite red kimono – a present from his boss for another job well done – looking out at his beautifully maintained little garden. He liked it here, at the edge of Thurlow Junction, close enough to the town without making him feel claustrophobic, and only a half-hour drive to the big city. His neighbours were half-decent, although he did tend to keep to himself, and the shops were within a short walking distance, a prerequisite for a man the size of Mr Sumo. Less time walking meant more time eating. But he had noticed recently that he was putting on a little, and it clearly wasn't muscle. Time to think about renewing that gym membership.

A blackbird, its yellow beak flashing in the sunshine, flew down and onto the bird table Mr Sumo had thoughtfully erected at the edge of the lawn. Yes, Mr Sumo could be very thoughtful when he wanted to be…

* * * * *

When Withers and Dawg got there, they were greeted by the sight of three police cars sprawled across the road, while a forensics van was up on the pavement, its back doors open, and technicians in white suits were going in and out of the house. An ambulance sat a little way off, its engine idling, two paramedics inside. Withers knew straight away that they were obviously not needed.

"What the hell!" he mouthed.

Dawg swung the car in beside one of the police vehicles and they both got out, just as Pat Rafferty, clad in crime-scene protective clothing, emerged from the house. He gave them a double-take.

"John, what are you doing here?"

"Came to see Mo Sanders." He looked at the activity beyond Rafferty and sighed. "Looks like we're too late."

"Several hours too late, pal. According to the man who knows, our Mo's been deceased for at least twelve hours." His Irish lilt seemed more pronounced than usual. "Wanna take a look?"

Withers donned a white suit and followed Rafferty into the house. There was police tape everywhere, as well as labels marking important aspects of the crime scene, such as fingerprints and small items that had clearly been disturbed during Mo's fight for survival, as short as it had probably been. Mo himself was lying on the sofa, looking as peaceful as a sleeping princess, save for the red marks around his neck and his tongue poking very slightly out of his purple lips. Withers took a closer look.

"So what was the killer after, Pat?"

"Good question, John. Your guess is as good as mine.

Nothing missing, by the look of it, and the place hasn't been ransacked. Looks like the guy just came in, throttled Mo here and left through the front door. Anyway, why did you want to see Mo? Not a friend, surely?"

"Never met him. But he is… *was* a sports agent representing somebody I want to talk to."

Rafferty looked puzzled. "Sounds very much like you've got yourself a case. I thought you were convalescing. What's going on?"

"We'll talk outside, if it's all the same to you," Withers said, making for the door. Rafferty wasn't too far behind him.

"So," said Rafferty, now standing on the lawn, enjoying the fresh air and gulping it in gratefully, "now you can fill me in."

Withers and Dawg stood beside him, still trying to put the story together. Withers said, "Have you heard of Learie Carmichael?"

"Name rings a bell."

"Jet Carmichael," clarified Dawg.

"Ah, yes, he's a footballer, isn't he?"

Withers said, "His mother thinks he's in trouble. Hasn't heard from him in four days… she's worried."

"He's a big boy, surely?"

"Normally, I'd agree," said Withers, "but she says that he always phones her, every day."

"But not recently," Rafferty surmised.

"Right. We're now also looking for his best pal, Bryn Owen…"

"Another player," Dawg elaborated.

"Thank you, Dawg. Mo Sanders was Bryn and Jet's agent."

"And now he's dead," said Rafferty with a whistle. "That's more than a coincidence and a half."

* * * * *

She was flushed. Never in her life had she done anything remotely like this. She felt like James Bond, Miss Marple and Lord Peter Wimsey all rolled into one; or possibly more like Bonnie Parker to Ty's Clyde Barrow, but without the violence. Dressed in her finest suit, with a bounce in her step, she entered the hallowed portals of the Mercurial Bank. It was, as intended, a building which stunned the visitor with its high ceiling and beautifully carved arches highlighting the craftsmanship that only true wealth can purchase.

As she approached the reception desk, she could see that the young girl didn't recognise her. "Hello," she said, "my name is Grace Templeman. I have an appointment with Mr Hargreaves."

The girl studied her diary and, with a deft tick using her expensive Mercurial Bank-engraved rollerball pen, registered Grace's arrival. "Yes, Ms Templeman, would you care to sit? Mr Hargreaves's secretary will be with you shortly."

Grace sat in one of the plush armchairs in the 'holding area', as they used to call it when she worked at the bank. They are probably more refined these days, she reflected. She picked up a copy of *Banking Issues* from the coffee table, and pretended to read it. Like everybody else, she thought with a smile. Nobody really reads this rubbish.

They had gone through the procedure carefully, her and Ty, so she knew exactly what to say, what to do. But that didn't make it any easier. She still felt that she was letting her former employers down in some way. Surely she should have gone straight to the police. That's what any sane person would have done. But Ty was so persuasive; and the money really could do so much good. She had turned it over in her mind so many times: she had pencilled in numerous worthy causes, each of which would benefit considerably from a financial injection. But she had to be careful. It all had to be done with such precision so that it was never traced back to her. My, she sighed to herself, retirement shouldn't be this complicated.

"Ms Templeman?" A very young, pretty girl stood before her, smiling. "I'm Pamela, Mr Hargreaves's PA."

Grace couldn't believe that such a snip of a girl could fill the shoes that she had once worn, and the thought depressed her. She had spent thirty years at the bank, and it took two-thirds of that time to work her way up to the dizzy heights of 'Chairman's Secretary', which now, apparently, is called 'PA'. Heavens, what is the world coming to?

"Yes, hello," she stuttered, regrouping her thoughts for what lay ahead.

"Please," said Pamela pleasantly, "if you'd like to follow me."

Grace didn't like to say that she actually knew the way, thank you very much, as it was only last year that she had retired, so the layout of the offices was clear in her mind. Instead, she meekly followed the stiletto-heeled, short-skirted PA through to the lift, up an almost never-ending number of floors and then through labyrinthine corridors, before coming to rest at the top-floor office that was once the domain of Leroy Figgis, but now housed Daniel Hargreaves, brand new chairman and CEO of one of the largest banks in the country. It was a sobering thought to Grace that this fine institution had been created by Leroy Figgis the First, great-grandfather of her Leroy, but now the family name had been usurped forever.

"Grace!" Hargreaves welcomed her with such warmth that she was slightly taken aback. He had been with the company for probably twenty years, working his way to the surface from some subterranean position deep in the bowels of the building. Rumour had it that he had started as a cleaner, but she knew that wasn't true. She had been on first-name terms with all the cleaners.

"Hello, Daniel," she responded, taking the seat he offered and looking round the room. It hadn't changed much since her day. There was still the huge portrait of the first Figgis, dressed in his mayoral robes, a ceremonial mace in his hand. All very grand. Grace also noted that her Leroy's smaller picture still hung behind the chairman's chair.

Hargreaves studied her, before saying, "So, how's retirement?"

"Oh, you know, never a dull moment."

"I can imagine." That was the pleasantries out of the way. "Now, Grace, what can I do for you?"

She had reached the point of no return. She could just say that she had missed the bank and that she wanted to have a nostalgic walk round, and to congratulate him on his elevation to the top job. Or she could plough on with the plan. "I want to write a book."

"Really?" He almost sounded interested.

"On Mr Figgis."

"Yes, that would be wonderful. So, you're looking for finance?"

Typical banker: all about money. "Oh, no," Grace assured him. "That won't be necessary. I have means."

Hargreaves tried to apologise. "I'm sure you do. Sorry."

She waved his words away. "Not a problem, Daniel. It's just that…"

"Yes?"

It's now or never! "Mr Figgis had a laptop…"

"Several, I would imagine," grinned Hargreaves, expecting Grace to chuckle.

She didn't. "Just the one, Daniel." She paused. "It has some things on it which could help."

"In your research, you mean?"

"Something like that." She smiled disarmingly. "Do you have it?"

"I'm sorry, Grace, but we don't." He saw her face drop. "He didn't have any family left, so all his personal effects were gathered together and sent to some out-of-town solicitors. I believe that our security department cleared it all before it went, so I doubt if you'd find anything of interest."

"Oh," she said, "you never know what secrets it might give up." She leant forward, her eyes sparkling at him. "I wonder, Daniel," she purred, "could you give me the name of the solicitors?"

* * * * *

Rafferty was in a different place. He was at a Genesis gig, or perhaps on the seventeenth green. Who cares! Anywhere was better than this stuffy office.

He looked out of the window for the umpteenth time, then tried to concentrate on the paperwork which was building up mercilessly on Withers's desk. He thought again about the sad demise of Mo Sanders, but his mind drifted, mainly because the sheriff appeared to have retaken control of the town of Bakerton and its environs when it came to crime. Rafferty was… well, a spare one at a wedding, he thought sadly. It really was time to get back to what he did best.

It was then that the sweet wrapper came into his mind. He had enjoyed the look on young Keene's face as he dropped the 'evidence' into the bag. Silly boy, he mused. Now, though, perhaps it was time to end the joke.

"Keene!" he bawled, "get in here."

It was only seconds before the officer was framed in the doorway. "Sir?"

Rafferty hesitated. Should he let him down lightly, or just say that the youngster must be a real prat if he thought for one minute that the wrapper meant anything at all. "Listen, Keene, it was nothing personal…"

"Sir?"

"I mean, I was just having a laugh…"

"Laugh, sir?"

"Dammit, Keene, the sweet wrapper…"

"Oh, yes, sir."

"Well, I was…" The words wouldn't come, and Rafferty sank into his chair, realising at last how childish he had been.

"I've already sent it, sir." Keene's face was the epitome of innocence.

"Sent it?"

"To forensics, sir. They've had it for a few hours now. I must say, sir, it was a job well done on your part."

"Thank you," was all Rafferty could say in reply. "That will be all."

"Yes, sir." Keene turned to leave. "You said something about a joke, sir."

Rafferty sighed. "Never mind, Keene. I think it's on me."

* * * * *

It had been a strenuous workout, by his standards. The thought of those extra pounds had weighed heavily on Mr Sumo, so he had indeed made his way to the gym, intent on regaining control. He had tried to get on one of their cycling machines, but his bulk had proved a hindrance, so he satisfied his inner thin man with a spell on the rowing machine and a brisk walk on the new treadmill they had installed, where a computer screen offered you various walks around the world, in real time, and with real people passing you on your journey. Mr Sumo chose the Japanese route, of course, but was disappointed when the other walkers failed to say *konnichiwa* as they passed. In fact, they appeared to totally ignore him.

After getting home and downing a litre of tap water to cleanse his system, he went to his laptop to check on any messages. He didn't find one from his boss, but there were ten messages, nine of which were spam, the other one being from Herbie, his some-time partner. *Hi, jerk*, it had said, *how about a beer tonight? Usual place?*

Mr Sumo wasn't that keen on Herbie, especially when he called him 'jerk', so he typed back: *Out with blonde with big tits. See you around.* He had smiled when he pressed Send. He was expecting to be doing something else tonight, but, sadly, it wouldn't involve a woman.

Now, after a hearty lunch and a long snooze on the sofa, he tackled his laptop again. This time, he was in luck, the message from his boss short and to the point.

Go ahead

He replied:

OK

and sank back onto the sofa, a wide grin on his face. He liked his job, and he performed it to the best of his ability. It was also a pleasure to get recognition for a job well done, and his employer was good at acknowledging his specific skills. Thinking back, he was a little disappointed that Mo had given up the information so quickly. He liked to tease the facts out slowly, methodically, using techniques he had picked up from numerous thugs he had met along life's highway. Although he was immensely strong, Mr Sumo preferred delicate touches and the more flamboyant process of eliciting details from his victims. Mo had let him down, squealing as he did so soon after Mr Sumo took hold of his throat. It just wasn't right. He deserved to die. And tonight Mr Sumo had another chance to exercise his considerable talent for murder…

* * * * *

He heard the key in the lock and went down the hall to meet her. She was rattled, Ty could see immediately. He stood back in the shadows as she entered her house, and he quickly closed the door behind her. "What's wrong?" he asked.

She sat at the dining table, not even unbuttoning her coat. It took a few moments for her to settle. "He hasn't got it."

"What do you mean?" Ty said.

She looked up at him, bewildered. "I thought this was going to be so easy."

Ty grinned. "Nothing is ever easy, Grace. Tell me."

"Daniel Hargreaves packed up Mr Figgis's things and sent them down to a solicitor in Thurlow. He's holding on to them while a private investigator looks into possible dependants. Leroy didn't have any immediate next of kin, so it could be a long process."

"Fair enough, but why Thurlow? What's the connection?"

Grace finally undid her coat and took it off, laying it carefully over the back of a spare chair. She had regained some of her composure. "A cup of tea, I think, Ty. Then I will explain how Mr Figgis came to be friends with Reginald Green, partner in Erin and Green, solicitors."

* * * * *

"I bought you something."

Withers gave her a long kiss on the lips and stepped aside, letting Judith pass, and then pinched her bum. Not PC, but it was sure a delight – for both of them. She wiggled daintily and laughed.

"What is it?" he asked, intrigued. "It's not my birthday."

"Does it need to be?" Judith responded, handing him the parcel, beautifully wrapped in a football-design paper. She couldn't resist the joke.

He ushered her into the dining room and waited as she sat at the table. "I'll open it later," he said, putting the parcel down and moving to the kitchen, where a rather tasty spag-bol was ready to be dished up. He filled two bowls, adding the parmesan, and carried them carefully into the dining room. Judith had already poured the wine that had been chilling in a bucket.

"Open it now," she said, excitement clouding her voice.

"Really?" he teased. "Can we not have supper first?"

"No!" she cried. "I can't wait!"

He picked up the parcel and turned it this way and that, shaking it, inspecting it, keeping Judith waiting until she sighed heavily with frustration. Then he opened it. He was speechless.

"Do you like it?" she asked, knowing very well that he had been searching for one of these for several months without success. It was volume six of the 'Real Crime: Forensics' series, *Three Women: The Jannette Isaac Case*.

Withers caressed the hardback as he pulled it gingerly out of the slipcase and opened it carefully. "Wonderful!" he purred. "Thank you so much."

"Chad Orwell told me you had been looking for it. He says you're his forensics apprentice!"

Withers laughed. "Hardly! But the subject does intrigue me. I do rather bend his ear sometimes."

"So I've heard!" she grinned.

Supper was forgotten. Withers sat beside Judith and flicked through the pages. The beautifully produced folio recounted the case, from some years ago, of Jannette Isaac, an English housewife who had poisoned her husband over a number of evening meals, and had appeared to have got away with it. However, Pam Wareing, a CID inspector, was like a dog with a bone, and her constant pressure paid off when forensics scientist Dr Joan Doney stepped in and carried out an exhumed post-mortem. Doney confirmed digitalis poisoning, and Wareing had arrested Isaac as she attempted to abscond to the Continent. Isaac said she had got the idea from Agatha Christie, and is now serving life in Holloway. The trio eventually became known as 'The Three Women' in the national media. It had been a *cause célèbre* in England at the time.

"Thank you," Withers said again, leaning over and kissing her. "I shall treasure it."

Judith smiled. "As long as it doesn't give you ideas! That spag-bol looks great. I'd hate to find rat poison or something in it!"

They laughed gently and lifted their glasses. "To us," Withers said.

"Yes," breathed Judith. "To the future."

Withers sank back in his chair with a contented sigh. Yes, he was going to have a future, and it looked more rosy each day. "Come on, eat your digitalis before it gets cold!" he said with a wicked pantomime grin.

Chapter Six

"Thanks for coming in, gentlemen. Please, take a seat."

Withers directed the two men to the chairs in front of his desk, and they sat, silently. It had felt strange this morning, coming into his office again after everything he had been through. His nerves had jangled and his throat had felt unusually dry, as if something was waiting for him as he turned the handle and entered. It was all nonsense, of course. The office was the same as it had ever been: small and tight, somehow, for a man of his size, but welcoming nonetheless. He had taken the briefest look out of the window, sat at his desk and picked up the framed photograph of Judith she had given him when he left the hospital. Dawg had kindly put it on his desk, ready for his return. He had smiled down at her and had sighed with contentment and not a little relief that he had overcome the first obstacle to returning to work.

Pat Rafferty, as usual, stood at the window, studying the visitors. He didn't know them, but he knew their names.

"Sheriff," said Barry Mason, "this is our first-team coach, Will Preston."

"Sheriff." Preston's voice was clear and strangely melodic, almost like that of a tenor practising his scales. Even with his limited knowledge of the game, Withers was aware that Altona City had one of only three English-speaking managers in the league, and he was thankful for that. The powers-that-be certainly wouldn't have wanted to pay out for a translator.

"Mr Preston, thank you for coming. You, too, of course, Mr Mason."

Mason shifted in his chair. "Your call sounded serious, sheriff."

"It is." Withers paused. "Maurice Sanders is dead."

Both men sat with their mouths open, clearly in shock. Withers knew instantly that this was news to them.

Mason gathered his thoughts the quickest. "What happened?"

"He was murdered. So now we have a missing player and a dead agent…"

Preston coughed nervously. "Er, it might be worse than that, sheriff."

Rafferty came to attention as Withers stared at the manager. "What do you mean, Mr Preston?"

The two football men exchanged glances, and Preston waited for his chairman to explain. Mason put his hands on the desk, as if that would offer him some kind of support. "We can't find Bryn," he announced simply, his voice trembling.

"Bryn Owen?"

"Yes. We've been looking for him since your visit, but…" His voice trailed away, lost in the desolation of it all.

Withers nodded. "Okay, Mr Mason. Let's start at the beginning. Tell me all about Bryn Owen and Jet Carmichael."

Preston took up the reins. "They were both in our youth system. Jet is about a year older, but they seemed to hit it off. Not surprising, really, I suppose, because they are both great players and they're not in competition for places. They became pretty inseparable… until Jet got his transfer."

"As we discussed yesterday," said Withers.

"Yes," confirmed Mason. "Bryn was happy to stay with us, for some reason. He could have gone on to greater things as well, if he'd set his mind to it. But something kept him with us."

"So, when was the last time you saw Bryn?" asked Withers, now making notes on the pad he had taken from his top drawer.

Preston thought about that one. "I don't know, getting on for a week, maybe." He shrugged in resignation.

"Do you not keep a check on your players, Mr Preston?" demanded Withers, amazed at the club's apparent complete lack of control. "After all, they are valuable assets, are they not?"

Preston shrank back a little. "Of course! But they are also young men, sheriff, and they need their space. Bryn has always been exemplary, and I expected him to turn up for training after a few days off. I just let it slip a little…" The last few words were so soft that nobody could hear them, but both Withers and Rafferty could see the pain in his eyes.

Withers eased back. "Okay, so you're saying Bryn may have disappeared at the same time as Jet?"

"It is possible," agreed Mason, his hand resting on the

arm of his manager for solace. "We don't know."

"He hasn't been his usual self," said Preston. "Not for a few weeks."

"In what way?" asked Rafferty.

Preston pondered. "I'm not sure. It was just a feeling I got. I tried to talk to him once, but he said he was fine. It wasn't affecting his game."

Withers sucked on his pen, his mind racing. "Could this be connected with Jet coming back to the club?"

"I never thought of that," admitted Mason, "but it's a possibility."

"They are close," Preston said. "If one of them was in trouble…"

"The other would watch his back," Withers finished. "As you do for a friend."

All nodded, and fell silent. Withers tapped his pen on his pad, the soft sound filling the otherwise silent room. Rafferty coughed, and a chair scraped, while the feeling of hopelessness came over them all.

Withers put down his pen. "What did they do in their free time? Clubbing, girls…?"

"Oh, nothing like that, sheriff!" exclaimed Preston, a thin smile on his face. "They aren't ones for the high life. They share a flat and keep pretty much to themselves."

"No adverse publicity, then," said Withers.

"None at all," agreed Preston. "They have been a joy."

Withers mused. "But something has changed."

"Yes," said Preston, looking first at his chairman, then at the lawman. "On that we *can* agree."

* * * * *

Ty stood in Grace's kitchen, waiting for the coffee to percolate. He was still amazed that she had even listened to him in the first place, let alone invite him to stay the night in her spare room. He hadn't mentioned Hector, afraid that the prospect might frighten her; and he assumed the Spaniard was still up on the Ridge, living rough and waiting for Ty's return.

The coffee was ready, so he poured some into a mug with a fox printed on it. He went to the table and sat down, caressing the mug thoughtfully. He knew that one of them would have to go to this solicitor in Thurlow, and he felt it should be Grace. She had proved a formidable woman, accepting him back into her life and helping him, even after everything that had gone before. He liked Grace Templeman, and he would see that no harm came to her.

The front door opened and Grace walked in, a shopping bag in one hand and her handbag in the other. "I thought I would treat you," she said with a motherly smile. "How do you fancy brunch?"

"Don't mind if I do, Grace," he said, returning a grin. "What are you offering?"

"Sausage, egg, bacon, hash browns, fried tomatoes. Is that enough?"

His grin turned to a chuckle. "More than enough! Thank you." The last two words were so sincere that Grace stopped in her tracks, looking at him. She didn't know what to say, so she rubbed her hand against his shoulder and began unpacking the bag and placing the food on the table. "Want any help?" he asked.

"No, it's fine."

She reached down into a drawer and came out with a frying pan. The sausages went under the grill and she poured oil into the pan. It all seemed so homely.

"So," she said, "what is the next part of your master plan?"

He sat there, looking at her. "You can drop out any time, Grace. I don't want you to feel obliged."

"I am obliged," she replied simply. "I'm obliged to Mr Figgis. I need to do what is right for him."

He nodded. "Me, too."

She put the bacon in with the sausages and the hash browns into the pan. "Well?"

He thought about it. "I want you to go see this solicitor."

Last night, Grace had told Ty about the relationship between Leroy Figgis and Reginald Green. They had been at university at the same time – not together, but crossing paths at certain campus gatherings and events, like debates and political discussions. They were both painted with the same conservative brush (with a lower case), and held high ideals and outlooks. To put it simply, they had just clicked. While Figgis blossomed into a banking magnate (due in part to his brilliant mind as well as to his father's legacy), Green had become a solicitor to the high and mighty, servicing politicians and pop stars with equal zeal. He made such a name for himself that he was able to open plush offices in three major cities, each operating under his strict rules. He kept in touch with Figgis, and they often met up for a bad round of golf or an evening at the opera. While Figgis had remained steadfastly bachelor, Green found the right woman and built up a family of three sons, all of whom were looking towards taking over one of the offices. Green then decided to take a back seat, so he moved with his wife Erin to Thurlow Junction, where he started his new company, Erin and Green, with a handful of trusted employees. That was when he handed the Mercurial Bank account over to number one son Neil; but he kept Leroy Figgis's personal account. "And that is why," Grace had finished, "everything belonging to Mr Figgis is in that office."

Grace returned to the cooker and checked the food, before putting halved tomatoes in the pan. "I should have known what you wanted me to do," she said.

"What other choice is there, Grace?" said Ty, shrugging. "This Green character must have Leroy's laptop."

"But how do I get it from him?"

"You ask for it," said Ty, as if it was the easiest thing in the world. "I take it you know Reginald Green."

"We have met, yes."

"Then it's easy. He knows you were Leroy's PA. We can try the same story again."

Grace grimaced. "Do I look like somebody who can write a book?"

"Hargreaves at the bank believed you. I have every faith, Grace."

"Really?" she said, pulling out the grill pan, with blackened sausages and shrivelled bacon throwing off smoke and a fierce burning smell. "More fool you!"

Then they laughed loudly and long.

* * * * *

Scotty's Diner had almost become their second home. It was the scene of their first date, and now it was the place where they could enjoy a five-minute break and share precious moments together. But there was more to it this time.

"So," Withers began immediately, "what can you tell me?"

Judith took a sip of her coffee and then removed her notepad from her bag. When she reached the right page, she smiled at Withers before beginning. "Bryn Owen is twenty-six, single, plays for Altona City." Withers knew better than to interrupt. "He has a sister, Morag, five years older, give or take a month. Parents both deceased." She gave an involuntary chuckle. "Sorry, John, I'm beginning to sound like you! Parents both dead in a plane crash twenty years ago. Bryn and his sister were brought up by an aunt and uncle in Thurlow. They are still in Bryn and Morag's lives, but on the periphery."

"It happens in families," observed Withers drily.

"Morag is close to her brother, I think. My sources tell me they meet often…"

Withers was amazed how much Judith could glean from her journalist contacts. She seemed better informed than he was!

"What does she do?" he asked.

Judith flipped a page on her pad. "Something in tele-sales. Mobile phones, I think."

"Okay," Withers said. "What about the relationship between the two players? I was told they were close."

"Very much so. I found a piece from the *Thurlow Echo* when they were teenagers. I quote, 'Both lads are inseparable now that they have signed deals with a big club, and their joy is obvious to all.' They even got a two-column picture."

She offered a photocopy to Withers, who saw two impressionable young boys holding a football between them, grinning at the camera. The world at their feet, literally, mused Withers. "So, what happened all those years ago for Jet to suddenly want to leave?"

Judith put away her notepad and caressed her coffee cup. "And what made him need to come back?"

Withers leant back in his chair. "But, more to the point, where are they both now?"

* * * * *

Rafferty didn't hear the gentlest of taps on the door, and was startled to see Deputy Keene swing in with a wide grin on his face.

Rafferty just stared for a moment. "What?" To be honest, he really couldn't care less, but he had to go through the motions, even if his manner was terse, to say the least. Well, he was only talking to a minion.

"That sweet wrapper, sir," grinned Keene even more.

"Yes?"

"We have a match."

Rafferty almost fell off his chair, before righting himself and adjusting his posture so at least he looked like a senior officer. "Ty Cobden?" he found himself asking, hardly believing the words had escaped his lips. This really was crazy.

Keene placed a sheet of paper on the desk. "Sadly, no, sir… but we have the next best thing."

"And that is?"

"The DNA matches the second man who was involved in the Leroy Figgis killings."

"I don't believe it!" Rafferty said, his face a picture of startled bewilderment. He'd only gone up to the Ridge to keep Keene quiet, and now here he was, the man who had found a major clue in an ongoing investigation. Man, this just made his day!

Chapter Seven

The flat was in a smart area of Thurlow, far enough away from the hustle of the small town, but close enough to the highway and all points east. It had taken an inordinate amount of time to get the search warrant, and Withers was silently fuming over the delay. He needed to be here yesterday, not sitting on his hands waiting for bureaucracy to take its due process. It was imperative that they moved at speed to find the two footballers and the killer of Mo Sanders, and it was a pity that officialdom did not share his motivation.

The building itself was constructed of stone, rather than brick, giving it a more intimate feel, and Withers was taken with it immediately, as he led Dawg, Rafferty and a couple of agents through the entrance into the lobby and over to the lift. That was on the small side, and five well-built men had difficulty cramming themselves in before the door closed. They ascended in silence, each trying not to move in case they touched something they shouldn't. After what seemed like an hour or more, they escaped through the open door onto the tenth floor and made their way to flat 10C.

Withers had secured a key, and now he turned it and stepped into the home belonging to Bryn Owen.

Donning their latex gloves at the threshold, the officers followed him in, each of them amazed at the opulence before them.

"Wow!" purred Dawg, eyes agog.

"Yes," said Withers drily. "How the other half live, eh?"

No expense had been spared in fitting out this wonderful home. Everything was of the highest standard, from the plush carpets to the Anna French wallpaper; from the state-of the-art sound system and television to the Giacometti-inspired statuary and other artistic items scattered around. The flat comprised a spacious lounge, a slightly smaller kitchen/diner, and two bedrooms, both en suite.

"Our boys have taste," noted Rafferty, whistling through his teeth.

Withers needed to be workmanlike. "Okay, Dawg, you take the left bedroom, and one of the guys can help you out." They obeyed immediately. "I'll take the other one, Pat. You can have a poke around here and in the kitchen."

Rafferty nodded, and got to work.

When Withers stepped into the bedroom, he knew at once that it belonged to Jet Carmichael. As well as a poster of Bob Marley, there was a framed collage of the young foot-baller taken from various matches, with the emphasis on his goal-scoring and him wheeling away with a wide grin on his face after executing yet another beautifully crafted score. Withers felt a cold shudder as he wondered where this gifted man might be.

The clothes in the built-in wardrobe bore designer labels that the lawman had never heard of, but he knew they were of the highest quality. Jet obviously liked old-style blazers of all colours, but with the chic cut of the fashionista. Silk shirts, too, were in plentiful supply, again representing all colours of the rainbow and tints and shades beyond. He must cut quite a figure when he goes out, Withers thought with some envy. Sadly, he himself was way too old to do any of this justice.

He was about to close the door when his eyes went to the row of shoes below the rack of shirts. Something had caught his attention, but he wasn't sure what it was. Getting down on his hands and knees, he pulled out each shoe, examining it and putting it to one side, matching the pairs as he did so. It was only when he lifted up one of Jet's black trainers that Withers realised what he had seen – it was a white business card, the corner of which had been poking out of the shoe, almost as if it had been deliberately hidden.

Withers studied the card and put it in the breast pocket of his shirt. Then he continued the search.

It was half an hour later when the group met again in the lounge. Dawg and his colleague had found nothing of interest; Rafferty had only a framed photograph to offer.

"Family?" asked Withers.

"Probably," said Rafferty. "Perhaps Bryn's sister. We can check it out."

"I found this," said Withers, offering up the business card. "It was hidden in the wardrobe."

"Hidden?"

"It looked that way."

"Why?" Rafferty was puzzled.

"Why indeed?" said Withers, slipping the card back into his pocket.

* * * * *

Ty had spent too much time at Grace's, he knew. It wasn't safe for either of them. But he had to get things down on paper. Leroy's codes and passwords.

He had decided, perhaps a little belatedly, that the length of his freedom was inversely proportional to the length of time he spent in the open, so it had become imperative that he pass on the details to Grace, in case anything happened to him.

She had sat transfixed, her eyes on her laptop as he pretended it was Leroy's and painstakingly went through the method of opening files, transferring huge pretend amounts and closing the accounts, while at the same time making copious notes which he hoped she would be able to understand.

She had halted him with a hand on his arm on a couple of occasions, asking pertinent questions, but generally Ty was impressed with her understanding of the procedures, and was quietly confident that, once she had Leroy's actual laptop, she would be able to manage the finances very well indeed.

"It all seems so simple," Grace said with a twinkle. "Money at my fingertips."

"Spend it wisely, Grace," Ty replied.

She looked up at him. "We haven't got it yet."

"We will. *You* will."

Grace closed the laptop with the sheets of paper inside. Then she stood and took Ty's hand. "I don't know why I trust you, Ty. But I'm glad that I do."

Ty gave her a warm smile. "So am I, Grace."

* * * * *

Back at the office, Withers sat at his desk, an extra strong mint helping him to chew over everything they had. Dawg stood in front of him, a sounding board for the sheriff.

"So, Dawg," Withers started, "Jet Carmichael left Altona City when he was fifteen."

"Yes, boss."

"Twelve years ago."

"Yes, boss." So far, so good.

"Why?"

Dawg gulped silently. "I don't know, boss. He did go to a better club…"

"Agreed," said Withers with a nod. "But surely Altona would have held onto him for a few more years? He'd have been worth a hell of a lot more then, wouldn't he?"

"Er, yes," said Dawg. "The club would have been able to see how well he was developing, even at that young age."

"Exactly!" Withers said, as if a knowledge of football clubs was ingrained in his psyche. "So we have to assume it was Jet's decision to move."

"You could be right, boss."

"And he must have been pretty insistent, too. Fifteen-year-olds don't usually get their way, do they?"

Dawg sighed. "I certainly didn't, boss."

"So, what we need is a list of those people who were at the club twelve years ago. It could be that one of them knows something."

"I'll get onto it straight away," said Dawg, turning on his heel.

"Good man. Meanwhile, I'm just popping out."

"Out, boss?"

"Yes," said Withers, rising, "I'm going to pay a call on the sister. She is expecting me."

* * * * *

Morag hated secrets. When she was seven, she had to pretend that her best friend Stacey wasn't responsible for tipping ink into the school aquarium to see if the fish changed colour. They didn't, but they didn't survive, either. Stacey was like that: not really destructive or spiteful, just enthusiastically inquisitive, a trait that Morag admired but did not possess herself. She was just plain old Morag, the accomplice.

Now, as she plumped up the cushions on her sofa for the third time in as many minutes, she had to hide the biggest secret of her life – and she still wasn't sure if she could handle it. She fussed around the vase of geraniums, manhandling the delicate blooms, and looked once more into the mirror above the television. She wasn't happy at what she could see. There were lines round her eyes, and her brow was furrowed with the worry of it all. Her cheeks were warm, a darker pink than usual, making the few freckles she had leap out at her. She grimaced and ran her hand through her hair. It felt so lank, unloved. Letting out a deep sigh, she went back to the cushions…

She was expecting it, but when the doorbell rang it still made her jump. She calmed herself as best she could and went to the door. With one last effort, she tried to control her nerves, and then turned the handle.

"Morag Owen?" enquired the tall man.

"Yes," she mumbled.

"I'm Sheriff John Withers, Bakerton police. This is Agent Rafferty…"

Morag gasped. "Agent?" She hadn't expected this.

"Purely unofficial, miss," Rafferty said, a smile on his face. He realised she was on edge, so a disarming Rafferty smile was definitely called for. He wasn't sure, though, if it had the desired effect.

"May we come in?" asked Withers.

"Yes, yes, of course." Morag had regained a little of her composure, and she ushered them into her lounge. She thought about the cushions, but decided they looked fine. The two men waited for her to sit in the armchair before they sat, almost in unison, on the sofa, each moving a cushion for comfort.

"Can I get you anything?" Morag offered, her mind still racing. On the telephone he had said it was unofficial, so why on earth would the sheriff bring a federal agent with him? Her secret became just that little bit more uncomfortable, and Withers could see something wasn't quite right.

"We're fine, thank you," he said, eyes firmly locked on hers. He could see the little spots of sweat forming over the bridge of her nose. "We're looking for your brother, Bryn."

"As you said on the phone, sheriff. But, as I explained to you, I haven't seen him for several weeks." She felt confident here, because that, at least, was the truth. "We don't keep in touch as often as we should." She paused, uncertain of how to proceed. She didn't want to over-complicate things.

"Yes," purred Withers with charm, "we appreciate that, but we are a little concerned…"

"Concerned?" Morag's mouth stayed open just a fraction.

"He appears to have gone missing."

Morag tried a short laugh, but it seemed to her to come out all wrong. "Ha, my brother often goes off on his own, sheriff." Again, she was speaking the truth, although she knew that this time everything was *so* different. She studied the lawmen and waited.

"Really?" said Rafferty. "In what way?"

Morag, losing the plot slightly, leant forward. "Sorry?"

"You said Bryn often goes off on his own. Can you give us an example?" said Withers.

"Well…" Morag stopped. Now was the time to begin to embellish the half-truths and downright lies, but did she have the confidence to pull it off? Her gaze went to the window, as if some answer might be found out there, but she knew she was on her own. It was now or never. "Well," she repeated, "he's always been a loner. He would often disappear for a day or two…"

"Did he have any special places?" asked Rafferty.

She could have told them about the old sidings down Thurlow Junction, where Bryn spent many hours with his boyhood friend Learie, but instead… "Nowhere in particular."

"And you have no idea where he might be now?" said Withers.

"No," she replied simply, and that really was the absolute truth.

"Thanks for your time, Miss Owen," Withers said, rising.

"Is that it?" Morag almost gasped.

"For now," Withers said, pressing his business card into

her extremely clammy hand. "If you hear from Bryn… or have anything else to tell us… just give me a call."

"Of course." Morag tried to keep her voice on an even keel. She was sure she failed miserably.

Withers and Rafferty made their farewells and stepped out into the crisp morning, the chilly wind lifting up a few fallen leaves from the silver birch in Morag's garden and the gravel path beneath their feet crunching as they made their way to the gate and their car beyond.

Rafferty was the first to speak. "Do we believe her, John?"

Withers shook his head. "She's hiding something, Pat. But what?"

"Only one way to find out."

Withers nodded and reached for his phone. "Dawg, drop everything. I've got a little job for you."

* * * * *

Hector had a dream. A recurring one. It involved an extremely well-endowed young lady by the name of Salome and… well, never mind. He had come across her photograph only a few weeks ago and had instantly fallen under her spell. But there was one problem: he had no idea who she was.

As well as his dream, Hector also had physical needs. He assumed it was because of his latino blood. Whatever the cause, being holed-out up on Copper Ridge did nothing for his over-active libido.

"*Senor* Ty," he sighed, "I need *coito*."

Ty looked at him with horror on his face. "Does that

mean what I think it means?"

"*Si*. Bang-bang. *Comprende?*"

Ty nodded. He had left Grace an hour ago, and now he and Hector were in a new hideout, safe from prying eyes for the time being. But it was getting harder as each day passed, and their close proximity to each other was taking its toll. Their tempers had been on short fuses for some time now, and it was clear that an explosion of some kind was imminent. It was only now that Ty realised what sort of explosion was on the cards.

"I'm not sure what I can do to help," he said weakly.

Hector was aghast. "No! No! I not need *your* help. I need…"

Ty held up his hand. "I know, Ector. I wasn't offering…"

Both men fell silent, embarrassed, before Hector offered a smile. "It is just that I dream of my Salome."

"I understand," said Ty, "but what can we do? You don't even know who she is. She's just a photograph."

Hector leered. "A very *big* photograph!"

They fell about then, laughing like schoolboys, slapping each other's backs and grinning inanely at each other.

Eventually, Hector said, "There is a bordello in Bakerton."

"How do you know that?" Ty spluttered.

"I listen. I hear men talk of such a thing. It is common."

Ty became serious. "So what are you saying, Ector? Don't tell me…"

"Oh, yes! I must attend. I must offer my services."

Ty didn't like to tell him that it was the women in such establishments who offered services, so he just sat back and looked at his companion.

Hector was much more animated now. "I will go and put the cock among the hens! I will feel relief and satisfaction. It will do me good, Ty. You could come," he added almost pleadingly.

Ty thought about it. Seriously. Then he said, "It's too dangerous, Ector. We could be spotted."

Hector was having none of it. "We will be in the bosom of a lovely lady. Who is going to see us? Ha! I will go alone." He stood, determined to have his way, literally.

"Okay," sighed Ty. "Do you know where it is?"

"Oh, yes, my friend. I have investigated. It is all in here," Hector said, tapping his head.

"If only it would stay there," Ty sighed in resignation.

* * * * *

The railway carriages looked eerie in the late-afternoon light, like some metal monoliths lined up for a giant's amusement. Their paintwork had faded, the rich burgundy of the original livery now appearing only sporadically through the rust and decayed wood panelling. The WR logo on the side of each one had all but disappeared, leaving only the outline of where it had been. All the windows had been smashed long ago, and as Dawg peered into one of the carriages, he saw that most of the seats had also been ripped out, by souvenir hunters or, more likely, vandals. The Western Rail company had abandoned the site at least forty years ago, and had done nothing with it, despite the urgent need of housing in Thurlow and the pleas of local councillors, who were always looking for a quick way into the public's good books and the chance of an even quicker buck.

Dawg winced at the damage. Like most people, he had a nostalgia for the train system, even though it had never operated in his lifetime. He read one or two of the words of wit scrawled on the walls of the carriage: somebody called Kilroy had been here; and, apparently, 'Ricky is as bent as a nine-bob note', whatever that meant. Dawg quickly moved on.

It had been a long afternoon. He had sat in his car at the end of Morag's road, waiting for movement. He had passed the time listening to the lunch-time show on the radio, where the host and his two guests discussed prostate cancer. Dawg had resisted the urge to feel himself. Instead, he had hummed along to the songs he knew, and ignored the rest. He had worked his way through a bag of jelly babies and wished he had bought some boiled sweets, because they last longer. He had settled back into his seat and his eyes had begun to droop, when Morag Owen had come out of her door. He had become immediately alert.

Now, he was trailing her through the disused sidings, keeping low and silent, his eyes on her every move. She knew where she was going, and her speed was sure and firm. He struggled to keep up with her.

Morag had no idea she was being followed. The thought had never occurred to her, although it should have done, because she was more worried now than she had ever been. The law was interested in her, and that was almost too much of a weight to bear. She raced on, desperate to end this.

Dawg had rounded a coal wagon that had been tipped

on its side, when the scream erupted. It was like nothing Dawg had ever heard before, and he stopped in his tracks. Without thinking, he drew his gun and walked forward, cautiously but at a gathering speed. The scream had morphed into a long, painful cry, and Dawg followed the sound.

He stopped when he saw Morag kneeling on the ground, something stretched out before her, her body wracked with sobs. He made his way to her side and knelt next to her, a comforting arm over her shoulder. They stayed like that for a minute, before Dawg slowly stood, took out his phone, and dialled.

"Boss, I've found Jet Carmichael."

* * * * *

Ty pulled the car to a halt two streets from the brothel. He'd had reservations ever since the subject first came up, but Hector had been very persuasive. Ty had only agreed on the condition that he would be in and out within the hour, as it were, when Ty would be waiting at this exact spot to make their getaway. Under no circumstances was Hector to talk to anybody, especially the girl, or give away any secrets that might compromise their position. Hector had thrown his arms in the air at that. "As if I would do anything to jeopardise our freedom!" he had said with feeling.

"Okay," said Ty, hands still on the wheel, "go and enjoy yourself. But be careful."

As Hector jumped out of the car, he gave Ty a cheesy grin. "I shall give her one for you, my friend. It is the least I can do."

Ty watched him almost dance down the street, but felt only foreboding as he wheeled the car round and started to drive back to the relative safety of their hideout. He wasn't to know that he would never see Hector again.

* * * * *

Chad Orwell was a thorough man. He had ensured that his forensic team covered every inch of the murder site, and now he stood beside Withers and Rafferty, a frown on his face. The District Medical Officer, a thin-faced man with a beautifully sculpted ginger beard and close-cropped hair to match, was talking.

"Cause of death is clearly strangulation. No other signs on the body that I can see. Somebody just choked him to death."

Withers grunted. "What did they use?"

"Oh," said the MO with a dry laugh, "just human strength, sheriff. Two very large and strong hands, that's all." He paused. "There is one thing that is puzzling me, though."

"Oh, yes," said Withers.

"There looks to be dried blood on his hands, and it's been smeared slightly across his forehead, as if he'd wiped it at some stage."

Withers understood the implication. "But you're saying that he has no injuries, doc. Therefore the blood must be someone else's. The killer's?"

"I'm afraid not, sheriff," the MO stated with complete conviction. "This is old blood. He had it on his hands days before he was killed."

Withers thanked him for the information, and turned to Chad. "Anything to add?"

The two had worked closely together on many cases in the two years since Withers had been made sheriff, none more so than the recent case of the General, and there was often a level of humour in their dealings. But not today.

"Nothing, I'm afraid, John. We picked up one or two fibres, probably from the killer's clothing, but I don't think they'll be much use. The perp wore gloves, so there are no fingerprints round the neck…"

Withers turned away, his mind trying to recreate the final moments of the talented footballer. He had burrowed into a good hiding place, but it had not saved him. Someone knew where he was, and it was obvious how they had found out. And it was also clear to Withers that the same monster had carried out both murders.

"The fact that Jet had not been tortured is significant," he said slowly. "They obviously didn't need to find out where Bryn Owen is, so that leaves two stark options. They've either got him already… or he's dead, too."

* * * * *

After dropping off Hector for his badly needed nookie, Ty drove around, trying to formulate his plan to get Leroy's laptop. Grace had worked wonders so far; in fact, she had gone way beyond anything that he could have expected, and his admiration grew. Leroy's millions would be in safe hands – if only they could get hold of them.

He parked up on Westdean Drive, a leafy little street a

stone's throw from the main thoroughfare, but far enough off the radar that he felt safe. After all, he only had half an hour to kill before his rendezvous with Casanova.

He took out the newspaper that Hector had bought earlier and scanned the front page. Nothing of interest there, so he opened it at random, stopping when he saw the name Judith Wiseman. Her column today concerned the slaying of a local sports agent, who had been strangled. He didn't bother reading it, but he lingered on her name. It was Judith he had written to after the demise of the General. Ty had made an impassioned plea that Leroy should be treated as the innocent party, despite the mention of drugs. Judith had published every word he wrote, which was unusual for a journalist, he assumed, and she had even added a few lines of her own about how image can be tarnished by lies and suppositions. Yes, here was another woman he could admire. How strange that, apart from Leroy, Ty could think of no man who even came close to the women in his orbit. Perhaps he was just exercising his feminine side.

A young lad strolled by, hoodie up and cigarette dangling from his mouth. He glanced through the window as he passed, oblivious to anything but the beat resounding through his head from the oversized headphones covering his purple Mohican. Definitely not someone to admire, chuckled Ty to himself. But, at the same time, he might just recall the strange man in the car if a passing policeman asked, so perhaps it was time to move on.

That thought was confirmed when he noticed out of the corner of his eye the twitch of a lace curtain in one of the houses. He folded the *Altona Oracle* and threw it onto the back seat, switched the ignition and pulled away from the kerb.

He might be a little early, but it was better for him to be premature rather than Hector.

* * * * *

Withers strode into the Incident Room and all eyes turned towards him. Some of them he knew, such as 'Magic' Newman, the computer geek from Bakerton, and Paula McFarlane, the civilian profiler who worked almost exclusively for the police. Others were complete strangers, drawn together by both Withers's immediate superior and Agent Rafferty, an eclectic mix of uniformed and plainclothes specialists who always came together at times such as this.

The 'Incident Room' was, in fact, the ground floor of an empty shop in central Thurlow, sequestrated through official channels purely to give the investigation a high-profile feel, considering the public clamour and media attention the death of a famous footballer would invariably attract. Here, the police were not only doing their job – they were *seen* to be doing it. Especially through the very large shop-front window.

The blinds had now been drawn, of course, but the general public could still see the constant influx of people, computers and documentation that crossed the threshold, and it was felt by the powers-that-be that this could only be a good thing. The run-of-the-mill coppers weren't so sure.

It had taken precisely an hour to access the premises and set up the tables, chairs and ancillary equipment needed to create a working control centre, so that it was up and running smoothly by the time the sheriff came back from scene-of-crime.

Withers nodded to the throng, who immediately returned to their tasks, seemingly doubling their efforts now that the boss was here. That wasn't really true at all, but Withers couldn't help the thought crossing his mind. He knew they all worked bloody hard all of the time, and that they would get him results, no matter how long it took.

He turned to Dawg, who was seated nearest the door. "Has anyone told his mother?"

"Yes, boss."

"Stupid question, but how is she?"

"Coping, just about. Debbie Perkins is acting as our Family Contact on this one. She's there now, and Maureen Pelham as well. They're going with Mrs Carmichael to identify the body."

Withers nodded approval. "Good." He looked around. "Is there a desk for me, Dawg?"

Dawg got to his feet and scurried ahead, leading Withers through the shop and into an office out the back. It reminded Withers of the first flat he had when he left home – a broom cupboard, almost. Someone had thoughtfully wheeled in a fold-away table which took up two-thirds of the space, and a pink plastic bucket chair was tucked under it. Hanging on the wall was a corkboard bearing the inscription 'Property of Bakerton Police Force' and pinned to it were photographs of Mo Sanders, Jet Carmichael and Bryn Owen, along with various assorted Post-it notes containing snippets which might be relevant to the case.

Withers thanked Dawg with a sarcastic aside, and pulled

out the chair, leaning on it and seeing the plastic buckle somewhat. He raised his eyebrows with disdain and sat down, the chair buckling a little more. He adjusted his buttocks, and the chair gave out a low, slightly rude groan, as if in protest. Withers stood. "Another chair, if you would, deputy!"

"Yes, boss," said Dawg, beating a hasty retreat, coming back only seconds later with an executive leather chair on castors and wheeling it almost reverently behind the table. Withers didn't dare ask where the chair had come from, but Dawg stepped back, at attention, as the sheriff performed a pantomime sit and wiggle.

"Ah, do you hear that, Dawg?" he said brightly.

"What, boss?"

"The sound of silence. My arse is satisfied. Thank you."

"My pleasure, boss," said Dawg with a straight face.

"I'm sure it is," agreed Withers. "Now, I believe you have a list for me."

Dawg produced a single sheet of paper from his pocket. "A short one, boss."

"Really?"

Dawg placed the sheet on the table and attempted to smooth it out. Withers brushed away his hands and pressed down on the paper, deliberately pushing out the creases with exaggerated strokes. "Carry on, Dawg."

"Yes, boss." Dawg gathered his thoughts. "When Mr Mason took over the club, there was a massive clear-out…"

"Of the deadwood."

"Er, yes, I suppose so, boss. Anyway, there are only three people left at the club from the old regime."

Withers studied the paper. "Michael Osborne…"

"Head groundsman now. Mr Mason promoted him two years ago."

"Mrs Jean Chivers…"

"Club Secretary. Been there since the year dot."

Withers made a short whistle which could have been a snort. "Ah, and our old friend Oscar Castle. What can you tell me about him?"

"As Mr Mason told us, Castle is the Academy Director – been in that position for the last six years."

"Before that?"

"He was one of three assistants. The club has since done away with the assistants, so Castle runs things on his own. He has overall charge of the youngsters."

"Does he, indeed?" muttered Withers. "Right," he said brightly, "after we have interviewed Morag Owen, we'll pay a little visit to Oscar Castle and the others."

* * * * *

As Ty settled his vehicle into a parking space at the pick-up point, he was surprised to see a police car race past, siren wailing, heading towards the street on which the brothel was situated. He thought nothing of it, although he did duck down as the car went by. No point in inviting trouble, he told himself.

He was thinking of having another look at the news-paper when a second police cruiser flashed by, blaring for all it was worth so that people realised they were on an import-ant mission.

Ty sighed and let his mind wander. Hector would be

along soon, and they could get back to their hideaway, and to the relative safety it offered. But it wasn't working. He had always been inquisitive, and it was almost too much of a coincidence that two police cars were heading in the general direction of where his accomplice might still be ensconced between the thighs of a buxom and lithe beauty who was giving her all for the cause. Something was telling Ty he should investigate.

He climbed out of the car, locked it with the fob and began walking down the narrow path, stepping into the road and back again as he negotiated his way past a mum with a three-wheeler pram. He didn't like those at all. Give him the old Silver Cross any day.

As he crossed the road and headed west, he saw a large crowd had gathered, and his heart rate quickened.

He stopped next to a thickset man who was craning his neck to look beyond the immediate throng. Ty could see his neck muscles straining to gain a better view.

"What's going on?" Ty asked with as much innocence as he could muster.

"Not sure," replied the man, annoyed that his concentration had been invaded. "Lots of coppers, though."

Ty tried to push through the crowd, but met much passive resistance. So, instead, he turned on to a side road and made his way to the far end of the brothel street, where, again, he met a knot of people. This time, though, he managed to move through them, until he almost had a view of proceedings.

"Damn, can't see a thing!" he blurted to himself, but loud enough for the woman in front to turn and give him a running commentary.

"There's a madman loose!" she said with feeling. "He's waving a gun in the air!"

Ty was stunned. Of all the times for Hector to go exercising his pecker, some maniac had to be running amok. "Good God!" he said with such feeling that the woman recoiled.

"A bloody foreigner, too!" she spat. "What is the world coming to?"

A very large penny dropped in Ty's mind, so much so that he swayed as he turned away, intent on getting back to his car and away. What the hell had Hector done now? It was a question that did not have an answer that Ty could reasonably formulate. As always, Hector was once again the bane of his life.

And it had become abundantly clear that, from now on, Ty was on his own.

* * * * *

The private hospital room was a haven of peace for Morag. When she had woken from her drug-induced sleep, she had been comforted by the fact that an armed policeman stood outside the door, and now she sat up in the bed, looking first at the sheriff, who sat on a chair a few feet away, and then at the beautiful woman who was perched on the bed beside her, holding her hand.

"Morag, this is my friend Judith, Judith Wiseman," Withers introduced them. "I thought it might be easier for you to talk to her, rather than just me."

Morag gave him a watery smile. "I need to tell you everything, don't I?"

Judith squeezed her hand. "Yes," she said. "We need to find…"

"Jet's killer," Morag finished for her. "I understand."

"In your own time, Morag," said Judith gently.

Morag cleared her throat and looked directly at Judith. "Mo Sanders phoned me. He said he was worried about Jet. He said he'd been strange for a while, but wouldn't talk about it. Mo thought I might be able to get to the bottom of it. Then Jet suddenly disappeared."

"How did you know Jet would make for the sidings?" asked Withers, drawing a scornful look from Judith. He just couldn't help himself from taking charge.

"We used to play down there when we were kids. It wasn't very safe… the carriages were a bit unstable… but kids don't care about things like that, do they?"

Judith smiled and nodded. She'd had her fair share of scrapes living on the wild side as a pre-teen.

"So you found Jet," said Withers. This time, Judith let it go.

"Not at first. I was scared for him, but I knew that if he was able to, that's where he'd go." Morag hesitated, feeling the nausea welling up inside again. "He was there on the second day. God, he looked a mess!"

"It's okay," soothed Judith, stroking Morag's hand. "We can take a rest, if you want."

"No. Thank you, but you need… *I* need to finish this." Morag sighed heavily and leant back on the pillow, gathering her thoughts. "He was exhausted, but he wouldn't go to the police. He begged me to keep quiet and look after him where he was. He was too frightened to come out. What could I do?"

Judith looked into her beseeching eyes. "This is not your

fault, Morag. You did what you could for him."

"Yes," said Morag, rallying a little, "I did. I took food to him and looked after him… as best I could." The tears were welling now as the memories played with her mind. "If only I had called you…" Her eyes were fixed on Withers, who squirmed in his seat. He hated being so close to death, especially when he, like Morag, could have done nothing to prevent it.

Judith broke the silence. "What did Jet tell you, Morag?"

"What?" She was miles away now, reliving the events and rearranging them in her mind so that one day she might possibly be able to come to terms with everything that had happened.

"How did he get to the sidings?" persisted Judith, her tone calm and measured. She was not a journalist now, just a concerned onlooker seeking the truth.

"He said they had been taken from Bryn's flat by two men with guns. There was no point in arguing with them." Morag paused. "The funny thing was, he said that these guys were very polite. They weren't at all threatening…"

"Apart from the guns, you mean," observed Withers with heavy sarcasm.

Morag locked eyes with him. "Yes, apart from the guns."

"Did Jet recognise these men?" Judith asked.

"No. He had no idea. They were black, but that was all he said."

"Did they say anything?" asked Withers.

"Nothing. Jet didn't have a clue what was going on."

"Okay," said Withers gently. Judith tilted her head to indicate that Morag should continue.

"Jet said they were in the cellar of this big house some-where – he knew it was in Thurlow, because when he escaped it wasn't long before he knew where he was…"

"Heading for the sidings," Withers clarified.

"Yes, but he'd been disorientated, so he wasn't sure of the direction he had started from."

"How did Jet escape?" Judith wanted to know.

"They overpowered the guard when he brought them some food, and they ran."

"Both of them?"

She nodded. "They were together, he said, until they got outside." She paused, her eyes wide and moist. "That was when…" Her voice tailed off, leaving Judith and Withers hanging.

"When… what?" asked Judith, squeezing Morag's hand a little tighter.

"When Bryn was shot."

Judith's gasp filled the ensuing silence, and Withers moved to sit on the end of the bed. Now he understood the blood on Jet's hands: it belonged to his best friend. He must have been in mental agony.

"How did he get shot?" he asked.

It was several seconds before Morag could arrange the words in her head, let alone force them out of her mouth. "They had got out of the cellar and through the front door. Jet said that was when Bryn was hit. He was sure Bryn wasn't badly hurt, but there was a lot of blood." Her voice broke and trailed off, her body shaking with the telling of her horrific story. She looked beseechingly at Withers. "They shot my brother."

Withers could find no suitable reply, so he shook his head gently and looked at Judith, who pulled Morag to her and offered her a comforting embrace. Morag eventually looked up, her face pale and wet from the tears. "I begged Jet to go to the police… but he said no. It was too dangerous. People might get hurt, he said."

"Family members," Withers whispered through gritted teeth.

"Yes, I think that's what he meant. He was worried about his mother especially."

Judith said, "Forgive me, Morag, but did Jet know what happened to Bryn?"

Morag steeled herself and sat upright. "He said that Bryn had fallen when he was shot and he helped him up. Then they ran. He assumed Bryn was behind him, but…"

"He wasn't," added Withers, understanding. "I think he knew he was going to be caught, especially as he had been wounded, so he deliberately went in the opposite direction. He gave Jet a fighting chance." There was no way of knowing if this was what really happened, but Withers hoped it might lessen the load for Morag.

She brightened slightly. "Do you really think so?"

"Your brother is a very brave man, Morag," said Withers simply, and he caught the thin smile playing around her lips. She needed all the help she could get, especially as it was clear to Withers that Morag had told Mo where Jet was, and that had led directly to the agent's and the footballer's deaths. Something which he hoped she would not realise too soon.

Now was the time for that question Withers had been

desperate to ask. "Jet mentioned a house. Did he say any more about it?"

"No, sorry," Morag said. "But it must be in Thurlow, mustn't it? Jet said so."

"I'm sure that's right," said Withers. "The only problem is the number of houses in the town. Most of the old ones have cellars or basements. We need something else to go on." He thought for a while. He didn't know how hard he should push this vulnerable young woman, but eventually he leaned forward. He had been formulating his theory from the moment Morag had mentioned the cellar and from the obvious closeness of the two footballers. Men who could share a dark secret, perhaps one which was strong enough for one of them to return to his old club if his friend called. Something from the past, when they first met as young, budding players…

"Morag, I'm going to ask you a very difficult question now, but you have to be absolutely honest with me. Okay?"

"Okay."

Withers paused, gauging the moment. He hated it, but he knew he had to ask the question. "Did Bryn or Jet ever say anything about being molested or abused as youngsters?"

Judith almost fell off the bed. Morag opened her mouth, but nothing came out.

* * * * *

Rafferty was feeling resentful again. There was Withers, swanning off left and right, trying to solve a couple of complex murders, while he was put in charge of a very run-down police station and a muffin of a deputy.

"Keene!" he screamed.

His door opened. "Yes, sir?"

"Is the prisoner ready?"

"Yes, sir."

"Solicitor present?"

"Yes, sir."

"Then let me vent my spleen on somebody else for a change."

Keene was extremely thankful for that thought as he followed Rafferty to the bowels of the old police station, down chipped concrete steps and badly whitewashed walls. It was like going into a labyrinth in a Greek tragedy.

They stopped at a solid door and looked through the small window. The room was remarkably well presented, considering, and was furnished with a new table and a set of four chairs. A security camera was screwed to the wall, the pictures of which were relayed to a small office up on the ground floor, where criminals could be watched for tell-tale twitches of guilt. A policeman stood in the corner, watching over a middle-aged woman in a tweed suit and a swarthy man who was lolling in his chair, nonchalantly whistling to himself. Rafferty would soon change that.

He noisily opened the door and went in. "Hector Lopez?"

"*Si*," Hector replied, not moving, not caring.

Rafferty sat opposite him as Keene closed the door. "My name is Rafferty, and this is Deputy Keene. You are?" he asked, looking at the woman.

"Prudence Fairchild," she replied in a clipped, professional tone, "duty solicitor."

"Lovely," Rafferty mumbled, as he laid out the paperwork he had carried down. "Now, Mr Lopez, you have been detained for causing an affray outside of…" – he scanned his documents – "the Starlight Club, and brandishing an offensive weapon, that being a hand gun."

"*Si.*"

"Would you care to tell me, in your own expansive way, what exactly happened?"

"*Si,*" Hector said, looking to Prudence for guidance. She offered him nothing. "It was Salome's fault. She would not come with me."

"Salome?" The name pulled a trigger in Rafferty's mind. "You tried to abduct a woman named Salome."

"No! No! I just wanted her."

Rafferty winced. "Isn't that the idea of this particular club?"

"No! No!" Hector exclaimed again. "I had to take her away from such a life."

"Using a gun?" Rafferty said sarcastically. "Tell me more, Mr Lopez."

Hector wanted nothing more than to open up about his affection for the lovely Salome. "Such a wonderful lady. She was in my dreams, but little did I know that she would be there, in that terrible place."

"The place you frequented, you mean?" Rafferty couldn't and wouldn't hide his contempt.

"I once saw her in a photograph, you see, and I fell from a great height. She is *hermosa.*"

"Her… what?"

"Beautiful, *senor*. A special one." Hector kissed the tips of his fingers and waved them in the air, as if sending a personal message to Salome herself.

"So, you're saying this, er, lady worked at the club?"

"*Si.*"

"And you first saw her in a photograph?"

"*Si.*"

"In that case, we're going to need a DNA swab, Mr Lopez," Rafferty said with a satisfied smile. He, too, had seen Salome in the photograph, back when he was investigating the killing of Leroy Figgis. Then, they had lifted DNA from the glass where a certain killer had taken delight in kissing Salome's nipple every night before going to bed. Now Rafferty knew that he had got that elusive second man wanted in connection with the killing – the man who had dropped the sweet wrapper. It had all been such a fluke, but wasn't that what police work was all about? Rafferty leant forward with a smug grin. "So, Mr Lopez, tell me what you know about Ty Cobden."

Hector froze, speechless.

Chapter Eight

Withers had dropped Judith off at the car park so she could get her car. They had driven in silence from the hospital, both too stunned to say anything. She had given him a peck on the cheek and raced off, bewildered. Withers himself had gone to the incident room, and now sat at his table, chewing over what Morag had eventually told him.

Dawg knocked on the door and came in. "You wanted to see me, boss."

"Yes, Dawg. Come in."

Withers had asked for the pink plastic chair to be placed on the other side of the table, and the deputy sat down gingerly and waited. He knew better than to pre-empt any conversation the two of them might have.

"I had a theory, Dawg…"

"Yes, boss?"

"And it would appear to have borne fruit. When Bryn Owen and Jet Carmichael were younger, one or both of them suffered abuse."

"Really?" asked Dawg. "How do you know?"

"To be honest, I don't *know*. It was just something that Morag Owen told me… and it fits in with the chain of events. She said that both Bryn and Learie… sorry, Jet, seemed to change about twelve years ago. Jet was around fifteen then, Bryn a year younger, and both were talented members of the Altona City boys' team. Morag couldn't get anything out of them at the time, but her suspicions then were much like mine are now. She's five years older than Bryn, so she was of an age to notice subtle or not so subtle changes in their attitudes. She approached the club, but they brushed her off."

"No proof?" said Dawg.

"Exactly. But no goodwill, either. They wouldn't even discuss it with her. The boys, of course, clammed up entirely."

"I'm not surprised," said Dawg. "The club could have made it very difficult for them."

"It's no wonder Jet got away at the first opportunity. Yes, it was a dream move, as you've said, Dawg, but it must also have been a breath of fresh air."

"But he came back," said Dawg. "Why would he come back?"

"Because," said Withers with feeling, "I believe it is happening to somebody else."

"What makes you say that?"

"Bryn had stayed at the club, an indication that it was Jet who had been abused."

"Yes," agreed Dawg.

"So what if Bryn had learnt that a young player now was being abused? What would he do?"

"Talk to his best friend about it."

"Exactly! And that is why Jet demanded a move back to Altona. He needed to be back at the club to stop the abuse from escalating. He knew what was involved, and he knew he had to stop it."

Dawg hesitated. "But this is just supposition, boss. We have no proof."

"No, we don't. But that's never stopped us in the past! We must dig deeper."

* * * * *

Grace couldn't believe the change that had come over Ty. He had pulled up to the house with screeching tyres and had raced up her path, almost battering down the door. His eyes were wide and his breath was hoarse as he slammed the door behind him and scurried into the lounge.

She followed him in, nervously rubbing her hands down her skirt. Was this the anger that he had shown the moment before he killed?

"What is it, Ty?" she asked.

He gathered his wits. "We haven't much time, Grace. We need to get this done."

"Why?" she asked, bewildered. "Whatever has happened?"

He plonked himself into the armchair and wiped a hand across his brow. He hadn't realised how much he was sweating. "You don't need to know all the details…"

She leant over him, gripping both arms of the chair and giving him a steely stare. "Yes, I do," she said through tight lips. "From now on, you tell me everything. Do you understand?"

Ty was beaten. Grace knew it, and so did he. He told her all about his first meeting with Hector, and how they had kept on the run together, moving from place to place, evading capture; and then the latest instalment, when it appeared that Hector had gone off the rails once too often and was brandishing a gun in the middle of the street. The one thing he didn't tell her was Hector's role in the murder of Leroy Figgis. That would have been a step too far.

"So what was he doing there?" she asked when he had finished. "And with a gun, too!"

He wasn't sure he should mention the reason for Hector's trip out. "I think he was just going to get some food for us," he lied. "But I honestly didn't know he had a gun."

"Did he shoot anybody?"

"I don't think so, Grace. The crowd seemed to be enjoying the spectacle, so I guess it was all pretty harmless." Ty realised how stupid that sounded, but there was an element of logic in it. If a gunman was running rampant through the centre of Bakerton it wouldn't attract an audience; rather, they would be scampering in all directions, intent on self-preservation.

Grace relaxed a little. "I assume," she said pointedly, "you expect him to spill the beans about you."

Ty shrugged. "I really don't know, Grace. But it's a distinct possibility. That's why we need to set Operation Leroy in motion immediately."

"Operation Leroy?" she asked, bemused.

"Well," he grinned, "I couldn't think of anything more James Bond-like to call it!"

Chapter Nine

The building looked out of place, nestling as it did in a small complex of six modern, brick-built offices in a cul-de-sac off the main street of Thurlow. The one that Withers and Rafferty stood in front of was actually a whitewashed structure with black *faux*-wooden timbers, trying for all it could to look like an Elizabethan building from the sixteenth century. A swinging sign, rather reminiscent of one hanging over an old tavern, proclaimed the occupancy of Erin and Green, Solicitors. A large quill sat behind the wording, emphasising, if that was needed, the historical aspect of the whole façade.

Withers and Rafferty exchanged a look, and entered, a small bell above the door announcing their arrival.

Inside was a world of difference. Although the plush carpet carried on the quill theme, the rest of the reception area was as modern as any office, with two sofas and a glass-topped coffee table to one side and a light-wood desk, extravagantly curved to add gravitas, directly in front of them.

A middle-aged woman, as poised as the surroundings and with a beautifully cut bob, knocking at least ten years off her age, smiled at them. "Good morning. How may I help you, gentlemen?" She had already taken stock of Withers's uniform, and thoughts were racing through her mind.

Reaching the desk, Withers took the business card from his breast pocket and put it down. "We would like to speak to someone, please."

The company had made a policy of using only generic cards, so there was no indication as to whom they might want to see. The receptionist smiled her warmest effort. "Of course. May I ask what it might be about?"

"Learie Carmichael," said Withers.

"Oh, we cannot discuss our clients, sheriff."

Withers could show patience when needed. "I appreciate that, Miss…?"

"Mrs Rawlings."

"Mrs Rawlings, right. Perhaps I could speak with one of your partners. This is an official enquiry."

He now had her undivided attention. "Of course. Yes. Mr Carmichael, you say? That would be Mr Marsland, then."

"Marsland?" echoed Withers. "Not Eric Marsland?"

"Why, yes. You know him?"

"I do," was all he could say, recalling the teetering idiot at Phil Lenier's wake.

"Please, take a seat. I will see if Mr Marsland is available."

"Thank you." Withers smiled at her, but she recognised a fiery warning within his eyes. Mr Marsland *will* see them, no matter what excuse he may try to invent.

Withers perched on the edge of one of the sofas, eyeing Rafferty, who was furtively ogling the receptionist.

"An attractive woman," Withers said, with a grin.

"What?" Rafferty stuttered. "I hadn't noticed."

"Of course not!"

"Anyway," reasoned Rafferty, feeling the warm flush

across his face, "she's obviously a married woman."

"Possibly." Withers waited. "But no wedding ring."

"Really?"

"Divorced, I would guess." Withers paused again, wallowing in the unease which his companion was feeling. "What do you think, Pat?"

"I wouldn't know…"

The conversation was brought to a close by the arrival down the spiral staircase of an extremely sober and professional Eric Marsland. Dressed in a made-to-measure pinstripe suit, white shirt and burgundy tie, he looked every inch the solicitor, his manner at once dominating and authoritative. His brogue shoes seemed to bask in the sunlight coming through the large window at the front of the office.

"Gentlemen, how can I… Ah, I believe you look familiar… sheriff."

"Indeed, Mr Marsland," said Withers, rising. "We met at the funeral of my colleague."

Marsland wilted visibly. "Of course," he said, his voice cracking. "I must offer you my sincere apologies, sir. My demeanour was far from…"

"Please, Mr Marsland, may we talk with you?" urged Withers, trying to put the man at ease.

"But of course. Please, follow me."

They went beyond the spiral staircase and into a large conference room, its opulence more apparent than that in the outer vestibule. This was a place of power. Marsland offered them seats one side of the oak table, while he sat on the other side, his face now drawn with embarrassment. "Again, I am so sorry…," he began to apologise.

"Please, Mr Marsland, we have urgent business," said Withers.

Marsland gathered himself and sat upright, once again the perfect solicitor. "Of course, sheriff. Now, how can I help?"

Withers's face was a mask. "We have some extremely bad news, Mr Marsland."

"You do?" asked the solicitor, his face suddenly ashen, his eyes wide. "Good God, it's not Maureen…?"

"No, no, she is fine, as far as we are aware."

"Oh, thank the Lord. I'd be lost without her."

Withers once again wondered at the strange relationship between them. Marsland was so obviously besotted, and yet she was… what was the word? Aloof? Unapproachable? Withers thanked his lucky stars that he had a straightforward bond with Judith. He chose his words. "I'm afraid that Learie Carmichael is dead."

Marsland sat back, shocked. "How? What happened?"

"He was murdered." Withers paused while the information sank in. He thought that Marsland's pickled brain might not be working at normal speed. "We found your business card in his room. I assume he was your client."

Far from falling apart, Marsland remained the consummate professional. "He was, yes. I had the pleasure of representing him from the moment he was elevated to the first team at Melrose. He's a Thurlow lad, you know." Marsland suddenly remembered that Jet was no longer with them. "He *was* a fine young man, sheriff. I am shocked."

"Mr Marsland, did Learie have any special instructions for you?"

Marsland frowned. "Why should you ask that?"

"Because I think that he had hidden your card, as if he thought somebody might go through his things."

"But you found it." Marsland paused, wary of overstepping the mark. "Surely he couldn't have hidden it that well."

"Fair point," agreed Withers. "But I think he wanted *us* to find it. Anybody else searching his room might have been looking for something larger, like photographs, for example."

"Photographs?"

"The point is, they wouldn't have been looking for a business card."

Marsland nodded. "Yes, I understand. Well, as it happens, about a week ago, Mr Carmichael dropped an envelope through our letterbox with a note for me."

"A note?" said Withers.

"It was an A4 envelope. When I opened it, there was the letter for me and another envelope, addressed to… the police."

"And you didn't think to pass it on!" exclaimed Rafferty, his face like thunder.

Marsland was not intimidated. "Mr Carmichael's instructions were specific, sir. I was to hold on to the envelope until he told me otherwise. As I say, he was very specific."

"We understand, Mr Marsland. Did you try to contact him?"

"I did, sheriff. I spoke with him briefly on the telephone the same day the letter came in. He emphasised his instructions once more."

"Did he sound all right?" asked Withers. "Was he worried, did he come over as frightened?"

"No, sheriff. He sounded as normal as usual. I asked him about the contents of the envelope for the police, of course, but he wouldn't say anything. He just reiterated his instructions. I placed the envelope in our safe and that was the end of the matter."

"May we have it, Mr Marsland?" asked Withers.

"Of course. Our obligations are sadly now at an end, I am afraid." He picked up his phone. "Mrs Rawlings, could you please go to the safe and bring up item LC469. Yes, that's right, 469. Thank you."

Withers noticed that Rafferty's breathing had quickened at the mention of the receptionist, and he smiled at the agent. Rafferty shrugged, as if he didn't have a clue what Withers was implying. They waited.

A gentle knock on the door heralded the entrance of the delightful Mrs Rawlings. Now that Rafferty could see all of her, rather than the above-waist picture in his mind of her seated at her desk, he was even more impressed. She certainly looked good for her age, dressed in a grey pencil-skirt and white blouse, the top two buttons unused, as if signifying something to Rafferty. He smiled at her as she entered, and she returned the gesture, making the agent even more uncomfortable.

"Thank you, Mrs Rawlings," said Marsland.

"Yes, thank you," said Rafferty, the smile a permanent fixture on his face.

"My pleasure," she told him, and he read so much into her words that he felt even hotter. He fought to bring himself under control, watching her as she left.

Marsland was speaking. "Although we no longer have

any legal responsibility over this, I would like to offer my services in any way that you may feel is required, sheriff. I liked Learie." His voice tailed off, sadness in his eyes.

"Thank you for your co-operation," Withers said, taking the offered envelope. "I shall certainly bear your offer in mind." He rose, forcing Rafferty to do the same, and made his way to the door. "Once again, Mr Marsland, thank you. We will take it from here."

Rafferty could only nod his agreement as they left the offices of Erin and Green.

He couldn't believe his eyes! There, emerging from the building, was Sheriff John Withers, striding away with another man, deep in conversation, oblivious to the two of them sitting in Grace's car.

Ty put his hand on her arm. "Not yet," he whispered.

Grace nodded. "Yes, Ty, I see him. I'm not as stupid as I look."

"I'm sorry," Ty mumbled. "I've been with Hector too long."

"What do you think the lovely sheriff wants with our solicitor friends?" Grace asked.

Ty shook his head. "I've no idea. Surely he hasn't got wind of our plan?"

Grace sniggered. "Of course not! Now, sit back and wait here for me – and please don't do anything silly."

She didn't know what had come over her. Here she was, talking to a wanted man as if she was the godmother. It scared her, but it sure as hell excited her, too. With a new-found vigour, she got out of the car, looked sharply at Ty, making him cower in his seat, and then she stepped smartly away, confidently closing the door and walking briskly into the offices of Erin and Green.

Mrs Rawlings offered her usual smile. "May I help you, madam?"

Grace equalled and surpassed her smile. "I wonder, would it be possible to see Mr Green? I was a friend of Leroy Figgis at the Mercurial Bank in Bakerton."

Grace had obviously said the magic words, as she saw Mrs Rawlings visibly succumb to her superior aura.

"I'm so sorry, madam, but neither Mr nor Mrs Green are in today. Could I ask the senior manager to speak with you?"

"I was hoping to see Reginald again, but never mind. Yes, I will speak to your manager. Thank you."

Mrs Rawlings picked up the internal telephone. "May I ask who is…?"

"Grace Templeman. I wish to discuss Mr Figgis's personal account."

Mrs Rawlings waited for the phone to be answered, then relayed what Grace had said. She put down the receiver, and almost immediately Eric Marsland came down the stairs, offering a hand to Grace.

"Ms Templeman, please come into our conference room," he said, directing her into the room that Withers and Rafferty had recently vacated. As it was, Marsland had only just got back to his office when the call came through and he had to turn around and retrace his steps.

Grace felt her knees tremble, but she was determined to see this through. Marsland indicated for her to sit, and before she could open her mouth, he said, "Mr Hargreaves at the bank has been in touch. You're in the process of writing a biography of Leroy Figgis, I believe."

Grace was dumbfounded. "Er, yes, that's the idea…"

"Capital! I so admire people who can write. I'm sure you will do a wonderful job."

"Er…," Grace stuttered.

"You think Mr Figgis's laptop might offer up some tantalising nuggets," he continued enthusiastically.

"Er, I hope so."

"No problem," purred Marsland, reaching behind the table and pulling up a laptop in a deep purple case. "I was expecting you, so I took this out of storage."

Grace stared at the case, not sure what to say or do next. Was it really going to be this simple? "Er…"

Marsland misunderstood her reaction. "I appreciate this might be a little disconcerting for you, Ms Templeman. I'm assuming you were close to Mr Figgis. An emotional moment, I'm sure."

"Yes, indeed," agreed Grace, desperately wanting to grab the laptop and race out to the safety of her car, but realising that she needed to be more circumspect. "Dear Leroy," she said with feeling. "I believe this will help me get to the heart of the man."

Marsland nodded. "Good. I'm glad. Although Mr Hargreaves did express his doubts that it would be of any help. The bank went through it very carefully before they sent it to us. Security, you understand." He looked at her with a wink. "Perhaps you have some hidden passwords that the bank doesn't know about."

Grace nervously shared his laugh. "I couldn't possibly comment," she said with a waspish smile.

"Of course not!" Marsland handed her the laptop, which she gripped tightly as she started to rise. "If you don't mind, Ms Templeman."

Grace froze in mid-movement. "Sorry?"

Marsland waved a piece of paper. "Perhaps you'd be kind enough to sign this receipt. We must keep the records straight, as you will appreciate."

As Grace hurried to her car, she was still amazed how she had managed to scribble her signature with such a shaking hand. She fell into the car, the laptop clutched close to her body, and she let out a deep sigh of relief and excitement.

Ty grinned at her. "You did it, Grace!"

"Yes, I did, didn't I?" she replied, still breathless. "Drive, Ty. I think I need a strong cup of tea!"

* * * * *

"Do you think I should phone her?" Rafferty's voice was almost pleading.

They were at the old railway station, long ago renovated and turned into a small parade of two classy antique and arty shops and a stylish, upmarket coffee house. Rafferty was pondering over a skinny latte, all style and no substance.

"I think," replied Withers, putting down his cup, "you should concentrate on the matter at hand."

"She did smile at me, though, didn't she?"

Withers looked up from his cappuccino and winced. "How old are you, Pat?"

"Yes, I know!" Rafferty conceded. "I'm not a teenager any more."

"Far from it!" Withers whispered under his breath. "Now, can we get on with the important subject?" he said aloud.

Rafferty reluctantly came away from his daydream and picked up the single sheet of paper Withers had taken from the envelope given to him by Eric Marsland. "So, we have a name."

"A rather obvious one, to be honest," said Withers. He read the brief note once again. "*It seems to be happening again. Talk to Oscar Castle.* Hm. I wonder."

Rafferty looked at him. "What?"

"He says 'Talk to Oscar Castle'. Not, 'Arrest the bastard', or 'Castle's the one'. There's no sense of guilt attributed here. He wants us to just *talk* to Castle."

"I see what you mean, John. But Castle must know something. He's involved somewhere along the line."

Withers drained his cup. "I agree. And there's only one way to find out."

* * * * *

Tea had never tasted so good, as Grace sank into the armchair, cradling the cup and still experiencing the high she thought a master criminal must feel at the conclusion of a big job. She looked across at Ty. "Thanks for making this, Ty. My hands are still shaking, so I don't think I would have been able."

"It's the least I can do, Grace. You were *magnificent*." The last word came out with such feeling that Grace felt more goosebumps on her already goosebumped body. She hoped this feeling of elation would never leave her.

"I've never felt like this before," she said. "It's scary."

Ty laughed. "Yes, it does give you a buzz, doesn't it? Doing something that is not quite illegal, but feels like it."

Grace became serious. "This is a heavy burden, Ty. I'm not sure I'm up to it."

Ty was at her side immediately. "Nonsense, Grace. You were born for this. Now," he said, as he pulled over the coffee table and took the laptop from its case, "let's boot this up and start changing the world, shall we?"

* * * * *

The first-team players were just going through the motions. News of the death of Jet Carmichael had been swiftly relayed to them, and they were in shock at the dreadful loss of one of their own.

Will Preston stood on the edge of the training ground, watching, his face ashen, his lips tight. Oscar Castle stood beside him, hands in pockets, the collar of his raincoat pulled up against the strong wind that was howling across the field.

"I can't bloody believe it," Castle muttered. "Not Jet."

Preston nodded. He was in no mood to talk. He leaned to one side and lifted his right leg, running it through with an air-kick, mimicking the player doing exactly the same thing on the pitch. It was a nervous reaction, something he did often when he was watching his team. Or perhaps he was just reliving his playing days, when he had turned out for East Chawton Rangers in the fourth division. That was the height of his playing career, because an injury cut it short at the age of twenty-six, and he turned to coaching and then management. Life had been a little more successful in this strata of the game.

"Good shot, Baz!" he shouted, his words lost in the swirling wind, as if that, too, was mourning the passing of Jet Carmichael.

"What happened, exactly?" Castle's words broke in.

"What?"

"To Jet. How did he…?"

Preston sighed. "I don't know, Oscar. Mr Mason didn't say. Just that he's dead."

Both men seemed to freeze at that last word, as if it was so final; which, of course, it was. They stood there in silence.

Gerry Asquith, first-team coach, had gathered the players together for man-to-man training, but he could see their hearts weren't in it, so he called it a day and sent them back to the dressing room. It was all too much.

Preston and Castle turned to go back into the warmth of the office, only to be confronted by the sheriff of Bakerton. They stopped in their tracks, but Withers was only interested in one man. "Mr Castle."

"Sheriff?"

"I need a word."

Castle was surprised, but stepped into line beside Withers as he made his way indoors. Preston stopped and looked on, wondering.

When Castle entered his office, he threw off his raincoat, hung it on a hook on the door and sat at the desk. "Yes, sheriff, what can I do for you? My time is precious."

Withers ignored him and pulled up a chair, sitting on it and staring at the football man. "I want to talk about Jet Carmichael."

"Yes," said Castle, waiting.

"When he was a youth player."

"Oh." Castle had not expected this. "In what way, sheriff?"

"When he was abused, Mr Castle."

Castle's face drained of any colour the wind outside had given it, and fell back into his chair. "How did you find out?"

"Jet himself."

"I don't understand."

Withers took out the note left by Jet and handed it to Castle, who read it and then wiped his eyes.

"It happened then… and it's happening now," Withers said, his jaw set and his nostrils flaring.

Castle suddenly realised what the lawman was implying. "What, you think it's me? Bloody hell, man, you're way off the mark." He jumped out of his seat, his face burning red with the anger welling up inside him.

Withers ignored it. "Mr Mason said himself that you are very close to your boys."

Castle spluttered. "Not like that! Shit, man, it's nothing like that! I love those boys, yes, but not…" He stopped, the words failing to come through. He sank back into his seat, defeated. "It's not like that…"

"Tell me about Jet."

Castle knew he had no choice. "It was about twelve years ago now. Jet came to me and said that someone was…"

"Who?"

"He didn't say. Too scared, I guess." Castle composed himself. "It was someone in the club, but it wasn't me."

Withers was inclined to believe him. "So, what did you do?"

"What do you think? I reported it."

"To whom?"

"Why, the chairman, of course."

"Mr Mason?"

"No, no! This was before Barry's time. It was the previous chairman. Arusi Akintola."

Withers had heard the name before. "The African businessman?"

"Yes," confirmed Castle. "One of the richest men on that continent, apparently. He held a major share in this club for five years before he sold up. I believe he then made a bid for the South African club Maritzburg Rangers. Not sure how he got on, but we never saw him again. He didn't even come back for any of our matches."

"Is that so?" Withers's mind was racing. "Tell me, Mr Castle, do you have any African or black players in your youth team at the moment?"

Castle didn't hesitate. He knew everything about his young squad. "Jojo Kone. His family came from Cameroon, but he was born here. And Jacob Dimka, who's Senegalese. Are they in danger, sheriff?"

"Quite possibly, Mr Castle."

* * * * *

The paperwork Rafferty's men had brought together was impressive. Withers sat at the desk in his office, leafing through the pages and tutting loudly every now and then. Rafferty stood at the window, as was his wont, waiting patiently.

Finally, Withers looked up. "Sounds like a piece of work, this Arusi Akintola."

"My thoughts exactly," agreed Rafferty. "Not the sort of person I'd want running my club."

"Mm. I hate to think what sort of club you'd be in, Pat!" Withers smiled.

"What was it Groucho Marx said? 'I don't want to belong to any club which would accept me as a member.' Sounds right!"

There was a knock on the door and Dawg leaned in. "They've arrived, boss. They're in the interview rooms."

"Thanks, Dawg," Withers replied. "With adult supervision?"

"Their parents."

Withers rose. "What about Dr Clarke?"

"He's been here a while. He's been watching every move."

"Good."

Withers had been seeing Dr Oliver Clarke for very nearly four years now, almost from the day he arrived in Bakerton. The death of his wife still lay heavy on him, and his odd chats with the psychiatrist had worked wonders, enabling him to get through the dark moments of his bereavement. Withers found the doctor a necessary sounding-board and a welcome ally against the melancholia which had at one time threatened to engulf him completely. Recently, as well as talking about Heather, his soul-mate who had been stabbed to death, Withers had also found it possible to talk with Clarke about Judith, his new love. Although Withers struggled at times, he was slowly unravelling the inner workings of his mind — and his heart.

When Withers and Dawg entered the first interview room, the sheriff gave a barely noticeable nod to the one-way mirror on the back wall. Oliver Clarke was out of view, watching and listening.

"Mr and Mrs Kone, thank you for coming. And you must be Jojo. I'm hearing good things about you from Mr Castle."

The boy was embarrassed and looked at his parents, not knowing what to say. His mother nudged him, and he replied softly, "Thank you."

Withers sat down opposite him and smiled. "Now, you're not in any trouble, Jojo. I just need some help, and you might be just the person. Would that be okay?"

"I guess so," the thirteen-year-old said, still not sure of his surroundings. Withers had, of course, briefed the boy's parents, but had asked them not to say anything. He needed the boy to respond naturally, without prompting.

"Are you comfortable? Would you like a drink? My deputy can rustle up a Coke, if you'd like."

Jojo pulled a face. "I'm not allowed. I'm in training."

"Of course. Sorry." Withers took a notepad and pen from the drawer in the table and prepared to make notes. It wasn't necessary, because the parents had agreed that the interview be recorded. They realised the seriousness of the investigation, even if they were scared that their son might be a victim of an outrage. Withers saw them hold hands, the father tense and protective. He would kill if someone was molesting his son.

"Right then, Jojo. Can you tell me when you joined the football club?"

The boy wriggled uncomfortably. He was nervous. "Dad signed the papers," he said softly.

"It was two years ago, sheriff," the father said. "Mr Castle was very keen to sign him."

"Thank you, Mr Kone," said Withers, scribbling something on the pad. He looked at the lad, who was nervously scraping a fingernail across the edge of the table. "So, Jojo, who else talks to you at the club?"

Jojo looked at his father and back at the sheriff. "Jacob…"

"Your friend, Jacob Dimka."

"Yes."

"Which adults?" Withers had to be sure not to prompt the boy. "Apart from Mr Castle."

Again, Jojo glanced at his father and back. "Mrs Chivers…"

"I know she is the club secretary," said Withers. "Who else?"

"Would it be better if we answered, sheriff?" asked Mrs Kone, fidgeting in her seat and fretting over her only son.

"I'm afraid not, Mrs Kone. We need the evidence to come directly from Jojo. So…" Withers leant forward and offered the youngster a conspiratorial smile. "Just between us."

"I talk to Bryn Owen. He's always checking that I'm okay. I like him." Jojo grinned. "He's a great player, too."

"So I hear," said Withers, waiting for more names.

"Jet spoke to me a few times, as well. Isn't it fantastic that he's back at the club?"

The room fell silent. Nobody had thought to tell the boy about Jet Carmichael, and Withers knew that now wasn't the time. "Any of the other first-team players?"

"Naw, they aren't very friendly. I have to clean the boots of Chas Killick, but he just grunts at me."

"Yes," agreed Withers, "I've got superiors like that."

Mr Kone smiled knowingly. "You should try working where I do!"

Withers now knew he had to tread very carefully indeed. "Tell me, Jojo, what do you and Jacob talk about?"

"Football." The boy made the announcement as if it had been the most stupid question anybody had ever asked him.

"Yes," said Withers, nodding. "Of course. But what else? Music? Girls? School?"

"Yeah, all of that," Jojo said, although he became a little sheepish. "Not so much girls, though. They're no good at football."

Withers knew it wasn't politically correct to agree, so he moved on. "Anything else?"

Jojo looked at his parents, who sat upright, holding their breaths. They knew what the sheriff was trying to prise out of their son, and they were petrified. "Is there anything else, J?" asked his father, his voice faltering. "You can tell us."

"I don't understand, Dad. What do you want me to say? We talk, that's all. Or we play games on our iphones. That's all," Jojo repeated.

Withers sat back. "It's all right, Jojo. I think we're done here. Thank you for coming down. Deputy Janowski will give you a tour round the station, if you'd like."

Moments after the Kones had left with Dawg, Dr Clarke came in. Withers couldn't fathom his expression. "Well, doc, what do you think?"

Clarke sat at the table on the seat young Jojo had occupied, and thought through his answer. "I'd say, on a probability scale, that he is not the target. The only time he became uneasy was when you mentioned girls. A natural reaction for someone his age. He responded well to your questions, and he never once flinched or showed signs of distress. I believe, as far as I am able, that he is safe, John."

"Amen to that!" said Withers with a heavy sigh. He paused, before continuing. "Look, doc, I know it's not protocol, and you have every right to tell me to go to hell, but…"

"You want me to interview Jacob Dimka."

"Well…," began Withers, choosing his words carefully, "it does make sense, even though it is not strictly by the book. I can okay it with his parents first. I'd be mighty grateful. You can study every aspect of his demeanour… much better than I could."

"Flattery, John, will get you everywhere."

"I hope so, doc. Because, if my hunch is right, then Jacob Dimka has got to be our latest victim."

* * * * *

Her fingers hovered over the keypad. "Are you sure about this, Ty?"

"Relax, Grace. Just type in the password."

She did as she was told, and was greeted with a display of numbers and symbols which meant nothing. She looked up at Ty and frowned.

"Good," he said soothingly. "Now type in this group of numbers." He pointed to a row of numerals he had previously written down on a piece of paper.

"This one?" she asked, still unsure that they were going to get away with it.

Ty nodded. "It's okay. Trust me."

She did. Tapping in the numbers, the screen erupted into another set of figures, but this time she could see that they were obviously bank accounts and sort codes. "How on earth did the bank miss all this?" she said incredulously.

"Don't forget, Grace, this was Leroy's *personal* computer. The bank had no reason to suspect there would be anything on it which might endanger them. And they were right. None of this has anything to do with the bank. You are merely about to re-disperse Leroy's private wealth."

Grace looked at the first column of figures. "Is this Leroy's account?"

Ty was once again impressed with her grasp of things. "Yes. Now click on the first line," he instructed.

The screen offered her a choice. "What now?"

"The first box. Type in the sort code for the good cause you have chosen. Then, in the second box, the account number. It couldn't be simpler."

She obeyed, and when a third box appeared on the screen, she knew what to do. She typed in two hundred – because this was only a small test run – and was about to press return when Ty's big hand covered hers.

"Wait, Grace."

She looked up at him. Had all this been a ruse? Had he set her up? "What is it, Ty?" she asked, her eyes pleading.

He grinned at her. "I just need to warn you… Leroy installed a little sideshow." He took his hand away and let her continue.

As the transaction took place there was the sound of a mini explosion and loud brass-band music playing, causing Grace to rock on her chair with excitement and pleasure. "Oh, Mr Figgis, you clever man. How spectacular!"

"There," said Ty, "your first charitable payment has taken place, completely anonymous. No one will ever be able to trace it back to you – or Leroy."

"Wonderful!" gushed Grace, completely overwhelmed by the whole experience.

"So, who was the first recipient of your generosity, then?" Ty asked.

Grace turned to look at him, her face suddenly serious. "The Police Benevolent Society."

Ty stood still. He understood. "You're trying to tell me something, aren't you?" When she nodded, he said, "It's time to hand myself in."

"I'm sorry," Grace said, knowing the words weren't really enough, "but yes, it is."

Ty embraced her for a long time and then made for the door, with Grace calling after him, "Leroy would have been very proud of you, Lucas."

As he stepped outside, he knew it was true… and that was the only thing that kept him going.

* * * * *

"Okay, Dawg, what have we got?"

Withers was once again chained to his desk by paperwork. He preferred the intimacy of his office to the goldfish-bowl atmosphere of the Incident Room; and he knew that if anything did develop over there, he was only a few miles away. He had a large espresso coffee in one hand and an even larger sausage bap in the other. It was lunch-time, and he had pushed the file on Arusi Akintola to the far extremity of the desk; not quite out of sight for the moment, but certainly out of mind. He had been looking at the new framed photograph on his desk, this one of Judith with him by the lake, the sun cascading over her auburn hair and onto her face. So beautiful!

Dawg had broken the spell by knocking and entering in the same second, a pile of papers in one hand. Now he was sitting opposite the sheriff; always a daunting prospect for him, as he still held his boss in awe and felt uncomfortable sitting at the same level. He coughed nervously. "Well, boss, you asked for details of Jean Chivers and Michael Osborne."

"I did."

"Jean Chivers…"

"The club secretary."

"Yes," said Dawg, annoyed that the sheriff always interrupted his flow. "She's on and off, really…"

Withers furrowed his brow. "Meaning?"

"She only works three days a week. Tuesday to Thursday."

"Okay."

"She's sixty-four. Widowed. Her husband died of a heart attack twenty years ago. He was quite a few years older. Her other interests are gardening and writing. She's had several short stories published."

Withers shook his head. "Just the facts, Dawg, not a bloody biography of the woman!"

"Sorry, boss." Dawg felt that he always seemed to be apologising, but it was just another burden he had to carry for working with the brilliant sheriff. Fortunately, the good considerably outweighed the bad.

"Next!"

"Michael Osborne. Forty-eight. As I said, he's the head groundsman. Started at the club as an apprentice. Apparently, he got on well with Jet."

"Did he now?" murmured Withers. "Married?"

"No, boss. Separated twelve years ago."

"Mm, twelve years, you say."

"Yes, boss."

Withers rubbed his stubble thoughtfully. "Neither of these characters are black, I assume."

"No, boss."

"Interesting." There was a long pause as Withers chewed over all he had been told. Finally, he slapped his hand on the desk as he rose, and said, "Right, let's pay a visit to Michael Osborne. He can tell us why his wife left him twelve years ago."

* * * * *

There was a spring in Rafferty's step, despite the fluttering in his stomach. He hadn't felt like this for at least fifteen years, not since a certain Miriam crossed his path with a wiggle and the alluring fragrance of Gucci Rush, with its hints of peach and vanilla. Heady stuff indeed. He knew that there was no reason he should be here – not officially, anyway – but he just couldn't help himself.

It was all her fault, of course. Mrs Ursula Rawlings. He had carried out a bit of detective work by checking the website of Erin and Green, Solicitors, and her pen portrait had been very illuminating. It didn't mention anything about divorce, naturally, but neither did it say that she enjoyed potholing with her husband, or anything else for that matter.

"She has two daughters, both in their twenties and now away from the nest. Ursula [what a lovely name, he thought dreamily!] likes the theatre and sings in a choir, as well as going to pub quizzes." Perfect!

Rafferty had been standing outside for almost twenty minutes, trying to be as nonchalant as possible while he attempted to peer through the frosted glass. He was having no luck. All he managed was to attract the icy stare of a lady who emerged from the building carrying a briefcase and who clicked her high heels almost in contempt as she went past him and headed for a rather smart Jaguar parked on yellow lines further down the road.

Rafferty felt the chill of her scorn wash over him, but manfully brushed it off. He was on a mission.

As he opened the door, Agent Rafferty felt more vulnerable than he ever had during his auspicious career. This was something else entirely.

He approached the desk, legs feeling sluggish, heart pumping. He saw immediately that Ursula was not in her place. That was taken by someone who, while attractive, was considerably younger and clearly was not his Ursula.

"Can I help you?" said the young lady.

Rafferty stumbled over his words. "I assume Mrs Rawlings is out the back. May I see her, please?"

The girl's smile was warm. "I'm terribly sorry, sir, but she's not in today."

Poor old Rafferty fled the building, defeated.

$$* \quad * \quad * \quad * \quad *$$

Withers and Dawg had only a short trip to see Michael Osborne. He lived in Nettlefield, the next village beyond Thurlow, and a couple of miles closer to the city of Altona. A short commute for the groundsman.

He lived in a mid-terraced red-brick house with a front door that opened directly onto the path, which gave the impression that here was an extremely small property. This was proved to be deceptive when Osborne welcomed them into a spacious lounge/diner with a kitchen off, and a clear view of a good-sized and stunning garden, as was to be expected of a man in the trade. The French doors were open, allowing a gentle breeze to envelop the room.

He looked good for his forty-eight years, thought Withers. He was slim, clean-shaven, with close-cropped hair and animated features. Life had been good to him, despite (or perhaps because of) losing his wife.

"Please, take a seat," said Osborne, and Withers was taken by how relaxed he appeared.

"Thank you," said Withers, sitting on the sofa, Dawg dropping himself down beside the sheriff with a thump. Withers gave him a look.

"Now," said Osborne pleasantly, coming to rest in one of the armchairs, "how can I help you, sheriff?"

"Thank you for seeing us, Mr Osborne. We are investigating the death of Jet Carmichael."

"So sad," said Osborne with feeling. "He was a great lad."

"So I hear," said Withers. "Did you have much to do with him?"

"In the early days, yes. Jet was just a child then, of course. He would talk to everyone. His talent didn't give him airs and graces. He would sit on my ride-on mower and we'd chat for a while about football. I knew he had ambition, and we both knew he was going places. It was a shock when he came back to the club, although I didn't see much of him. He was a star by then, so no fraternising with the workers." Osborne stopped. "Oh, don't get me wrong. Jet hadn't changed; it was just club policy, I suppose. They had helped to put him in orbit, and they wanted to keep him up there."

"Actually, we are more concerned with his early career. We're talking to everyone who was at Altona City when Mr Akintola was chairman," began Withers, but he stopped, shocked at the look on Osborne's face. The man had gone quite pale, and was drawing in his breath, so that his cheeks appeared hollow and gaunt. He looked as if he might crumble completely. "Are you all right, Mr Osborne?" Withers asked, concerned.

"Akintola!" Osborne spat, the spittle dripping from his mouth. "I'd hoped never to hear that name again."

Dawg leant forward in case the other man slid off his chair. "Would you like a drink, Mr Osborne?"

"What? No, I'm fine. It's just…"

Withers took his time. "I'm sorry, sir, if this upsets you, but we are investigating Jet's murder – and possibly another very serious crime. What can you tell me about Akintola?"

Osborne gathered himself. "It was a long time ago…"

"Twelve years," prompted Withers gently.

"Yes. Dawn and I… that was my wife," he explained, the sadness heavy in his voice. "We were happy until Akintola and his son got close."

"His son?"

"Name of Dume. Strange man."

"How old was this Dume?" asked Withers, intrigued.

"I don't know, maybe twenty-three, twenty-five. Good looking, too."

"In what way was he strange?" said Dawg.

"It's difficult to put into words, really. He was just… weird. His father doted on him. Told me once that the name Dume means bull, and his son lived up to it, he said. I didn't ask!"

Withers nodded. "So what was the father like?"

"He was a slimy bastard!" Osborne said with venom. "Came sniffing round my wife. He was pretty near old enough to be her father; but he was smooth, I'll say that for him. I couldn't say anything because he paid my wages, but I could see her being turned. I was sick to the stomach." Osborne stood and paced the room, the resentment and anger welling up inside. He went to a framed picture and picked it up, staring at it. When he turned back, Withers could see it was a photograph of a couple on their wedding day. "I've kept this, but God knows why," he said, tears rolling down his face. "Dawn walked out on me. She went to him, but he dropped her almost immediately… and disappeared. It was only later that I found out he'd run off back to Africa. Good riddance, too!" he finished, the breath expelled from his body as he sank back into the chair.

Dawg and Withers sat in silence, surveying this broken man. Finally, Withers said, "Do you have any idea why he went back to Africa?"

Osborne stared at him. "I don't give a damn, sheriff. He went – and Dawn never came back to me."

Chapter Ten

Don't you just hate it when one of your best-laid theories hits the skids? You're merrily rolling along, piecing it all together with that oh-so-smug look on your face – and then it all goes pear-shaped. Withers felt like that now, as he digested what Doc Clarke had just told him.

They were in the interview room, after Withers had been summoned so that the good doctor could outline his findings following his chat with young Jacob Dimka.

Withers looked lost. "You mean…"

Oliver Clarke sat at the table, putting his notes into his holdall. He would type them up later. "I mean, John, that – as far as I can reasonably assess – Jacob Dimka is not, nor ever has been, the victim of abuse, either physical or emotional. He is a bright young man who has been raised in a stable and loving environment. There is nothing in his attitude or his mannerisms that would indicate any kind of molestation."

Withers had been standing by the closed door, just waiting for confirmation that he could go out and arrest Arusi or Dume Akintola – or both. Instead, he slid into the seat beside Clarke, his mouth set, his mind racing. "I don't understand, doc?"

Clarke had finished filling his bag, so he turned all his attention towards the sheriff. "I'm sorry, John. Your theory looks dead in the water."

Withers rubbed a weary hand over his face. "I was so sure…"

"You need to rethink this," offered Clarke, clear in his mind that there was nothing he could do. He stood, ready to leave, until Withers grabbed his arm and jerked him back down again.

"Hold on, doc. Can you give me a minute?" He looked beseechingly at the medical man. "I need to pass something by you."

"Fine," said Clarke. "Fire away."

Withers took a while to start. "Okay. I believe that either Arusi or Dume Akintola abused Jet Carmichael as a boy."

"You have no proof, I assume, but carry on," said Clarke, amusing him.

"Jet confided in his friend, Bryn Owen. They told Oscar Castle, the youth team director, who went to the football club hierarchy; but no one wanted to know, of course, because the abuser was the chairman or his son." He paused, the cogs whirring. "But then the Akintolas left the country in great haste…"

"Right," said Clarke.

"But it doesn't fit, doc. Arusi had just started an affair with the wife of one of the ground staff. Why would he leave?"

"Perhaps the husband threatened him?" offered Clarke.

"I think not. He is a very weak man. Yes, he was angry – still is – but not violent." Withers remembered Osborne's tears. "I think Arusi panicked when Oscar came to see him."

Clarke was immediately onto his wavelength. "He needed to get his son out," he said flatly.

"You're damn right he did – because Dume was the abuser."

Clarke looked blank, and waited.

"And they've got to be connected with the deaths of Mo Sanders and Jet, and quite possibly Bryn as well. So that leaves only one question. What are they up to?"

* * * * *

The two men stood facing each other, the scowls on their faces as dark as their skin. They were in the penthouse suite of the Altona Nightingale: the most luxurious set of rooms in the flagship hotel of the group, owned by a consortium comprising African and Chinese companies, one of which belonged to Arusi Akintola, in a round-about, tax-dodging way.

The son was dressed in a three-piece Savile Row suit, while the father wore just a bathrobe.

As Dume had entered, he had passed a slender, heavily made-up woman of tender years, her skin smooth and pale. She had eyed him knowingly, offering him a wink and a seductive smile. She didn't have a clue who he was, but he bore a slight resemblance to the old man who had just bedded her, his wrinkled fingers playing over her body and his soft voice offering her the world in return for her favours. She had met men like him many times before, but somehow this one seemed more sincere. She had actually enjoyed the encounter, and she thought this younger version might give her a little more of what she craved, and with a lot more verve. Dume ignored her.

Now, as they both stood in the bedroom, he studied his father, and didn't like what he saw. He felt he was a dinosaur, a relic of an almost colonial time, a yes-man to Europeans who had swamped his country, destroying its culture and its very breath. His father had worked for the invaders, cow-towing to their every demand; but at least Arusi had moved up, eventually securing the first of his small companies, before expanding at such a pace that he had earned the nickname 'Whirlwind'. Dume had a grudging respect for his father, as well as a deep loathing that tended to overshadow the love that was buried deep inside him. He looked round the room. "I suppose," he sneered, "you're going to say, 'One day, my son, all this will be yours'."

Arusi didn't answer. He, too, had hatred in his eyes. He remembered when this son of his was born: the delight and overwhelming excitement of that day had remained with him for the first twenty-five years – until it was washed away with the knowledge of what he had done, and what he was truly capable of. If he hadn't been so hardened over the years, Arusi might well be shedding a tear for the offspring he had lost.

Finally, Arusi said, "Why are you here, Dume?"

Dume stepped closer, his breath heavy on Arusi's face. "I want you out of here, father." The last word was spat out with such spite that Arusi retreated a pace, gripping the teak desk and holding back his anger, but only just.

"I am here for only one reason, Dume… to stop you."

The son laughed long and loudly, the sound reverberating through the suite like the wind of a hurricane, growing in intensity, about to explode into such a destructive force that it would annihilate all before it. "You came to stop me? And yet your first thought is still to fuck white women young enough to be your daughters. Have you no shame?"

Arusi ignored the barbed words. "I knew you had come here, Dume. My people have ways of finding things out. But I don't understand why. There is nothing here for you."

Dume pulled out the dainty chair from the vanity table and perched on it back to front, leaning his arms across the chair's back. It was an incongruous sight. "Sit down, father," he demanded. "We need to talk."

Arusi sat on the edge of the bed. "Have we anything to talk about?" he asked softly, almost with resignation.

Dume grinned wickedly. "What I meant to say was that I will talk… you will listen. And obey." He paused, allowing his words to penetrate. "I came back here for one reason. When I have fulfilled that, I will go home. I will go home to take over your businesses. You, father, will 'retire'. Do I make myself clear?"

"What are you intending?" asked Arusi.

"It is something you should have done years ago. I am just settling a score. For the family honour."

"Ha, you have no honour!" screamed Arusi, getting off the bed and pushing Dume's chair. The younger man was taken by surprise, fell forward and ended up sprawled on the floor. When he got back up, his face was murderous, his eyes like slits of hatred.

"You will regret that, old man," he promised through clenched lips.

Arusi took the offensive, moving forward and leaning into his son's space, crowding and flustering him. "You killed

Jet, didn't you? And what about the other boy? Is he also dead? Tell me, Dume, what other evil have you done?"

After a second, Dume gave a brittle laugh. "Whatever I have done, you cannot disown me. It is your job to protect me. You are my… *father*."

"Yes, I am," Arusi sighed. "I protected you then. I got you out of the country, out of harm's way. Even after what you did, I still believed in you. I thought you would change…"

"Change?" boomed Dume, grabbing his father round the throat with two big, powerful hands. "I am what you made me, father. Just remember that. I am my father's son!" He released his grip, so Arusi staggered back against the desk and fell into the chair, emotionally exhausted.

"Yes," he sighed with regret, "I created you, but the evil within you is entirely of your making. I will not let you touch any other innocent children."

The blow from Dume was swift, and Arusi slid across the bed and onto the floor, dazed and bloodied, his lip split.

"You will not stop me, father," Dume sneered down at his prostrate father. "I promise you that."

Chapter Eleven

Although he was only ever temporary, Pat Rafferty had been a great asset, not least because he had saved Withers from the mad General. Now he was plying the sheriff with information, gathered by his agents both at home and overseas. Withers was getting the full dossier on Arusi and Dume Akintola, and it made interesting reading.

Withers was at his desk, pawing at the sheets of paper before him, while Rafferty was giving a running commentary.

"Arusi came back into the country two weeks ago. His private jet was cleared into Delcine International, so he is legit. Not so sure about his son, as there is no record of him arriving."

Withers looked up. "Really?"

"There are quite a few ways an illegal can get into the country, John, or hadn't you thought of that?" Rafferty grinned. "Or perhaps he's not here at all."

"Oh, he's here," said Withers. "Believe me."

"In the short time I've had the pleasure of knowing you, I have to say that you have usually been proved right."

Withers eyed him with a twinkle. "So, it's been a pleasure, has it, Pat? I am honoured."

"That's enough!" laughed Rafferty. "I don't want it to go

to your head. I'm an agent, you're only a lowly sheriff. Just remember your station in life!"

They shared a rare moment of silent friendship, before they got back to business. Rafferty continued, "Arusi is holed up in the penthouse at the Nightingale in Altona."

"Swanky!" purred Withers, a touch of envy in his voice.

"I suppose he has every right. One of his five companies, AAMedia, has a two percent stake in the hotel chain. Cost him twenty million, apparently."

"AAMedia, you say?"

"That's the company he used to secure shares in the football club. He also has fingers in clubs across Africa and, of all places, Ecuador."

"I was told he tried to get in at Maritzburg Rangers in South Africa," said Withers, remembering something about football for probably the first time in his life.

"That was a fiasco, John," said Rafferty, pulling a piece of paper from under the pile on the desk. "They sent him away with a flea in his ear and egg on his face."

"The mind boggles," beamed Withers. "What happened?"

Rafferty studied the piece of paper in his hand, a press release from Maritzburg Rangers. "Ah, here we are. It says: 'Following the approach by Mr Akintola's company, AAMedia, to become a stakeholder in this club, the government of South Africa has advised us that Mr Akintola is not considered a suitable person to be allowed to conduct business within this country. It is therefore with regret that we have informed Mr Akintola that his approach has been rejected.' So, he is not welcome."

"There must be a reason, Pat."

"Oh, yes," said Rafferty, pulling out another sheet. "AkinTin *versus* The State. Another of Akintola's companies was involved in a fraud case a few years back. It was something to do with exporting tin from their South African mine through a central African conglomerate, and trying to avoid huge tax bills while picking up profitable government grants. Akintola wasn't cited personally, but the government took the unusual step of banning him from ever operating in the country. He went to court over his attempt to buy into the football club, claiming that it had nothing to do with his tin-mining venture. The court threw the case out."

"Good for them!" said Withers. "But it just means he comes back here."

"You can't expect to win them all, John."

Withers opened a drawer, took out an extra strong mint and leant back in his chair, sucking thoughtfully. Rafferty waited.

"So," said Withers eventually, "let's get back to the present. Arusi tried his luck in South Africa, without success; but why did he come back here? There was no way he was going to get back into Altona City; and no other club would entertain him."

"Apart from the hotel chain, he has only a small portfolio of companies here. Certainly nothing big enough to keep him occupied for any length of time," said Rafferty.

"Agreed. So he returned for some other reason. And that brings me back to Dume, his son."

"Go on," said Rafferty, his interest roused.

"Dume is here somewhere. I know it! Arusi came over to *stop* his son."

"Yes," agreed Rafferty excitedly. Then he stopped. "But if he hasn't started over with another black youngster at the club, what the bloody hell is he here for?"

"A good question, Pat, and one his father might be able to answer. So let's pay a visit to the Nightingale. I don't get to see many penthouses."

* * * * *

Surveillance. It sounds such an exciting word, cloaked in mystique and suspense, the world of espionage and spies, the Cold War and political shenanigans. Mr Sumo's mind was running riot – but it was only to ward off the boredom.

He was sitting in the back of a Ford of some kind. He wasn't good at car names, but he thought it might be a Focus. The seat was sumptuous, but then it needed to be to accommodate his frame. The windows were tinted, so he could look out, but nobody could see him, unless they pressed their nose against the glass, which is something the average person wouldn't do on a regular basis. He took a large bite of his sandwich, drawing a loud tut from his associate.

Arnie sat in the driver's seat. He was big and black (how come most black men are tall, Mr Sumo thought in passing), and he was dressed in a dark blue polo, pale blue slacks and dark blue boat shoes. A study in blue. He turned to Mr Sumo and gurned. "What the hell, Rich? You know the boss doesn't approve."

Mr Sumo allowed Arnie to use his birth name – but only on sufferance. Arnie was his air-inverted-commas superior, so Mr Sumo let it go. He shrugged his massive shoulders and took another bite. With his mouth oozing mayonnaise, he said, "Come on, Arnie, give us a break. We've been here for hours. I'm starving."

Arnie was athlete-slim, his biceps rippling under the short sleeves of his shirt. His face, too, was lean, his features pronounced. A young Sidney Poitier, perhaps? "Okay, but you clean up the mess," he said with a wave of a large hand.

"What mess?" demanded Mr Sumo. "I'm eating the lot!" He beamed at Arnie with twinkling eyes. Despite their difference in the pecking order, he liked Arnie. It also made him feel like he was in a scene from *Driving Miss Daisy*.

They both looked out of their respective windows. The view was the same: the Nightingale Hotel. It had been the same for the last four hours: the two doormen coming in and out, welcoming and waving goodbye, with immaculately white-gloved hands, to their guests; porters scurrying around with suitcases, vanity cases, and assorted nut cases, each of whom bellowed orders and demands that their luggage be handled with the utmost courtesy and respect.

Mr Sumo felt sorry for the staff. After all, they didn't have the job satisfaction that he enjoyed. He still couldn't believe that he had been head-hunted. There he was, working for the Kilburn brothers, when his current boss came in and whisked him off his feet. Well, to be exact, it wasn't his boss at all – it was Arnie. Mr Sumo had never actually met his new boss, and didn't have a clue what he looked like. He assumed he was black. He *knew* that he was rich, considering the amount he was passing Mr Sumo's way. Only right, mused Mr Sumo, when you think of what I've done for him.

Now, while welcoming the money, he resented having

to sit in this car and watch the world go by, waiting for some guy to come out of the hotel so they could follow him. Arnie had said it involved the boss's father, who they needed to keep a very close eye on. That wasn't a problem for Mr Sumo – but all this waiting was!

"What the hell…?"

Mr Sumo stirred at Arnie's voice. "What? What is it?"

"Cops… and lots of them."

Mr Sumo could see them now. They were piling out of a couple of vans, and had been obscured by a double-decker bus which was just easing out of a stop and back into the traffic. "What are they up to, Arnie?"

"Beats me," said Arnie, straining in the seat to get a better view. "They're going into the hotel."

In all its one-hundred-and-two-year history, the majestic Nightingale Hotel in downtown Altona had seen nothing like it. A swarm of policemen made their way, two by two, through the engraved glass of the revolving door and stood in the foyer, obviously meaning business.

Withers looked up at the ornate ceiling, feeling that he could almost be in a place of worship. He sighed at the extravagance of it all – the sweeping staircase with the burnished gold-effect banister; the *faux*-Georgian chairs and rich mahogany coffee tables; the deep-pile carpets in the most audacious of maroons; the air of lavish expense, which seemed to have been thrown around like confetti from the hands of Croesus himself. Withers couldn't help it, but he sighed again.

"What is the meaning of this?" A dapper little man, officious and gelatinous, stood before Withers, his face flushed with anger and nerves. His hair-style was straight out of Bertie Wooster. He stood, legs slightly apart, in a way that he assumed was dominant, giving him the edge. It didn't, and not only because he barely came up to Withers's shoulder.

"My name is John Withers. Sheriff of Bakerton," Withers said, deliberately slowly, so that the other man could digest every word. "And you are?"

"Marshall," spluttered the man.

"Is that Mr Marshall, or Marshall Something?"

The man blinked wildly, his nerves getting the upper hand over his anger. "Calvin Marshall… manager."

"Ah," said Withers, "the top dog."

Marshall marshalled a little courage. "What do you want, sheriff?" his quivering voice demanded.

"An illegal immigrant."

For not the first time in his life, Withers was stretching a point. And not only that, but he was way out of order. He had approached the Altona City police chief for permission to mount a joint raid on the hotel, in the firm belief that Dume Akintola would be in the premises, or, at the very least, his father would know where he was. Withers came up against a brick wall. Under no circumstances, stressed the chief, would he sanction such a venture. And no, Withers would not be permitted to go in on his own. So, Withers had called in sufficient favours to be able to gather together enough men from Bakerton, Thurlow and one or two other small towns – and go in anyway.

Marshall was stunned. "What do you mean?"

"Just what I say, Mr Marshall. We have reason to believe

that there is enough evidence to justify a search of these premises."

Marshall looked around, seeing the surprised staff and the even more startled guests, and leant in to the sheriff. "Please, can we do this quietly?"

Withers ducked his head to the manager's level and whispered, "Take me to the penthouse, Mr Marshall. I'll be as quiet as you like."

Withers followed the shuffling steps of the disgruntled manager as they made their way to the lift, Dawg in close attendance. No words were exchanged in the lift, and Marshall only spoke when they reached the door to the penthouse suite. "I'm not happy about this."

"Shame," said Withers, his face as neutral as possible.

"Mr Akintola won't be, either," continued Marshall, his voice simpering. "He is one of the owners of this establishment, you know."

Withers nodded, and indicated that Marshall should ring the bell. A soft, melodious sound wafted up from the bell, and Withers thought how fitting it was for the surroundings. The place was a candyfloss of splendour and indulgence.

The bell sounded again, before the door opened, revealing a tall black man, dressed in an expensive suit and black brogues so clean that they almost reflected the man's underwear up his trouser leg. Withers noted immediately the bulge under his left arm, but let it go. The man was security – why shouldn't he be armed?

"I'm sorry…," began Marshall, but Withers cut him short.

"Sheriff Withers to see Mr Akintola. Urgent."

The man hesitated, eyeing the two policemen and dismissing the manager with the wave of a slender finger. He stood aside and closed the door after Withers and Dawg had entered. He had said nothing. He disappeared into an adjoining room and returned moments later with Arusi Akintola, who was similarly dressed, but without the firearm.

"Gentlemen," he said, his voice velvety and welcoming. "Please, take a seat."

Withers took up the offer, while Dawg stood by the door, hands clasped in front of him. Mr Security stood behind Akintola's chair, watching through hooded eyes.

Akintola cleared his throat. "So, Mr Withers, what can I do for you? It must be serious, for you to disrupt the hotel as you have done."

Withers was nothing if not blunt. "I'm looking for your son."

Akintola knew this, of course, but it still came as a shock. He was not used to people being so forward. "My son?"

"Dume. Have you forgotten about him, Mr Akintola?"

Mr Security bristled almost as much as Akintola, but neither moved. Akintola thought for a second. "I will assume that was a little joke on your behalf, sheriff. However, I did not find it funny. Why do you want Dume?"

There was a tension in the room that seemed to radiate, like a current running through exposed wires, the energy spraying everywhere.

"I believe he is an illegal immigrant," said Withers.

"Really?" Akintola scoffed. "Is that all?" Mr Security grinned at that.

"No, Mr Akintola, that is not all." Withers paused, gauging the reactions of both men as he continued. "I wish to talk to him about the abuse – and possible murder – of Jet Carmichael, the murder of Mo Sanders, and the abduction of Bryn Owen."

"Really, sheriff? On what grounds are you making these wild accusations? Do you have evidence?"

Withers was well aware that Akintola knew that he didn't have a shred of evidence. But that didn't stop him. "I will get the evidence, Mr Akintola. I will destroy your son, and everything he stands for."

"You have said enough, Mr Withers. You will leave now," said Akintola, starting to rise from his chair. Mr Security straightened.

"I have two other questions for you first."

Akintola stopped. "You are persistent, sheriff, I will say that for you." He sat back down. "Very well, I will play your little game. Ask away."

"Why is Dume back in the country?"

"I have no idea. I was not aware that he is. You must understand, sheriff, that since my divorce from his mother, I do not see so much of Dume these days. He is his own man."

Withers gave a thin smile with no warmth. He knew Akintola was lying. "His own man," he said quietly, sick to the stomach. "Tell me, Mr Akintola, why did you spirit your son away all those years ago?"

"Spirit him away? Really, sheriff, you have a strange way with words. We returned home, that is all."

Withers was like a dog with a very juicy bone. "After he had abused Jet…"

Akintola jerked upright. "Careful, sheriff. You are close to the edge now."

"Then sue me! We both know what Dume is, Mr Akintola, don't we? Is that why you took him home? To stop him? Perhaps you're not a bad father, after all. You got him away – but was that to protect him, or some other poor defenceless boy?"

Akintola burst from his seat as Mr Security began to reach for his gun, but Dawg was ready, shaking his head.

Mr Security said, "That is enough! Mr Akintola will not be answering any more of your questions. We would like you to leave." The scowl on his face became a mask of hatred. "Now!" he added through thin lips.

Withers weighed up his options. He was already out on a jetty, dangling over the edge and towards deep water when his boss got hold of him; but there was so much more to find out. He ignored the hovering security man and stepped round him. "Mr Akintola, I am requesting your presence at Bakerton police station. Now!"

Mr Security's face broke into a sneer at the inflection of the sheriff's voice on the last word. It sounded like piss-taking to him. But Withers hadn't finished. "If you refuse, I have enough men downstairs to insist. The choice, sir, is yours… but the hotel's reputation might suffer if you make the wrong decision."

Akintola had gathered himself together, and he waved away the security man. "It is all right, Benjamin. I will go peacefully with the nice sheriff." He gave a weak smile. "Please arrange for my lawyer to attend me."

"Yes, sir," said Benjamin, the daggers in his eyes directed at Withers.

The Ford Focus was rocking. Mr Sumo was struggling to peer out of the tinted but misted window, his breath leaving rings on the glass. All he could see, in between the passing traffic, were two policemen standing guard, waving away anybody who tried to enter the hotel.

"Bloody hell!" he whispered. "This is what you call surveillance!"

Arnie shushed him loudly. He was rapidly talking into the hands-free phone, giving the person on the other end a running commentary on what was unfolding. "Yes, boss, they're still in there. No, nobody's come out yet…"

"Hold up!" said Mr Sumo, with relish. "Something's happening."

"Yes, boss, there is somebody coming out. Wait… sir." In the excitement, Arnie almost forgot who he was talking to.

Mr Sumo didn't recognise the people emerging through the revolving doors, but most of them were in uniform. The only people who weren't were two black men, dressed like company directors, and one of whom was animatedly on his mobile phone. They both held their heads up high.

Arnie, on the other hand, knew who they were. "Yes, boss, I can confirm… it's Benjamin Mbabo and… and… your father."

Mr Sumo thought the voice on the other end sounded mighty angry as he roared back, "Follow them. Then, when they are released, you will set our terrier onto Benjamin. My father must be taught a lesson."

"Yes, sir," said Arnie. He switched off the phone and

turned to Mr Sumo. "You understand what you have to do, Rich?"

The terrier on the back seat knew precisely what was required, and he smiled at the prospect.

Chapter Twelve

Arusi Akintola had been in the holding cell for over an hour when Withers got the expected phone call. He was surprised it had taken so long.

"John, what the hell are you playing at?"

"Sorry, sir," he replied in his best servile voice, "is there a problem?"

"You know damn well!" bellowed his chief, before softening just slightly. "My arse is on the line as well as yours, you bloody fool."

Withers gripped the phone tighter. "I'm just doing my job, sir," he said.

There was a pause, before a more subdued chief came back. "Since when has your job been to piss off the Altona City police chief, disrupt the entire staff of a respected hotel and cause an international incident by arresting an African industrialist?"

"I didn't arrest him, sir… I invited him in for questioning," said Withers flatly.

"Do you think the press will see it that way, man?" snapped the chief.

"Probably not, sir."

"No is the correct answer." The chief paused again, this

time making a point. "There have been repercussions, John. Serious ones. Top level. My head is on the block."

"Mine, too, I'd imagine," said Withers lightly.

"No, John. Just your bollocks! And if you want to keep them, I suggest… no, I *insist* that you release Mr Akintola immediately with a grovelling apology."

The line went dead with a resounding silence as Withers said, "Yes, sir."

After spending nearly an hour in the waiting room, Benjamin Mbabo finally left his master in the police station with the lawyer and stepped out into the busy street. He was not happy being here, preferring to be at home in Nigeria with his wife and children. He had come to this god-forsaken country because he was a good servant, and because he liked Arusi. He had worked for the businessman for many years now, firstly as the dogsbody and then taking over as security consultant when the previous incumbent found the job too stressful and absconded, taking a few thousand Nigerian naira with him. Benjamin's first assignment had been to track the culprit down, which he did remarkably swiftly, returning with the money and one of the man's fingers as a memento. Job well done, promotion assured.

Benjamin could do nothing now for his boss; that was in the hands of the lawyer he had phoned as they left the hotel. He looked across the road at Scotty's Diner, chewing over the idea of getting himself something to eat; but in the end he just shrugged and began strolling down the road in search of a taxi. He would take full advantage of room service before Arusi was released, as he surely soon would be.

His footsteps resounded noisily on the pavement as he weaved his way through the shoppers and office workers leaving for home, so he didn't hear somebody behind him, getting closer. There was a Ford Focus parked beside him, its engine ticking over.

As Benjamin got level with the car, he felt a very heavy push, and he fell through the car's open door and straight into the back seat, where he came face-to-belly with a giant. He struggled, but his arms were being crushed against the side of his body, a smiling Mr Sumo looking down at him.

Arnie slammed the door shut and ran round the car, climbing into the driver's seat. "We're going for a little drive, Benjamin," he grinned. "I see you've already met my associate, Mr Sumo." He threw the car into gear and eased it into the road, causing a cyclist to swerve and almost fall off. He shrugged off the abusive language that filtered through his half-open window and drove on.

Benjamin stared into the face of Mr Sumo, and knew things were not going to end well.

* * * *

TRANSCRIPT OF AN INTERVIEW WITH
MR ARUSI AKINTOLA
Thursday, 6th October

Those present: Mr Arusi Akintola; his lawyer, Mr Dominic Hall; Sheriff John Withers, Bakerton Police Force; and Deputy Douglas Janowski, Bakerton Police Force.

SHERIFF WITHERS: Mr Akintola, do you agree that you came to this police station of your own volition, without threat or coercion? [Pause] Please, sir, for the sake of the tape, answer each question. A nod will not register.

AKINTOLA: Yes.

WITHERS: Thank you. You are Arusi Akintola, resident of Surulere, Lagos, Nigeria?

AKINTOLA: Lagos, yes. I was born in Surulere, but I now live in the city.

WITHERS: You were married to Ruth Akintola, but are now divorced. Is that correct?

AKINTOLA: Yes.

WITHERS: You have one child… a son, Dume?

AKINTOLA: Yes.

WITHERS: Can you please tell me what connection you have with this country?

AKINTOLA: I have business interests here…

WITHERS: Business interests?

AKINTOLA: I deal in iron ore, tin and steel, as well as holding a stake in one or two commercial enterprises.

WITHERS: Such as the Nightingale Hotel.

AKINTOLA: That is one, yes. As you very well know, considering you invaded the premises today, sheriff.

WITHERS: Believe me, Mr Akintola, if I wanted to invade one of your properties, I would do so with more than a handful of officers. And, as *you* very well know, I am following a legitimate line of investigation.

[Pause]

WITHERS: Tell me about Altona City Football Club.

AKINTOLA: I am a fan, sheriff. What can I say? I had

to try my hand at running the club, so I became chairman. I think I was reasonably successful, don't you?

WITHERS: Was your son involved?

AKINTOLA: In the club? No.

WITHERS: But he was with you at the time.

AKINTOLA: Yes.

WITHERS: Why did you leave Altona, Mr Akintola?

[Pause]

AKINTOLA: No comment.

WITHERS: You left rather suddenly.

AKINTOLA: No comment.

WITHERS: Did your son leave at the same time?

AKINTOLA: No comment.

WITHERS: Was he the reason you left?

AKINTOLA: No comment.

[Knock on door. Door opens]

WITHERS: For the benefit of the tape, Deputy Keene has entered the room.

[Inaudible conversation. Door closes. Pause]

WITHERS: Mr Akintola, I'm afraid I have some bad news for you. Your security man, Benjamin Mbabo, has been abducted.

AKINTOLA: What?

WITHERS: We are, of course, using every means at our disposal to find Mr Mbabo. [Pause] Mr Akintola, are you all right?

MR HALL: My client is clearly distressed at this news, sheriff. May I suggest we continue this interview at another time?

WITHERS: Mr Akintola, are you happy to carry on?

AKINTOLA: Yes, yes. Please, may we continue?

WITHERS: If you are sure.

AKINTOLA: Yes, yes, I am sure.

WITHERS: Very well. We were talking about your son, Dume. Did he leave Altona at the same time as you?

AKINTOLA: No comment.

WITHERS: Why did you leave, Mr Akintola? [Pause] Was it something you did?

AKINTOLA: No… comment.

WITHERS: Was it something your son did?

AKINTOLA: No comment.

WITHERS: You were having an affair with Dawn Osborne.

AKINTOLA: No comment.

WITHERS: Did this affect your son?

AKINTOLA: No… comment.

WITHERS: Was he jealous?

AKINTOLA: No… comment.

[Pause]

WITHERS: Mr Akintola, did your son have anything to do with some of the players at Altona City?

AKINTOLA: No comment.

WITHERS: Youth players like Jet Carmichael?

AKINTOLA: No comment.

WITHERS: Is that why he is back now? To molest more youngsters?

AKINTOLA: No… comment.

WITHERS: Where is he, Mr Akintola? Where is your son?

[Pause]

WITHERS: What is he up to?

[Pause]

WITHERS: If people are in danger, we need to know.

[Pause]

WITHERS: Tell me, Mr Akintola, is your son responsible for the abduction of Benjamin? Is he here to commit a serious crime?

AKINTOLA: No comment. No comment!

[Mr Akintola breaks down. Interview ends at 3.34pm]

* * * * *

Benjamin felt nothing but pain and resignation. He knew that he was about to die, and the thought was comforting in a way. At least it would take away the pain.

He had been pinned to the floor of the car by the big man's foot and taken for a ride. Now, he was pinned to the ground by the big man, but this time he knew there was no getting up. He was acquainted with Arnie, who stood above him, smirking and puffing on a thin cheroot, like some guy out of *Django Unchained*. Oh, yes, he knew Arnie, all right. They had spent time together in the cesspit they called their village back in Nigeria. They even went to the same school, and it was Arnie who got him the dogsbody job with Arusi, before Arnie moved over to Dume's side. That's all you're good for, Arnie had said: licking the boss's boots. Well, Benjamin had proved him wrong. Boy, had he! Not that it made the slightest difference now. He could chalk up an imaginary point, but it was Arnie who was about to taste final victory.

The big man moved slightly, easing Benjamin's pain just a little. He had been sitting astride Benjamin, a thick leg either side, and had fixed Benjamin's arms backwards as he lay face down in the dirt. Benjamin could taste the gravel as he swivelled his head sideways, attempting to look into his eyes. He wanted to face his tormentor. The pain in his left arm was severe, and any movement engulfed him with nausea and agony. He knew that the arm was broken, but then again, what did it really matter in the great scheme of things?

"What do you want?" he said, in between taking great gulps of air.

Arnie took out his cheroot and blew a circle of smoke. "We've been told to teach your boss a lesson."

The big man laughed at that, and leant closer to Benjamin, so that he was almost horizontal on Benjamin's back, and his garlic breath filled the air around them both. "Yeah, a lesson he's not going to forget."

Chapter Thirteen

Dawg and Rafferty watched in silence as Withers paced the room. They could see that the sheriff was chewing over something, and whatever it was, it appeared to be sticking in his throat, judging by the faces he was pulling. Dawg had learned long ago to melt into the background until something erupted from Withers. He didn't have to wait too long.

"Akintola was trying to tell us something."

The others waited.

"Everything changed when I told him about his security man being taken." Pause. Silence. "It's on the tape."

Rafferty said, "What's on the tape, John?"

"Listen to it," said Withers, almost barking the order. "Switch it on, Dawg."

Dawg reached for the recorder and switched it on. There was a long beep, and then…

Mr Akintola, do you agree that you came to this police station…

"Fast forward, Dawg," urged Withers.

… benefit of the tape, Deputy Keene has entered the room.

Pause.

Mr Akintola, I'm afraid I have some bad news for you. Your security man, Benjamin Mbabo, has been abducted.

"Right," said Withers excitedly. "Akintola was clearly

upset that his man had been taken, but he refused to terminate the interview. Then something strange happened. Despite agreeing to continue, he still gave the usual stock answer. Now listen, Pat."

The tape ran on, but Rafferty failed to see what was so clear to Withers.

"Like you said, John, he just keeps saying 'No comment'. As per usual, when we interview crooks."

"But it's *not* the same, Pat," said Withers, bouncing on the edge of his seat. "Don't you see, Akintola is helping us! Whether or not he meant to, I don't know. Just listen!"

Mr Akintola, did your son have anything to do with some of the players at Altona City?

No comment.

Youth players like Jet Carmichael?

No comment.

Is that why he is back now? To molest more youngsters?

No... comment.

Rafferty leant against the window, stroking his chin. He still couldn't see it.

"Damn it, Pat!" bellowed Withers, annoyed that he was the only one who understood the implication. "He paused."

"He paused?" said a bewildered Rafferty.

"Good God, man. Listen!"

They played the same part of the tape again and Withers stopped the machine with the swipe of his big hand. "My question was, 'Is he back to molest more youngsters?'. What did he say?"

"No comment."

"But that's the whole point! He didn't say 'No comment'.

He said, 'No… comment'. There was a distinct pause between the words. It was almost as if he was saying 'No'. And that pause was only in some of his answers."

Rafferty rewound the tape and played it again, his ears close to the machine. Did Withers have a point? Of course he did! There *was* a distinct pause in some of the answers. Akintola appeared to be sending them coded messages.

Withers said, "I think the abduction was the last straw. Akintola knows that his son was responsible, and he wasn't prepared to defend him any longer – but nor could he bring himself to shop him to us. He left it for us to work out."

"Which you have," beamed Rafferty.

They played the tape again, this time making a note of Akintola's responses. It was like a Yes/No game from the TV.

Withers summarised. "So, what have we got? Akintola tells us that Dume *did* violate Jet, but that's not why he has come back this time. 'No… comment', he said. So there is something else on his agenda – and we need to find out what it is."

* * * * *

Surveillance, Part II. It was the same car, the same two men seated in it. It was almost like a sequel. Just a different location.

Mr Sumo slouched in the back, thinking of his next snack. He should go for something light – Ryvita, perhaps, spread with low-cal cream cheese with just a hint of smoked salmon. Oom, delicious! Are you kidding? No, Mr Sumo was salivating over a triple cheeseburger and double fries, swamped with ketchup and mustard, and accompanied by the largest strawberry shake he could get his hands on. That's right, Mr Sumo was normal.

He sat up and looked out of the window. "Say, Arnie, why are we here?"

Arnie answered without looking up from his paper. "Orders, Rich. That's all."

"Yeah," said Mr Sumo, "but why here?"

Arnie put the paper down on the passenger seat and swivelled to face Mr Sumo. "Come on, Rich, you know better than to ask questions. We're the do-ers, not the thinkers. Right?"

"Right," agreed Mr Sumo, still baffled.

"You get your money," said Arnie. "That's all you need to think about."

"Okay," said Mr Sumo dreamily. "So, do *you* know, Arnie?"

"What?"

"Why we're here?"

Arnie had returned to his newspaper, but now he swivelled back again. "Of course I bloody know. Shit, man! One of us has to know. And it's me. So just shut the hell up and let me read my paper."

Mr Sumo waited a few seconds. "Yes, Arnie," he said finally, returning to the thought of his sizzling cheeseburger. He just couldn't understand why they were outside a school.

* * * * *

The cocker spaniel had lost interest in the ball. Instead, it was racing across the field, hunting down the fluttering leaves and picking up twigs that fitted its jaws but were far too long and unwieldy for it to run, so that it tended to move in a comical stop-start fashion, as it attempted to adjust its grip while maintaining maximum momentum.

"Rosie!" its owner shouted hopefully.

The dog, of course, ignored her. It was enjoying itself too much to consider obedience lessons. This particular branch, however, was proving too much of an effort, so the dog dropped it and decided it would be more fun to chase its own tail.

"Rosie!" the call came again, as the lady picked up the ball in exasperation and began to track her dog.

The spaniel, sensing its owner's imminent arrival, took off once again, this time heading for the corner of the field, where it was sure it had seen a rabbit.

There was something there, definitely, and the dog began to sniff it and gave up a yelp of confusion. This was no rabbit.

The owner, breathless and annoyed, hurried to the scene as fast as she could for a sixty-plus-year-old. She stopped, gasping and wheezing, and looked down on the body of a man. She gave a yelp far greater than that of her dog.

The man, to her, was clearly dead. He was sprawled in an unnatural position one side of the gateway leading into the field, as if some strong force had lifted him up and hurled him over the gate. His arm was badly bent and his face, although dark in the late afternoon shade, bore marks of a terrible beating.

The woman gathered herself together and bent down, pushing her inquisitive dog to one side. She touched the man's forehead, which was beginning to cool, and then leant against his chest, ignoring the blood on his shirt. She felt a slight movement, as if his heart was fighting to bring him back. Without thinking, she took out her mobile phone and dialled. There was hope after all.

Although he was in no position to know it, Benjamin Mbato was an extremely lucky man. He had been the recipient of the one redeeming feature of Dume Akintola: his conscience. Through all his hatred of the world and its inhabitants, Dume had finally grasped the principle that something was stronger than the loathing he felt for certain people in his country – it was his love for his father. Simple. When it came down to it, Dume could not destroy his father by killing his closest friend, even if Benjamin was still only a lackey in Dume's eyes. That was why he had demanded that Benjamin be left alive. How was he to know that Mr Sumo went further than he should have, and that Benjamin was now much closer to death than life?

* * * * *

As well as being the second most beautiful woman he had ever met – although he would never ever tell her that! – Judith was also a trampoline for his musings, enabling him to bounce through his ideas and offering sharp and pertinent sugges-tions and observations when the need arose.

For the last hour, though, work had been far from their minds. They were now sitting on the floor in his lounge, their backs against the sofa, so close that their bare legs were touching and their naked toes were dancing together in a post-coital waltz. Withers wore just his boxers, while Judith had on her knickers and his dressing gown draped over her shoulders in a vain attempt at modesty, although Withers was convinced that the one escaping breast had been offered as a fitting reward for his masterful performance in the bedroom. Or was it just a costume malfunction?

They clinked their wine glasses together, took a sip of the cheap white plonk, and she nestled her head into his chest.

"Happy?" he asked, his voice croaky with feeling as he stroked her auburn hair.

"As happy as you, I would think."

"That's pretty damned happy, then!"

There was a silence between them for a minute. Then, "My friend Karen has been in touch."

Withers looked down at her. "Karen?" he queried.

"Karen," she repeated. "South African Karen."

"Oh," he said brightly, "*that* Karen." It was clear by his tone that he had never heard of her. Judith playfully dug him in the ribs.

"She works for the *Argus*. I told you."

No, you didn't, thought Withers, his lips sealed.

"She's in Cape Town, remember?"

Withers nodded, still clueless.

"I asked her to have a look at Akintola…"

He was alert now, gently pushing her away so he could look into her eyes. "You never said."

"Didn't I?"

Withers grinned. "I would have remembered *that*!"

"Ah, I have your full attention now, do I?" she said, a mischievous smile on her face.

"Always, my darling. And not just in bed."

"Well," she teased, "that's a first!"

They reached for their glasses, which they had put on the coffee table, and brought them together. "To us!" breathed Withers. "In and out of bed!"

Judith gave a gentle chuckle. "I'll drink to that!" she whispered, and they settled back into their comfortable position.

"So," said Withers eventually, "what about Karen?"

Judith sighed. "We've gone past our moment, then? That split second when you are Casanova rather than Columbo."

"I'm sorry you had to fall in love with a policeman. I can't help it."

"Neither can I," she said with feeling, then paused. "Anyway, Karen has emailed…"

"Karen in Cape Town."

"Yes. Don't interrupt!"

"Sorry."

"She has contacts in many African countries, one of whom is in Nigeria."

"And?" He was getting excited again, but not in that way.

"Allegedly…" She stopped when he gave her a frosty look. She returned the favour ten-fold. "*Allegedly*, Dumo has a reputation for liking young boys…"

"Young *black* boys," Withers put in.

"Probably," she said, non-committedly. "Also, the Akintola family have been involved in a blood feud with each other. It's to do with cousins falling out over land rights and tribal succession."

"Who will be the next chief, you mean."

"Something like that."

The conversation had reached a temporary conclusion, as Withers thought through what Judith had said. "All of this is fine, but it doesn't explain why the Akintolas are here. What are we missing?"

Judith took his hand. "Karen is still investigating, John. She senses a story for her, as well as answers for you."

"Let's hope she fast-tracks it, then. For all our sakes."

Chapter Fourteen

Dawg felt the full force as Withers burst through the door the next day. He was used to his sheriff's strange ways, but this time the bit was well and truly between his teeth as he threw off his hat and went into his office.

"Dawg!" he hollered, impatient to get moving on the case. The deputy was barely through the door before Withers began barking at him. "Tell me, what do you know about tribal wars?"

Dawg, taken aback, stopped in his tracks. "Er… Zulus, boss?"

"For your information, son, that was a colonial war – the British *versus* the native Africans."

"Oh," mumbled Dawg. "What about the Apaches and the Sioux?"

"Ah, you're getting warmer! Although you need to stay in Africa."

"I do?"

Withers sat down and took a bundle of papers from his jacket pocket – the emails Judith had received from Karen. "To be specific, the Kanuri tribe of Nigeria."

"Akintola?"

"Indeed," confirmed Withers. "Arusi is in line to be the tribal chief, with Dume obviously his heir. I believe that the son would like to jump the queue…"

"What, kill his father, you mean?" said Dawg.

"I don't think so. At least, not just yet. There is somebody else who has a stronger claim…" Withers flicked through the pages. "Kashim Okele. That's all we have at the moment, so I'd like you to look into it. See what you can find out about Mr Okele. I'm not sure it will do us much good, but it's worth a try."

* * * * *

The Ratcliffe Academy, Connaught Road, Altona. An exclusive finishing school for well-rounded and adjusted young men, if you believe the hype in their brochure. In reality, it was just a private school with connections.

Founded eighty years ago by knight of the realm Sir Henry Ratcliffe, who had settled in Altona some years earlier, its mission statement (not that they called it such in those days) was to encourage educational and physical achievements in the young people who passed through the hallowed gates. To that end, they offered Blue Ribands for academic success and Verdants for sporting prowess. Winning a Ratcliffe Verdant for rowing or rugger was almost akin to gaining a Blue at Oxford or Cambridge.

The school's first pupils had been the offspring of Ratcliffe's well-heeled friends and acquaintances, two of whom went on to become high-flyers in government. That was the making of the school, as other, more affluent, parents offered up their progeny for the 'Ratcliffe Experience', as it came to be known. First, there were the European aristocracy, followed by the Arab sheiks and then the oriental mandarins. Now, the school was home to a wide cross-section of the children of the rich, the latest of whom seemed to be the sons of African princes, industrialists and highly successful criminals, the last of whom naturally covered their tracks so carefully that the school apparently had no idea where the fees had really come from.

Mr Sumo knew none of this, of course. All he knew was that he had orders to sit outside the gates and while away a few hours just… watching. With Arnie.

The Ford Focus was again parked opposite the school and further down the road, as inconspicuous as possible, but close enough for Arnie to scrutinise every face that went in and out. He was looking for someone in particular, Mr Sumo guessed.

"What *are* we doing here, Arnie?"

"Come on, Rich, you know better than to ask questions."

"Sorry." Mr Sumo fell silent. He returned his gaze to the school. It really was a magnificent structure, its high stone walls reminiscent, in Mr Sumo's eyes at least, of a medieval castle, its narrow, arch-topped windows eminently suitable for firing arrows out of. Mr Sumo liked that idea. His eyes moved down to the crazy paving of the courtyard beyond the fence, and the small office where the short, tubby man with the large moustache and dark blue suit sat, only coming out when someone approached the beautifully ornate gates. Then he would direct them either through the archway which, presumably, led to the belly of the school, or round to the left, where Mr Sumo knew there was a car park. He had been here before, after all.

A couple of older pupils, in muted green gowns and an air of superiority, breezed past the office, ignoring the gatekeeper, and out through a small side gate, and Mr Sumo watched as they sauntered down the road, a touch of envy clouding his eyes.

Although he would like to have attended a school such as this, it was patently obvious to all concerned – his parents, teachers, social workers, probation officers and police – that it could never happen. However, Mr Sumo had excelled at some things. His dissection of a live frog in the playground had been roundly applauded by the other pupils, and he was unsurpassed when it came to teaching people not to pick on his friends. He even sent 'Get Well' cards to the hospital afterwards.

Now, as an adult, his skills lay in only one direction, and he knew he was a true master. Inflicting pain had become second nature to him, so when he had been asked to carry out a 'scrub' – a wonderfully graphic euphemism for a killing – he had no qualms whatsoever. He took to it like a duck to the proverbial. After six 'scrubs', he felt secure in the knowledge that he could do anything; and he was particularly proud of the fact that he had removed from this earth one of the greatest footballers in the country, if not the world. What a shame he wouldn't get the credit he deserved for it. Perhaps, he thought very seriously, he should write his memoirs: tell the world his story. What a Pulitzer Prize winner that would be!

"Rich!"

Mr Sumo jumped.

"Wake up, man!" hollered Arnie, trying to throw his arm

over the seat to prod the big feller.

"What? What is it?" Mr Sumo asked, still slightly dazed.

"We have action," said Arnie. "Belt up!"

Mr Sumo straightened himself and attempted to fasten his seatbelt. It didn't fit, of course. No belt in any car would ever go round him. He threw the belt away in disgust and peered out of the window. "What's going on, Arnie?"

"Look, just over there," said Arnie, pointing to a black limousine pulling up outside the school gates. "The boss said it would be along some time."

Mr Sumo grunted. "At least we didn't have to wait too many days," he said with relief. This could have gone on for weeks. "So, what's with the limo?"

"It's our target, Rich, my man," said Arnie with a wide grin. "Or, more to the point, it's the start of our next adventure." Arnie punched some numbers into his mobile and after several rings, a voice came over the speaker.

"Yes?"

"Arnie, boss."

"Go on."

"The limo has arrived… just like you said."

"I knew the boy would be let out for a day some time. Do you see him?"

Arnie peered through the window. "Not yet, boss."

"Okay," the voice said, "you know what to do when he does come out."

"Yes, boss." As Arnie said this, a small black boy, dressed in a dark suit and with a verdant green tie, emerged through the arch of the school, stopped and waved at the limousine, before running to it and jumping in through the door being held open by a tall black man wearing a chauffeur's cap.

As the limo pulled out gracefully into the traffic, an insignificant Ford Focus took up station a few cars behind.

* * * * *

The answer was staring him in the face, but still Dawg hadn't picked up on it. He studied the computer monitor closely, reading about Kashim Okele and the history of the Kanuri people. Kashim himself had apparently been named after the post-independence leader Kashim Ibrahim, an icon in the Kanuri world. Okele's son, ten-year-old Sani, had been given the name of a former military leader. Now, the son was overseas, attending a prestigious school with impeccable credentials for developing young boys who go on to great things, particularly in the political world.

Dawg wasn't sure how any of this was relevant, but he knew better than to keep anything from the sheriff, so he set the printer in motion and watched as the pages flopped into the tray.

The phone call beat Dawg to it. They were back in the Incident Room, and, as he knocked on the cupboard door and entered in a fluid movement, the telephone was ringing. Withers nodded to his deputy and indicated for him to wait, before lifting the receiver.

"John…"

Withers smiled, despite himself. "Hi," he said silkily. "Everything okay?"

Judith told him she was great, and he had to agree

wholeheartedly, before she continued, "I've been looking through some of our reports on Kashim Okele."

"Okele?" Withers echoed, and Dawg looked up and waved his paperwork at the sheriff. Withers ignored him. "What about Okele, Judith?"

"It's about his son."

"His son?" repeated Withers, and Dawg again waved his papers, this time with more gusto. Withers waved an arm back at him, as if to say, 'Just wait!'.

Judith said, "It's all supposed to be hush-hush, but it's an accepted fact that he has been sent abroad to a boarding school."

Withers spluttered down the phone. "School?"

Dawg took a step backwards. It was clear that Miss Wiseman had control of this particular angle.

"Nobody knows for sure, but my sources are convinced he's at the Ratcliffe in Altona," said Judith. "I've got their number, if you want to check it out."

Withers felt like blowing her a kiss, or something else entirely. Could it all be coming together at last? He wrote down the number, thanked her, pressed his hand down on the telephone, then dialled. "The Head, please. This is urgent," he said sharply.

"Who is speaking, please?" a refined female voice asked.

"I am Sheriff John Withers, Bakerton Police. I need to speak to the Head."

"I'm awfully sorry, sir, but the Head is…"

Withers snapped. "I need somebody in authority, madam. NOW!"

The line crackled as the refined lady had obviously put the phone down and raced off to find a suitable person to face the flak. Seconds elapsed before, "Hello, how can I help?"

Withers was still on adrenaline, his voice booming and authoritative. "You are?"

"Mr Dawson, Deputy Head."

"You'll do. Now, tell me, do you have a Sani Okele at the school?"

"I'm sorry, sir, I am unable to divulge…"

"Listen to me, Mr Dawson, *sir*, if you don't answer my question, I will arrest you for… something, anything! Do you understand?"

"Er, yes, sir." Mr Dawson's voice quivered with fear. "I can confirm that Sani is…"

"Good! Now this is what I want you to do. You will take Sani to your office and keep him there until I can get to you. Okay?"

"No, sir. I mean, that's not possible, sir."

"Explain?" roared Withers, exasperated.

Dawson took a deep breath. "Sani is no longer in the school. His mother's chauffeur picked him up a short while ago. She is visiting…"

"Never mind that! Where was the car heading?"

"I believe Mrs Okele is currently residing at the Altona Palace Hotel…"

"What car is the boy in?"

"Er, I'm not sure, sir. Although I believe it is some kind of limousine…"

Withers slammed down the phone and turned to his deputy. "Dawg, get some cars out to the Altona Palace Hotel and look for a limo on the way. I think Dume is about to play his hand."

* * * * *

It wasn't so much a car chase – more a car procession. The limo purred through the streets of Altona, its occupants unaware they were being tracked, while the Focus shadowed it from a safe distance. Maintaining contact was easy through the city, but when the limo eventually hit the countryside, the smaller car would struggle to keep up.

Although the Palace Hotel bore an Altona address, it was, in fact, about seven miles out of the city, much closer to the airport, which supplied the majority of its clientele. Miriam Okele would have preferred the opulence of the Nightingale, as befitted her status, but knew that was out of the question, bearing in mind that her old friend Arusi had a stake in it and her husband would not have approved. She still found it strange that they had all been so close at one time, with Arusi almost a father-figure and Dume and Kashim like brothers. How the world changes.

The boy talked excitedly about his mother, who had flown into the city the previous evening and who was going to spend a couple of days with her son before jetting back to Lagos, stopping at Harrods in London on the way for essential supplies. She did the trip three times a year, but was extending it this time so she could see her only child, who had been sent away in order to strengthen the family's hold on the situation back home.

"Is my mother here, Peter?" the boy asked gleefully, knowing the answer already.

The chauffeur chuckled. "Oh, yes, Sani. She flew in

yesterday and is waiting for you at her hotel. She has presents, I believe," he added, encouraging the boy's excitement.

"Presents! Put your foot on the gas, Peter!" Sani used one of the many Americanisms he had picked up from too much television back home. Peter chuckled some more, pressing his foot down just a little to show how willing he was to obey his boss's son.

Mr Sumo craned his neck – what there was of it – to look past Arnie and out through the windscreen at the posh car they had been following for a couple of miles.

"Where are they going, Arnie?" he asked.

"Let's just say, Rich," replied Arnie, "they aren't going to get there!"

"You have a plan?"

Arnie grunted. He always had a plan. And if he didn't, then he knew his boss would have one. "Just wait and see," he said. "And stop rocking the car. We'll be in the next lane if you don't sit still!"

"Sorry."

The limo took a left off the ME26 and onto the city circular, a two-lane highway that allowed traffic to filter in and out of the city, as well as to bypass it completely. It was a faster road, and the limo began to pull away.

"We're losing it!" said Mr Sumo with some concern. He was enjoying this new adventure and didn't want it to end.

"Relax, Rich," said Arnie, smoothly pulling out and over-taking a slower car. He was obviously a slick driver, a fact not lost on Mr Sumo, who eyed him with a little more respect. "We'll get them in the end."

The road swept left and Arnie lost sight of the limo for a few seconds, causing more consternation on the back seat. Then they were in contact once more, and Arnie eased back on the pedal, trying not to rouse too much suspicion. In the back, Mr Sumo was almost wetting himself with the excitement.

Eventually, the road turned into single-lane, and the limo was forced to tuck in behind a pick-up which seemed to be able to manage a speed barely into double figures, while at the same time belching out toxics from its exhaust and noise pollution from its cranky old engine. In stark contrast, its radio was blaring out one of the hits of the moment which pundits laughingly call R&B. Some people of a more discerning age remember proper R&B, when it *really* stood for Rhythm and Blues.

Arnie had anticipated the road narrowing, and had positioned the Focus a few hundred yards back, but still keeping the limo in view. He knew exactly what was to come, because his boss had talked him through it several times. It was crystal clear.

The limo indicated a left turn and glided almost silently onto a secondary road, this one with potholes and deep cracks where the council had failed to carry out any kind of repair. The road wasn't exactly 'unadopted', but it wasn't far short, and when the Focus followed the limo, Mr Sumo was thrown around even more, adding to his lack of well-being and ratcheting up his anger level a few notches.

They were now the only two vehicles in sight, and Arnie timed his move perfectly, pulling out, overtaking, and then slamming on the brakes, so that both cars slid to a halt, skidding on the uneven surface.

Arnie was out in a flash, pulling a revolver from his shoulder holster and waving it at the limo. Peter the driver locked the doors and was in the process of getting out his mobile when the windscreen shattered and the bullet caught him in the shoulder, throwing him back against his seat. The boy screamed and fell to the floor, some of the glass covering him as he cowered in the footwell.

Peter watched spell-bound as a huge man made his way to the limo and threw a fist at the driver's window. As it fell apart from the force, Mr Sumo calmly reached over and unlocked the door, throwing it open and dragging out the wounded driver, who fell helplessly to the ground, groaning.

Then, with surprising tenderness, Mr Sumo opened the back door and lifted out the frightened boy. As he carried Sani to the Focus, he kept his hands over the boy's ears, hoping that he wouldn't be able to hear the two shots that rang out across the silence of the countryside.

* * * * *

It was like an episode of *This Is Your Life*. Only much more important. Withers had called his forces together for a meeting, but had decided that both of his offices were too small, so had chosen somewhere much more civilised.

They were in Dawg's place, each of them sipping coffee and tasting a slice of Kitty's Victoria sponge, the one with apricot jam. Very nice, enthused Withers to himself, as he fought off the urge to ask for seconds. He took a gulp of the coffee instead.

Dawg and Rafferty sat on the sofa, the latter politely nibbling at his cake without enthusiasm. Sweetness was not his thing. Dawg, on the other hand, tucked into his wife's cooking with gusto, a wide grin stretching through the apricot, aimed only at his wife. She smiled and sat down opposite, just a cup of coffee in her hand.

Judith stood before them, a red book cradled under her arm. She had got to work immediately after Withers had phoned, searching the internet and her contacts for everything she could find regarding Dume Akintola and Sani Okele's father, Kashim. The vast majority of it was common knowledge, gleaned from Nigerian websites and newspapers; but Judith had also culled information from the most obscure angles, giving her a comprehensive dossier, which she now held. They sat before her, a spell-bound audience, waiting for the show to begin.

Judith opened the loose-leaf folder and took a breath. "This is the story of Dume and Kashim," she announced theatrically, drawing a groan from Withers. She really ought to be in am-dram, he decided, just not today!

"Please, Judith…," he pleaded.

She nodded and continued, "Dume and Kashim are cousins. They grew up together, attended the same schools, the same gangs, the same university of life that moulded them into the people they have become, almost identical in outlook and politics." She could have added that some observers might have seen them as twin sons of a corrupt Nigerian political movement, or just two young men with anger and revenge in their blood.

"Kashim, the older by four months, took the lead, as he had always done," said Judith, "and for the most part Dume fell in with the hierarchy, content to offer a subservient role to support his great friend. It worked well, and the pair, along with others of like-mind, created a cell of secrecy which spread through the country like wildfire and offered them riches beyond their comprehension."

"So they didn't begin as equals," said Withers.

"Oh, no," said Judith. "Kashim came from a family with far more standing in the community. He was destined to be chief one day."

"So what about Arusi, Dume's father?" asked Withers.

"Respected, yes, but not on the same level. Arusi was a businessman, not a statesman. Kashim's father held sway, and it was clear that Kashim himself would follow in his footsteps."

Now, Dume bestrode the earth with a sense of empowerment and control, masterminding business and criminal activities with equal relish, his reputation spreading far ahead of him.

Kashim, in contrast, had stayed at home and honed his political skills at meetings and councils, rising through the ranks until power came to him legally and through the ballot box. He was now a high-flying politician, his past misdemeanours largely forgotten by a grateful people who had seen their employment prospects rise as the economy soared. He could do no wrong, even as he continued to do wrong, while nobody of importance seemed to notice, or bothered to do anything about it.

He had married young, to a daughter of one of his rivals, thus taking away any threat that might have been forthcoming; but after three years his wife had died in a mysterious fire, and he appeared heartbroken. His sympathy level increased ten-fold, enabling him to win yet more votes. He was on the up.

Judith took a breath. "It was at this time that the two men, so close before, began to drift apart. Kashim had the authority to offer million-dollar contracts, and Dume naturally assumed at least one of them would come his way. A reasonable expectation, one would think. But not to Kashim. By now he was wary of Dume's reputation, and felt it more politic to offer the contract to Arusi, Dume's father, an all-together much more acceptable face of business."

"I assume Dume was not impressed?" said Withers.

"And you'd be right," said Judith. "Dume was catatonic with rage. He refused to attend Kashim's second wedding to Miriam, a woman who had grown up close to both boys, and began a subversive campaign to get the politician removed from office. It came to nothing, but the split was a chasm, and the two never spoke again. Kashim moved ever upwards and consolidated his standing, proclaiming the start of a new dynasty when his son was born. Dume just seethed and plotted."

"Until he could get his revenge," said Withers.

"Which," agreed Judith, closing her folder, "appears to be what is happening now."

Chapter Fifteen

Withers hated carnage. Not particularly on any personal level, but because it never reflected well on his policing or his control of criminality in the Bakerton area.

He had been called away from Kitty's apricot sponge by an urgent phone call. The limousine had been found.

Now, he stood slightly apart from Dawg, as they surveyed the havoc wreaked so obviously by Dume's henchmen.

Chad Orwell and his technicians were combing the immediate vicinity of the limousine, while the medical officer was making copious verbal notes via a hand-held recorder as he leant over the body of the chauffeur, crumpled as it was beside the car. His voice sounded tinny, monotonous, and Withers stepped away, deep in thought.

Orwell approached. "Nothing to report yet, John," he said, shrugging.

"I doubt you'll find much, Chad," said Withers. "This was just a smash and grab. But they didn't have to kill the driver," he added sadly.

"He would have been a witness."

"Yeah," was all Withers could think of saying. He went back to stand with Dawg, and silence descended once again.

Finally, Dawg said, "Where do you think they took the boy, boss?"

Withers didn't have a clue, but Thurlow kept preying on his mind. He turned to his deputy. "That's the whole point, Dawg. They *took* the boy. They didn't kill him here."

"No, boss."

"They obviously want to keep him alive, so they must have somewhere to take him. Perhaps the same place as Bryn Owen."

Dawg was wide-eyed. "You think so, boss? I thought we assumed Bryn was dead… like Jet."

"Maybe, maybe not… We have to live in hope."

Chapter Sixteen

He couldn't open his eyelids. Or his mouth. That was the worst part. His lips seemed to be glued together, parched and cracked. He could hear himself mumbling, the incoherent sound escaping through the narrowest of gaps, whistling past his teeth and vibrating on his tongue. Then he groaned and tried to move. Sickness overtook him, and he stayed still until the movement in his brain stopped enough to register something. *Anything.* He heard movement – no, that wasn't strictly true – he *sensed* movement. Close. A soft murmuring, a higher-pitched sound than he had been used to. He tried again to open his eyes, struggling with all his might to break the seal that was holding them fast. He was winning. Yes, the lids were moving, and he gave one final, monumental push, so that the dim light began to penetrate his left eye, and the truth of where he was finally came back to him. He stopped struggling, waiting for a miracle. His right eyelid opened slowly – and he saw a black face.

"Are you all right?"

He couldn't answer, of course, but just grunted a noncommittal sound, neither all right nor very bad.

"I am Sani," the boy said.

Grunt.

"Why are we here?"

Grunt.

"Who are you?"

He worked up a small amount of saliva and tried desperately to lubricate his mouth. His tongue began to poke out.

Sani moved away and quickly came back with a bottle of water that had been thrust into his hand as he was pushed into the room. He poured a little of the water onto the sleeve of his shirt and offered his arm to the man's mouth. He sucked greedily, his lips beginning to move apart. "More!" he whispered, and Sani brought the bottle up, tilted it gently over the man's lips, so that he could finally drink. A miracle indeed.

Sani waited patiently. He had still not recovered from his ordeal, and he was relieved that he would not be in this dank, dismal room alone. The man might not be much company at the moment, but at least he was here.

"That is enough," Sani instructed. "We have only the one bottle. You must not drink it all."

The man wanted so much to drain the bottle, but he obediently put his head back, taking in deep breaths until he felt strong enough to respond. "I'm Bryn," he croaked, his voice breaking.

"Why are we here?" Sani said again, his eyes large with fear and the knowledge of what had happened. He still had the sound of gunfire in his ears, the death of Peter etched into his brain. He knew it, even though the big man had tried to protect him as he carried him away from the car. He reached out to Bryn and clasped his hand, the tears falling freely. Bryn squeezed back, and they stayed locked together for several minutes.

Bryn indicated that he needed more water, but Sani kept hold of the bottle, offering only enough for a dribble to form on Bryn's lips. Bryn understood and nodded, his tongue massaging the liquid through the dryness and down his sore throat. "Thanks," he said softly.

"Your leg?" Sani said, pointing. "What happened?"

Bryn could not move, could not even feel his leg. "Shot."

Sani gasped. "It is bad. You need a doctor."

Bryn couldn't help himself – he laughed, or at least tried to. "Tell that… to who… whoever is holding… us." The effort wore him out, and he fell silent, still wondering why he couldn't feel his right leg. Surely it had only been a flesh wound?

For the first time in days, Bryn felt the warmth of company, someone close by who could offer him a crumb of sanity in a bleak, dank world. He held on to the boy's hand. "Thank you," he mumbled.

Sani was astounded. "For what?"

"For being here." Even as he said it, Bryn could see how incongruous it sounded. "Sorry, that doesn't help, does it?" He took a series of gulps, trying to get the saliva to lubricate his aching throat. As he shuffled his body against the wall, darts of pain ran through his leg.

"You must stay still," urged Sani.

"Yeah," Bryn sneered, "that will really help."

"My father will rescue us."

Bryn tried to laugh. "Got super-powers, has he?"

"He will find a way."

Bryn rested his head against the wall and fell silent. They both knew the boy was talking nonsense.

* * * * *

CCTV cameras can give up results remarkably quickly, if you're lucky. It was less than an hour since they had returned to the office, and already Dawg was racing in to see Withers with good news.

"We've got them, boss!" he exclaimed excitedly. "CCTV shows four cars leaving the ME26 after the limo, and we have traced all owners. There is one of particular interest…"

Withers nodded. "Someone who has a connection with Altona FC, I'm guessing."

"Well, yes, boss…"

"Had to be, Dawg. There was always going to be a link with the club."

"Maybe so," said Dawg triumphantly, "but I bet it's not what you're expecting." He handed over a sheet of paper, and Withers read it, surprise rising like sunrise over his face.

"Any idea where this Focus is now?"

"The boys are pinpointing as we speak. We've got CCTV of it going into Thurlow, but that's about it. The only thing we know for definite is there are two occupants. They came over very photogenic on one of the cameras."

"ID?"

"One black, unknown to us. The other is a white guy named Richard Towers. Bloody great big fella, he is, too. Wouldn't like to meet him in a dark alley."

"What sort of record does he have?" asked Withers.

"Sketchy, at best. He worked at one time for the Kilburn brothers in Altona, but hasn't been seen lately. Police have spoken to him in the past regarding GBH and such like, but nothing has stuck. Rumours abound that he has also acted as a hitman for the brothers, but that's all they are… rumours."

"Do we have an address?"

Dawg drew an index card from his breast pocket and glanced at it. "He's lived in Thurlow for a few years now. Got a bungalow on the outskirts."

"No basement, I suppose?"

"No chance, boss. It's a tiny place, apparently."

"So the boy won't be there." Withers pondered. "Okay, I don't expect this Towers to be home, but send a patrol car out there, just in case. Make sure they're armed, Dawg. We don't want to take any chances." Both men thought of Phil Lenier, and Dawg nodded solemnly.

"Meanwhile," said Withers, standing and whisking his jacket from the back of his chair in one move, "we'll pay a little visit of our own."

The house that Withers was looking for was one of three terraced properties in a hamlet almost equidistant between Thurlow and the city. It was small, but was immaculately well groomed and put the other two houses in the block to shame. Here was a fastidious owner, Withers surmised, using his deep police brain. There was a car outside, but it wasn't a Ford Focus.

Withers knocked on the door and took out his warrant card. Dawg stood behind him, hand resting on the handle of his gun. You can never be too careful.

The door opened to reveal the sweetest little lady Withers had ever seen. She couldn't have been any taller than five feet, and she wore a beige cardigan over a white blouse with a lace neckline and a green tweed skirt. Her smile was disarming, despite her obvious puzzlement at seeing two large policemen at her door.

"Yes?" she asked.

"Mrs Jean Chivers?" said Withers, his voice reflecting the surprise he felt. Was a hardened criminal standing before him? He thought not!

"Yes," she said, the smile still in place. "And you are?"

"Sheriff John Withers, ma'am. And Deputy Dawg… er, Doug Janowski. From Bakerton."

"Oh, how nice. Would you like to come in?"

Both men reverently took off their hats and stepped inside, waiting in the hallway as Jean closed the door and led them into a small, snug reception room. It was like something out of *Brideshead Revisited*, but on a much smaller scale. The walls were covered in flocked paper depicting some kind of exotic flower which Withers did not recognise, and one large gilt-framed original painting hung on each of the four walls, each depicting a landscape in a particular season, in the style of Constable, or perhaps Gainsborough. The carpet, a little tattered at the corners, it had to be said, used to be a deep burgundy, by the looks of it, but footfall and sunlight through the large bay window had weathered it alarmingly. In the corner sat an upright piano, on which stood an oil painting of a young lady dressed in Regency finery.

Jean caught Withers studying it. "A self-portrait, sheriff. Of course, I was much younger then. And in fancy dress, I hasten to add. I don't want you thinking I'm *that* old!" Her laugh tinkled like a babbling brook falling over smooth pebbles. It was warm and atmospheric. Withers was hooked.

"You are an artist!" he exclaimed.

"Of sorts," she agreed modestly, although he could see the work was of a very high standard indeed.

"The landscapes," said Dawg, "are they yours, too?"

"They are. Painting is my second love."

Withers nodded at the piano. "Music must be first, I imagine."

"Oh, no, sheriff," Jean said with feeling. "Altona football club comes above all else."

"Silly me," said Withers with a grin. "Of course it does!"

Jean fussed around the men, inviting them to sit on the two-seater sofa and offering liquid refreshment. "I only have tea, I'm afraid," she apologised. Both declined. "Now, sheriff, what can I do for you?" she asked, after finally finding a spot on the edge of an armchair and brushing down her skirt, as women of a certain age tend to do, Withers assumed.

He wriggled uncomfortably, as the sofa had clearly not been designed for two brawny men. "We believe you own a Ford Focus, ma'am."

"Yes, I do," she said evenly. "I lent it to a dear friend."

"May I ask who?"

Jean chose to ignore the sheriff's poor grammar, although she did make a mental note of the fact that young people these days are not educated to a sufficient level. It was very sad. "Of course. Dume Akintola has use of it. It is in safe hands."

Withers felt the irony of 'Dume' and 'safe hands' being put in the same sentence, but let it pass. He decided to be brutal. "The car was involved in a serious incident today, ma'am."

"Really?" Jean was visibly shaken, and she moved even closer to the edge of the chair. "What happened?"

"I can't say… but we are currently searching for a Richard Towers in connection with the incident. Do you know the name?"

"No, sheriff, I'm afraid not. I was unaware that Dume had been offering my car to a third person. I am disappointed."

Withers decided to attack from a different angle. "You know Dume from the football club, of course."

"Indeed," agreed Jean, relaxing just a little. Mention of her darling club did that to her. "He is the son of the former chairman, who was a lovely man, too. Very attentive."

To all the women, Withers thought to himself. "Did you spend much time with Dume?"

"Oh, yes. He is a very handsome young man, and he often took me out for cocktails and dinners. He was like a son to me, sheriff. So kind and thoughtful. He was also very close to the players, especially the young ones."

Both Withers and Dawg sat up at this statement. "You knew he was close to the boys?" Dawg spluttered, before Withers could make a similar comment.

"But of course, young man. It was I who introduced them to him. He was deeply interested in their development, especially the ones from his own ethnic background, as you would imagine. I used to drive the boys over to Dume's flat sometimes. It was the least I could do, considering the sterling work his father was doing for the club. I believe the boys benefitted greatly from the association."

Both Withers and Dawg were speechless for a moment. It was clear that Mrs Chivers, the club secretary, had been pimping out young boys for the gratification of an evil paedophile – and she didn't have a clue!

"Do you know why the Akintolas left, Mrs Chivers?" said Withers, no longer feeling that he could call her ma'am. Although she was completely innocent in all of this, she had become tainted. He could not look on her in the same reverential way. He did, however, decide not to enlighten her as to the results of her actions. It would serve no purpose.

"Not really. I know Mr Akintola senior was considerably attracted to Mrs Osborne – you know, Michael's wife – and she even left her husband because of it. All very sad," she added with the slightest of nods, as if she herself had been affected.

"Very," agreed Withers with more feeling than Jean Chivers could imagine. "Just one more question, if I may?"

"Of course," beamed Jean, eager to help the nice policeman, as she did with everyone who crossed her path.

"Where can we find Dume Akintola?"

"Oh, that's easy! He'll be staying at my brother's house."

Withers was stunned. "Your brother's house?"

"Well, my late brother, to be exact. He died last year, and I haven't had the heart to put the property on the market. You know how it is, I'm sure. But yes, Dume will be there. I gave him the keys when he first came to see me about three weeks ago. He told me he needed somewhere large to entertain his many friends that he hadn't seen for some years. I thought it was a wonderful idea, so I mentioned it to some of the players."

"Like Bryn Owen," Withers said softly.

"Oh, yes. I told Bryn, but he didn't seem particularly

happy about it. I thought perhaps he was still jealous, the silly boy."

"Jealous?"

"You know what it's like, sheriff. When one boy is being favoured over another. It wasn't Learie's fault that Dume liked him more, now was it? One would have thought that Bryn might have grown out of it by now."

Withers frowned. "I know it wasn't jealousy, Mrs Chivers. It was something much more."

Jean looked bewildered, not understanding what the sheriff could possibly be saying. However, she continued to smile, as that was her answer to everything.

"Mrs Chivers, where is your brother's house?" asked Dawg, taking out his notepad and pencil.

"It's in Thurlow," she said.

"I bet it's got a basement," said Withers, not needing an answer from the sweet little old lady.

* * * * *

Ty was going to miss this place. He had parked the car up on Copper Ridge, close to the estate of properties that oozed nothing but opulence and luxury – but not close enough to arouse suspicion. The last thing he needed was a set of prying eyes getting too interested in a man just sitting in his car, minding his own business.

The houses and bungalows appeared to have been built in layers, each one set within the hill, and each more grand than the one immediately below it, as if some kind of pecking order had been created, so that the mansion at the very top, complete with its massive glass-fronted verandah, was the icing, the epitome of success, the very pinnacle of power. Ty liked the look of that place, and he sighed: even the couple of million he had made from Leroy wouldn't hold down a mortgage, let alone secure the deeds of a house like that.

His mind wandered to Grace. He had left her hours ago, playing with her new toy and making lists of worthy causes. Ty smiled. He was glad that she had decided to trust him, had joined him in the adventure, and now she was reaping the rewards. He knew he had done the right thing. Leroy's legacy was in safe hands.

He had taken a detour around the Western Lake before coming up to the Ridge. That had been cathartic in some way, his troubled conscience easing somewhat as he drove, window down, the stiff breeze blowing away his cobwebs. Yes, it was magical around here, and he would be sorry to leave…

So there he was, back at the beginning. The reason he was sitting here, hands on the wheel, phone untouched in his breast pocket. He had found that it wasn't so easy after all. Of course he had known that it wouldn't be. His future could be condensed into the next few moments, and he was reluctant to pursue it. This was like knowing the second you are going to die, some time in the future, and not being able to do anything about it. But he could! It was in his hands. He could turn the key, drive away, hide for the rest of his life.

Or, he could make that phone call…

* * * * *

The raid on the bungalow belonging to Richard Towers produced nothing but a bright red kimono large enough for a family of four to camp under and a fridge full of strozzapeti pasta. As Withers had expected, although the type of spaghetti had surprised him. He was a tortellini man.

Now he and Dawg were racing into Thurlow, siren blaring, Dawg gripping the wheel of the patrol car and listening to Withers on the radio.

"Suspect Dume Akintola possibly at Cherry Tree House, Green Road, Thurlow. All cars proceed with caution. Our ETA is twenty minutes. Wait for us!"

Withers sat back in the seat and shared a look with Dawg, as if to say, 'Here we go again'. Neither spoke for several minutes.

The crackle of the radio disturbed the silence. "John, it's Pat."

Withers responded. "What's up, Pat?"

"A blast from the past, buddy. You're not going to believe it."

"Try me."

"Think back to the General," Rafferty said cryptically.

"He's dead."

"Yeah, but who isn't?"

The penny dropped so quickly that Withers half expected to win a cuddly toy. "Ty Cobden," he said through gritted teeth.

"The one and only," said Rafferty.

"So, what about him?"

Rafferty waited a second. "He wants to hand himself in, John."

"You've spoken to him!"

"I have. But he wants you."

Withers was dazed. "What do you mean?"

"He will only surrender to you."

"That's cobblers! I haven't got time for this, Pat. If you're still in contact, tell him to shove his head up his arse and walk it into the station." Withers was beginning to fume.

"No can do, John. He's not on the line any more. He just left you a message: 'I'll meet you at the love seat at four.' How romantic!"

Withers squirmed. "Very funny! Goodbye!"

Dawg looked at his sheriff, noticing the bloodshot face and the anger in his voice. "What do we do, boss?"

"We proceed as planned. Cobden will have to wait."

When they got to Cherry Tree House, Withers was pleased to see that the three squad cars had parked a reasonable distance from the house. He didn't want them to go in gung-ho and lose any of his valuable men. He sought out Deputy Baldwin, from Altona, who had been seconded to act as Withers's eyes and ears if the sheriff was elsewhere. Baldwin was a tall man, an inch or two over his superior, but not quite so broad. He had what some people might call a 'lived-in' face, with wrinkles creasing through other wrinkles, and a murder of crow's feet surrounding both of his penetrating brown eyes. His slicked-back jet-black hair (from a bottle, everyone guessed) was parted at the left and he carried his hat in a chubby left hand. He greeted the sheriff with a smile. "All ready, boss."

Withers nodded and surveyed the scene. The house was,

fortunately, detached, with a fair sized garden which swept round the building, allowing some cover for the approaching officers when Withers gave the order. He was informed by Baldwin that two men were covering the back door from a position outside the fence, so it was unlikely that they would be spotted. As ordered, everyone had their guns in hand, ready to throw the safety catch as they went in.

"Any action?" whispered Withers.

"Not since we've been here," replied Baldwin in hushed tones. "Ten minutes or so, boss."

"Okay." Withers eyed the windows of the house, looking for tell-tale movement. There was nothing. He breathed deeply. "Right, I want four men to get into position under those windows. *Silently*," he emphasised needlessly.

"Yes, boss," said Baldwin, before dashing away and passing on the order to a group in a huddle behind one of the cars. They were Group A of the elite, each one picked personally by the chief of police several years ago to form the 'super-cop' unit, as it became known. Every one of them would have made it into the SAS or the Marines without any trouble, or even the famed US Navy Seals.

Withers watched as they moved off stealthily, trailing their sub-machine guns and snaking their way over the fence and through the garden, their eyes, like Withers's, always on the windows.

The sheriff let out a relieved breath when the unit was in place, two men crouching below each window. They took furtive looks through the glass, then signalled an all-clear.

If protocol was to be observed, Withers should shout out a warning. But what the hell! There was a young boy's life at stake. The next two minutes were crucial. If there was anybody at all in the house, then the element of surprise was going to be the main weapon in Withers's armament. They had to get in, overpower all armed or unarmed suspects or civilians, and secure the place so that a thorough search could take place. *Without loss.*

"Go, go, go!" he screamed, and watched as Group B charged forward with a Blackhawk ram, up the path and, in one strike, broke through the door and then stepped aside so the armed unit Group C could force their way in. At the same time, the unit by the windows smashed the glass and also gained entry, forming a three-pronged attack.

Withers could not wait. Pistol raised, he followed the men into the house, his eyes quickly adjusting to the darkness of the hallway as he heard the familiar "Clear!" when each room was secured. Then he heard movement. A scurrying sound, as somebody was making a hasty retreat towards the back door. His men were in pursuit, shouting a warning and funnelling through the house as fast as they could. Beyond them, Withers could see two men as they charged through the door, firing erratically as they did so.

"Police! Stop!" shouted an officer outside, before a fusillade of bullets fell away to silence. Time seemed to stand still.

"Clear!" the same officer screamed, his voice on edge from the adrenaline pumping. "Two suspects down!"

Withers pushed past his men and out through the back door. The garden would have looked welcoming in the soft sunlight and gentle breeze, except for two bloody corpses sprawled on the grass. Withers ran over to a policeman who was being strapped up by a colleague. He had been shot in the arm, and was clearly in some distress.

"Sorry, sir," said the officer in charge of the unit. "We tried to take them alive."

"I understand. Take care of your man," said Withers, turning back to the house with a grim look on his face. Now was the moment he had been dreading. Was the boy in the cellar? Was he alive? "Clear the way!" he shouted, before heading into the hallway and the stairs leading down to the basement.

With one hand hopelessly searching for a light switch in the dark, and the other holding his gun and pressing against the wall, Withers eased himself down into the cellar, Dawg in his shadow. The only sound he could hear was the distant murmurings of his officers above, clearing up the rest of the house and making it safe for civilians to enter. Non-combatants like forensics and paramedics.

Withers reached the concrete floor and stopped, listening. It was a big house, so the cellar stretched out before him, its nooks and crannies offering inviting places for other, unaccounted gang members. He gripped tighter to his gun, wary of the slightest movement in front of him. Slowly, he stepped forward, feeling the flaking plaster on the walls and sensing the faint smell of petrol and oil from times long past.

He knew he should have sent down the specialist armed unit, but since when did Withers follow the rule book? He had his own to go by. He wanted the lad alive, and it was his job to ensure that happened, regardless of any personal cost.

He edged forward gingerly, senses taut, eyes peeled through the murk of the darkness. Then, he heard a soft groan, and stopped, trying to locate where it came from.

"Sani?" he whispered, hopefully. "We're police," he tried to reassure what he hoped was the schoolboy. He was rewarded with another grunt, although there was no meaning to it. It was just a sound of deep pain.

Withers moved more quickly, panic almost forcing his legs on. He feared the worst.

There was a dark figure on the floor, legs outstretched, back against the wall, head lolling forward. Withers and Dawg were at his side immediately. It wasn't the boy. He was too large for that.

"It's Bryn," sighed Dawg, as Withers carefully lifted the fallen head.

"Yes," he said simply. "In a bad way, too. Get a medic down here now!"

Dawg hurried away as Withers took out his handkerchief and gently wiped the sweat from Bryn's forehead. Both men were shivering, but for two very different reasons.

"Bryn, can you hear me?" said Withers. "Do you know where Sani Okele is?"

It took a while as Bryn licked his lips and built up enough strength to reply. He looked up at Withers and said, "Sani… gone."

Chapter Seventeen

Surveillance, Part III. Mr Sumo had been devastated as he had watched from a safe distance the ransacking of his beloved bungalow by the men in uniform. He had dabbed away some tears with a lace handkerchief, and vowed to get his own back. Arnie had stood beside him, holding the big man back – although they both knew that Mr Sumo could have easily broken away if he really wanted to. Actually, all he felt like doing was curling up in a heap on the ground. He was being violated.

It was then that Arnie's phone had rung and they were suddenly racing off, Mr Sumo disappointed through his anger that he could not fulfil the urge to rip those policemen limb from limb.

"We need to be quick," Arnie had screamed, as he jumped into the car – a green SUV driven by a black guy named Gil, who Mr Sumo had never met before, and took an instant dislike to. The Focus had been abandoned some time ago.

"The boss is very angry," Arnie had said as the car sped away, Mr Sumo gripping the seat in front. "We need to move the boy. The cops are getting too close."

It wasn't long ago that Mr Sumo had been looking

forward to going home after another successful mission. They had delivered the boy to the big house and received a handsome bonus from the boss. He was going to cook Arnie a nice meal to celebrate. Probably pasta. They had even bought an expensive bottle of chateau-something to toast their good fortune. But then the cops had arrived at the bungalow before them. It was luck, really. They could have been inside, toasting their success, when the bastards turned up. That would have been awkward.

As it was, there was barely time for them to get to Cherry Tree House and remove the boy before Sheriff Withers and his men arrived.

Now, the three of them – Arnie and driver Gil in the front, Mr Sumo draped across the back seat – were staking out Cherry Tree House from a road some distance away. Their orders were simple: watch and report back. Arnie had done that several times, keeping the boss fully informed, especially when they heard the gunfire. Now they just waited. Meanwhile, the boy was safely contained in the boot.

* * * * *

It had never been Dume's intention to occupy Cherry Tree House himself. He hated the thought of anyone being able to track him down through a wagging tongue or a word out of place. Jean Chivers had been an asset all those years ago, even if the old crone didn't have the sense to realise what was really going on. She had served her purpose admirably then, and now she had supplied a suitable bolt-hole for the two footballers and the boy. But even that was crumbling.

The police had raided first the bungalow and then Cherry Tree House. When Arnie had telephoned, Dume had gone into a blind panic. His plans were being demolished, one brick at a time, and there seemed to be nothing he could do about it.

They had got the boy out by the skin of their teeth, having to leave Bryn Owen to be dealt with by the two guards who had been living in the house. Dume could only hope that they had disposed of the footballer before he could talk.

* * * * *

Any child could tell you that there are seven colours of the rainbow, but Mr Sumo could see only one – red! His eyes were shrouded in the thickest red mist he had ever known, as the anger he felt towards the sheriff of Bakerton threatened to overwhelm him. He gripped the seat in front with his massive paws, creating huge dents in the *faux*-leather.

"Steady on, pal," said Gil the driver. "This is my car. Mind how you go."

Mr Sumo leant forward so that his lips were so close to Gil's ear that he could feel the breath tickling him. "You ain't no pal of mine, *pal*! You're just the hired help. And you'll treat me with respect. Understand?"

Gil, less than half the size and with a quarter of the power, sank back into his seat. "Sure. Whatever you say."

Mr Sumo let his threat hang in the air, making sure that both men understood who was the boss at this particular moment. Then he gave a short, raucous laugh and slapped

Gil on the shoulder, sending him forward against the steering wheel. "Good man. Now, let's just see where that fucking sheriff goes next, shall we?"

Chapter Eighteen

It was ten to four, and Withers was heading towards the Western Lake in his beloved MX5, grateful that he had found Bryn Owen, but despairing over the African boy. Bryn had been in a bad way, and on first inspection it looked doubtful whether they could save his leg. To Withers's unmedical mind, gangrene would be setting in and there appeared to be nothing they could do. It was a crying shame. Two fine young footballers, destroyed in two very different but final ways. Withers hoped beyond reason that Dume still held the boy, and had not dumped him in a ditch somewhere. That thought made him shiver anew.

What he didn't need now – of all times – was a distraction. And Ty Cobden was certainly that. He had been a prickly thorn from the moment Withers began the investigation into the murders of Leroy Figgis and his associates. What was it, barely a month ago? Ty had escaped the law by a whisker, but now here he was, offering to hand himself in. It just didn't make sense.

Withers pulled into the lake car park and drove to the far end, *his* end. He had felt the connection the moment he first set eyes on the placid blue water and the matching blueflag irises which grew around it, the whole area also dotted with the wonderfully red cardinal flowers. It had almost taken his breath away. He knew Heather would have loved it, and he always felt her presence whenever he sat there, the strains of the day washing away as his memories came to the surface. This was her place as much as his, and he felt that fact so strongly that he had never thought to bring Judith here. One day, perhaps. But not yet.

He sat on the seat, unwittingly rubbing his fingers over the chiselled initials and love-hearts carved into the wood. A living history of past romances. It summed him up exactly.

He watched spell-bound as, in the distance, a middle-aged man pulled from the water his motorised model of *The Cutty Sark*, or some other high-masted schooner, shook off the excess water, and tucked it under his arm with some difficulty due to its size, finally walking off to a second car park on the other shore. The magnitude of the lake demanded two such parking areas, especially during the summer season.

Withers scanned the horizon, as he always did. He was fascinated by the cadmium blue of the sky and the formation of the clouds, as well as the reflections speckled on the water. He should have been an artist. Then he heard the snap of a twig, and thought nothing of it. It would be Ty coming to sit next to him.

Instead, a huge arm went round his throat and lifted him in one movement, dragging him backwards over the bench and into mid-air. He felt his glasses being dislodged, but that was the least of his worries. He had never felt such pressure before, and his breath was catching in his windpipe, unable to escape. He knew, more than anything else, that he had only moments to live. He had to do something.

He kicked out at the man's legs, hoping to deliver a direct hit on a shin; but Mr Sumo was not letting go. To counter-balance Withers's extra height, Mr Sumo was leaning back, creating a curve so that the sheriff's feet could no longer reach the ground, no matter how hard he tried to stretch his toes.

Withers fumbled for the pistol in his waist holster. He managed to unfasten the holster catch, but the position of his body was such that he couldn't quite reach the butt of the weapon to withdraw it. Mr Sumo gave a snort of derision at the sheriff's feeble attempts to save his own life, and squeezed a little more. He was enjoying himself immensely. The red mist had lifted enough for him to wallow in his revenge, and he was going to make the most of it. He even contemplated the idea of letting go of the lawman, so that he could start the whole process all over again. He was playing with a feeble animal, and there was going to be only one winner.

Withers tried one more kick back, this time feeling the satisfying thud as his heel connected with bone, and a short gasp erupted from the lips of his attacker. It was enough. He wriggled down enough to reach his gun, but there was no way he could withdraw it from the holster. He had only one chance. He leant back so that Mr Sumo could grab him again, but at least it meant they were so close that Withers could try his suicidal idea. He pulled the trigger.

Mr Sumo released his grip with a scream of pain and reeled away, looking down at the hole in his shoe. He couldn't see it, but he could feel the blood pumping out of his foot and filling his sock. The red mist was now physical as well as mental, and he shrieked like a banshee as he looked daggers at the sheriff. Death was going to be *so* painful for him.

He reached for the sheriff but only managed to brush his collar, so that Withers could twist away and try to get his gun into action. But he was too slow. For a big man, Mr Sumo was remarkably agile, and he pounced, crashing into Withers's right arm and sending him sprawling across the grass, the gun slipping from his grip and bouncing harmlessly away. It was no longer a fair fight.

Withers struggled to his feet and blinked away the pain. His glasses were long gone, but at least his target was big enough for even his poor eyes to see. He rushed forward, hoping to catch Mr Sumo off-balance. However, the big man stood firm, and grinned as Withers bounced off, falling back to earth with a crunch. Mr Sumo scooped him back up and spun him round, ready to continue the strangulation process. Man, was he enjoying this – apart from the throbbing in his foot.

It was only a heartbeat later that he felt another sharp stab of pain, this time round the back of his head, and he released the sheriff with a surprised gurgle, before turning to see another man wielding a large clump of tree, which then caught him on the temple and sent him crashing.

Ty looked at Withers. Withers looked at Ty. They both looked at Mr Sumo, before shrugging and launching themselves at the huge figure trying to get up. The three of them rolled down to the water's edge, arms and legs flailing, punches hitting and missing, curses filling the air. The feel of the water seemed to stir Mr Sumo, and he staggered to his feet, lifting Ty with him and hurling him up the shoreline, before turning on Withers, who was still gasping for air and trying to clear the water from his eyes. He felt the strong grip and gasped aloud as he, too, was sent tumbling up the grass slope, the two men like human bowling balls coming to a halt beside each other.

Mr Sumo stormed after them, crunching his knuckles with menace and roaring oaths about what he was going to do to them, some of which involved dismemberment.

The mad man was heading for Withers, who shrank back, knowing what damage could be done. He threw a quick glance at Ty, but he appeared to be totally out of it. This was going to be one-on-one, and the bookies weren't going to be falling over backwards offering much cash on a police victory. It was odds-on for the bad guy.

Withers felt himself being pulled up, and he waited for those strong arms to engulf him again. Perhaps it wouldn't take long. It might soon all be over. In some small way he hoped that it might… but then again. He could see his gun glinting in the grass, tantalisingly close but more than an arm's length away. As the huge arms enfolded him, he slipped down and wriggled for all his worth, struggling to escape the clutches of this monster. It was working! He could feel the grip loosening as the arms changed position to exert more pressure on the sheriff's throat. It only needed one final push – but that came from an unexpected source. Suddenly, the big man was growling in pain and letting go of the sheriff, who fell to the ground and scrambled away, seeing out of the corner of his eye the sight of Ty riding on the back of Mr Sumo, his fingers clawing at the monster's eyes, as they both revolved on the spot, like a human corkscrew.

Withers reached for his gun as Ty was thrown into the air, and Mr Sumo was suddenly bearing down on the sheriff.

"That's enough!" Withers spat through gritted teeth and deep gasps for air. Mr Sumo ignored him. On he came, arms outstretched, face contorted in anger and pain. Withers had raised his gun, but the big man engulfed him, arms flailing, the destruction of the lawman his only reason for being there.

A shot rang out, the sound deadened by the mass of fat, bone and muscle surrounding the barrel of the gun. Mr Sumo stopped, even looked down at his belly with a startled expression, before taking a step back and, finally, accepting his fate. He sank to his knees and rolled over, clutching the wound and trying to scoop the blood back into his failing body.

Withers and Ty stood above him, gagging for breath. "What the hell was *that*?" said Ty. "Felt like we just fought with Dr Jekyll's alter ego."

"And only just won," admitted Withers. "Thanks for your help."

Ty nodded. "I'd like to say it was a pleasure."

Both men grinned widely, and Withers shook Ty's hand. "One thing's for sure: I couldn't have done it without you."

"So, what's the story?" asked Ty, retrieving Withers's glasses and handing them to him.

"It's a long one. Perhaps I'll tell it to you one day."

Withers was about to call Dawg when he noticed movement behind them. He looked round, just in time to see a black man running away, scrabbling up the grassy bank and out into the car park. Withers knew he had to give chase.

"Can you stay here, Ty?" he shouted as he sprang into

action. "I'll phone my deputy."

Ty looked startled. "Yeah, sure," he said, confused.

"Thanks again," Withers said as a parting offering, before climbing the bank and racing to his car.

He threw the Mazda into gear and pulled out behind a green SUV containing two men, both of whom were deep in animated discussion. They did not look at all happy.

Withers plugged his phone into the hands-free and dialled. Moments later, Dawg's laid-back voice came over the car.

"Dawg, it's me."

"Yes, boss?" Dawg was suddenly alert.

"You need to get out to my seat by the lake." Everyone in the station knew about Withers's seat. It was always treated with the utmost respect. "Bring an ambulance, too. There's a very large body to clear up."

"Right, boss." Dawg sounded baffled, but knew not to question the sheriff. It always came out right in the end.

"Oh, and another thing…"

"Yes, boss?"

"There will be someone else there. I've sworn him in as a special deputy in the field. So treat him with the utmost respect. Okay?"

"Yes, boss."

The two cars sped through the Bakerton countryside, the rolling hills eventually falling away as the urbanisation of the town engulfed them. Withers wasn't sure if the men in front knew he was in pursuit, but he hoped not, and he kept a reasonable distance, allowing other vehicles to overtake him and tucking in behind them, his eyes always trained on the suspects. He knew they had to be something to do with the big man, and by extension with Dume himself. Perhaps they would lead him straight to the boy.

He was constantly on the phone, dictating his movements to Deputy Keene, who had already informed him that Dawg was on his way to the lake, an ambulance in close attendance. Withers instructed Keene that no other car should be despatched yet, in case they spooked the suspects. He would call for back-up when he was good and ready.

The SUV turned right onto the Thurlow road, and Withers smiled. He could see light at the end of the tunnel. This case started in Thurlow, and it was surely going to end there. He indicated right and eased past a Hilux on the inside lane and swerved into the exit, the MX5 giving a throaty roar of approval as he went down through the gears. He felt like putting on Django's *Swing Guitars*, but that would just be indulgent. He needed to concentrate, not be wafted away into some dark, smoky French jazz club, where sinewy women and beret-wearing stevedores locked hips together over cheap whisky and Gauloises cigarettes. That could wait for another day.

The traffic was building up as they approached the town centre. Withers had time to glance at the parades of shops and the people strolling along in the late-afternoon sunshine. He saw couples hand-in-hand, and elderly folk on their mobility scooters; he saw youngsters gathered outside a coffee shop, mobiles glued to their ears, despite standing next to their friends. He wondered what sort of society was being bred, and felt a certain amount of despair. It had all been so different in his day. But didn't everyone say that?

He almost missed the SUV turning into a side road, and had to quickly readjust his steering in order to follow. He cursed his lack of concentration, and struck the steering wheel in frustration. He couldn't lose them now.

The SUV glided to a stop outside a pretty little two-storey house set back from the road. The man in the passenger seat jumped out and clearly said something to the driver, before the car sped off again.

"Shit!" Withers was in two minds. He pressed his phone. "Keene, get an unmarked car into Thurlow as soon as you can. Pick up on a green Nissan Qashqai, reg number…"

After priming Keene, Withers stepped from his car and approached the house. He removed his hat and put on his windcheater, despite the weather, so that his uniform would not advertise his status. His revolver was safely locked into place, and he thought fondly of the hole in his holster through which he had shot the mad-man with a delicate aim worthy of an Olympian. You don't have to be mad, but it certainly helps in this line of work.

The house looked peaceful, practically inviting. It was in a leafy, almost pastoral street, its neighbours of a similar construction and equally benign. The wooden façades were brightly painted, lending an air of a Swiss canton or perhaps a Bavarian village. Withers was impressed.

He tried to look unobtrusive as he leant into a Portuguese laurel hedge, which stood at least eight foot tall, his eyes straining to look for any movement in the house. There was none, so he edged closer. He ducked under a window and then looked back, his eye going straight to a mirror on the far wall. Through it, he could see the man in an adjoining room. He appeared to be rummaging through the drawers. Withers winced. Either the guy was a very bad burglar, or he was picking up incriminating items ready for a quick exit. Withers knew which was probably the correct answer, and gave himself a Brownie point *and* a gold star. Being a lawman was *so* easy.

He made his way past the front door and down the side of the house, silently opening the gate and coming into a nicely lawned back garden, complete with a swinging hammock and a rather garish pink flamingo, which did nothing to enhance the overall ambience of the place. The patio doors were closed, of course, but Withers could see the man more clearly now, moving from the bureau to the bookcase, pulling out volumes and taking things from them. Withers could see it was money. The man had used his library as a bank, and now he was making a very large withdrawal. Definitely going on a trip.

The man briefly looked up, and Withers slid back out of view. Time to make a decision. There was no chance the patio doors would be unlocked, and even he wouldn't be stupid enough to throw himself through them. That only happened in really bad movies. He could go back to the front door and just ring the bell. "Hello, I'm selling you a timeshare somewhere not so nice. Twenty-plus years to enjoy with the rest of the scum." No, that didn't sound appealing, either. Withers could probably take him without too much trouble, but there must be something better…

He retraced his steps to the front. He could wait there until the man came out; or – he saw another window. It was closed, but a gentle tap with the butt of his gun might just do the trick. It did more than that. Withers thought the cracking of the pane might have been heard in Nigeria itself, but he had no time to think about it. He pushed the broken glass away, pulled the latch and opened the window, climbing through the gap with as much agility as a forty-year-old man could muster. He crawled over a sink and into the kitchen, landing on the balls of his feet and swivelling as the door opened. Arnie was caught completely by surprise. He had heard the noise and had come to see what had caused it, but he never expected to be confronted by a burly police-man, and he fell back as Withers took a swing, connecting with a jawbone.

There was a moment of utter bewilderment as Arnie sat up, rubbing his chin. "Who the hell…?" he managed to splutter, before Withers was on him, grabbing and punch-ing, intent on total domination. Arnie grunted loudly as the wind was expended from his body, but he managed to roll over, taking Withers with him, so that Arnie was now in the superior position. He threw a punch which whistled past Withers's ear, but the next one connected, making the policeman really angry.

"Police!" he screamed.

"Up yours!" Arnie responded, launching another attack.

Withers parried and grabbed Arnie's wrist, his grip vice-like. He pushed upwards, sending Arnie back, until they were both sitting, their arms entwined, like some mad fertility dance. Or death-dance, perhaps. Neither blinked, their eyes locked. Arnie was frothing at the mouth with the exertion and knew he had to do something to break away.

This policeman was much stronger, even if he was at least ten years older.

Arnie leaned to one side, causing Withers a moment of confusion. It was enough. Artful and wiry, Arnie released his grip and sprang up, making Withers let go of his other arm. Arnie aimed a kick at the man on the floor, connecting with his shoulder. Withers gave a groan of pain and rolled over to avoid another kick. He especially needed to protect the wound in his side. At the same time, Arnie was at the sink, struggling to get the drawer open.

Split-second decisions don't come round very often, but Withers now had to make one. If he went for his gun, it would take, what, six seconds to remove it and aim? How fast can a desperate man move in six seconds? Damn fast. He'd be on the sheriff by then, stabbing down at a prone figure, the gun barely out of the holster. Bad choice. So, it had to be option two.

Withers didn't actually need to think through the scenario. His experience and training told him immediately what to do. He bounced to his feet and charged, catching Arnie off-guard as he began to raise the knife. Withers sensed the weapon slice into his jacket, but also felt the satisfying thump as his good shoulder bowled Arnie over, pushing him against the sink and forcing him down to his knees. Withers kicked out immediately, his boot connecting with a falling chin, and Arnie was gone, a crumpled figure on the kitchen floor.

Withers regained his breath, rubbing his bruised shoulder. Then he looked at the damage to his jacket, before stooping down and scooping up the knife. He threw it in the sink and dragged the unconscious man into the lounge, man-handling him up onto the sofa, before removing Arnie's mobile from his pocket.

Then he drew his gun and waited…

Arnie woke up fifteen minutes later, cuffed and bewildered, his chin hurting and his mind in turmoil. As he focused, he saw Withers eyeing him – and brandishing a gun. It was all over.

"So, my friend," said Withers, "we need to talk."

Arnie attempted to open his mouth, but nothing came out. He gulped down some air, and tried again. "I am saying nothing."

"That's a pity," sighed Withers. "Now I might have to shoot you while evading arrest."

Arnie's eyes flew wide open. "You can't do that!" he protested, all the time feeling so vulnerable. Perhaps this mad policeman might just do it.

"Believe me, after what I've been through today, I could pull this trigger quite easily. First, I had your big mate trying to strangle me, and then you offering me the sharp end of a kitchen knife. I'm beyond self-control. Man, you are *sure* going to talk!" It was the longest speech Withers had made in a while, and he leaned back in the armchair, caressing the gun.

Arnie licked his lips and tried to rub his aching chin, the cuffs causing him problems. He shrugged. "I have diplomatic immunity," he said.

"Sorry, chum. That won't work. Just because you're a foreign national, it doesn't mean you can hide behind politics.

I have reason to believe that you are an extremely dangerous criminal, and I would be within my rights to put a bullet in your back as you run away. It would be my word against… Oh, sorry, you wouldn't have a word, would you? You'd be pronounced dead at the scene. What a tragedy." Withers stood and leant over his prisoner. "There is another way…"

Arnie was beginning to understand that his choices were very limited. Judging by the dark look in the sheriff's eyes, Arnie realised that he might just do something stupid. Arnie decided the risk was too great. "What do you want?"

Withers sat back down, holstering his gun. He thought Arnie might open up a little more without the added pressure of hard metal being pointed in his direction. "Name?"

"Arnie."

"More."

"Arnie Bello."

"Good," said Withers. "And you were with the big guy?"

Arnie nodded. "Mr Sumo. We worked together."

It was Withers's turn to nod. "You're doing great, Arnie. Your mother would be very proud of you." He paused. "Just to let you know, I've instructed my deputies to pull in the driver you were with. So… all we need now is your boss's name."

Arnie squirmed. He had known the question was going to come, but that didn't make it any easier. "He'll kill me," he mumbled.

"Not if we get to him first," reasoned Withers gently.

"Is that likely?" asked Arnie hopefully.

"Depends how quickly you spill," said Withers. "After all, it's your life. As well as a young boy's," he added cuttingly.

There was a heavy silence as Arnie deliberated. It wasn't much of a choice, really: years in prison for murder, or a very painful and drawn-out death at the hands of a madman. "Dume Akintola," he said.

"Thank you. I just needed confirmation. Now, how do you contact him?"

"Phone. He has a special one to stay in contact with us."

"Does he now? Text or talk?"

Arnie hesitated. "Both. But I'm not talking to him!"

"No, you're not. That would be plain stupid. You'd give the game away, and we'd be back to square one. Well, I would be. You'd be in a body bag." Withers gave him a sickly smile. "So, it's a text, then." He took out Arnie's phone and waved it at him. "What's he under?"

Arnie squirmed, reluctant to go down this path. "I need some assurances…"

"Of course you do. What's he under?"

"Mechanic."

Withers scrolled into the contacts and pulled up the 'Mechanic' number. "Now, my friend, this is the moment of truth. If we don't get through to Dume, you don't get through the next minute. Understand?"

Arnie nodded. "It's him. Honest."

Withers chuckled. "Honest? Man, you don't know the meaning of the word."

Arnie squirmed a little more. "What are you going to say?"

"That's not for your delicate ears, chum. You just sit tight, and I will conduct business from here on in."

Withers stepped out of the room with a thin smile on his face, while Arnie just sat there, like a good little boy.

* * * * *

The SUV was being driven erratically, frantically. Gil had seen in his rear-view mirror a sports car stop exactly where he had dropped Arnie, and his pulse was racing. What to do?

Arnie had told him of the demise of the big man: he couldn't confirm he was dead, but Arnie was pretty convinced. "It was like Kilimanjaro tumbling down," Arnie had said. "A great mass spread across the ground, still, unmoving." Arnie had a way with words, and Gil had no doubts that his report was accurate.

Now, Arnie looked to be in trouble, too – and there was still the boy in the boot. What to do indeed?

He gripped the wheel with ever more sweaty hands, and could feel the dampness on his forehead. Dammit, he was a driver. That's all! Not a bloody hoodlum or gangster. That sort of thing was down to Arnie and the big man who he didn't like. Good riddance!

His narrow eyes kept darting from the windscreen to the rear-view mirror, expecting at any moment to see a wailing police vehicle getting closer… and closer.

He could dump the boy and run. Hell, that was one possibility. But not a good one. He knew from Arnie and the others the extent of the power of his boss, and he didn't hold out much hope of getting away with it. Think again, you fool.

He could never harm the boy – that was not in his DNA – so the only option left was to deliver him, as they had initially been instructed.

There was, however, one problem: only Arnie knew who and where the boss was.

* * * *

After a squad car had picked up Arnie, Withers began to set his plan in motion.

He had no intention of texting Dume; he would have smelled a rat in an instant. No, there had to be another way.

Withers took out his own phone and dialled the number on a business card. After a few seconds, a female voice came on the line, and Withers said, "Mr Marsland, please."

"Who shall I say is calling?"

"Sheriff Withers."

"Ah, sheriff. I believe your colleague was looking for me."

"Was he now?" said Withers, a smile on his face. Good old Pat.

"Perhaps you could get him to call me," said Ursula Rawlings.

"I most certainly will. He speaks very highly of you, Mrs Rawlings." He thought he could almost hear her blush on the other end of the line.

It took a very short time for Eric Marsland to be connected. "Sheriff?" he said questioningly, not expecting to have heard from the lawman again.

"Mr Marsland," drawled Withers, "you did say that if I ever needed your help…"

Chapter Nineteen

Gil was at the end of his tether. He had parked up, out of sight – at least, he hoped so. His head was in his hands, his breathing fast and furious. He had never felt so drained, so hopeless. He could hear the boy struggling in the boot, and he had half a mind to let him go.

It was at that moment his phone erupted. He sat there frozen, unsure of what his next reaction should be. Then, robotically, he took the phone out of his pocket and listened.

"Gil?"

"Yes," he spluttered.

"Where is Arnie?"

"Who is this? How did you get this number?"

The voice was strong, authoritative. "Listen to me, Gil. Where is Arnie, and do you have the boy?"

Gil squirmed a little more. "I dropped Arnie off. He asked me to, said I should pick him up again later."

Gil didn't like to add that, after the death of the big man, Arnie had panicked and was planning to do a runner. He had merely gone home to pick up a few things; then they were going to drop the boy off and Arnie would disappear. Gil had intended going round the block and then returning to Arnie's house, but the arrival of the man in the sports car had ruined that plan. He thought it best not to mention any of this.

"I don't seem to be able to contact him," said the voice. "Lucky he gave me your number, eh, Gil?" the voice said with heavy emphasis.

Lucky? Yeah, thought Gil sadly. *Very.*

"Do you still have the boy?" the voice repeated, more urgently this time.

"In the boot."

"Good. Now tell me, Gil, exactly where you are. I will send someone to collect the boy."

Gil wondered if he was doing the right thing when he spoke again.

* * * * *

Eric Marsland listened intently as Withers explained what was required.

They were in Withers's car, heading towards a showdown which Withers wasn't a hundred percent sure he could win. His shoulder hurt, and he stretched to ease the pain, flexing muscles that ached with age and exertion. He wasn't sure which of the two caused him the most grief.

The sheriff still wasn't convinced that Marsland was the man for the job, but he needed someone who at least sounded like a legal eagle and would stand scrutiny.

"Can I depend on you?" he asked, casting a quick look at his passenger.

"Absolutely, sheriff. I understand what is required." He almost added that he was definitely stone-cold sober, and that he would never let him down, but thought better of it. There would be no logic in reminding the sheriff of his inebriated state the first time they met. He needed to maintain trust.

Withers pulled the car up outside the Nightingale Hotel, where a valet in full dress uniform slipped into the driver's seat as Withers held the door open. As he prepared to take the car to the underground car park, the valet was well aware of Withers's scowl, implying that he should guard the motor with his life. The valet nodded, knowing full well that every client gave him the very same look. Quite often, it was clear that the car was held in higher esteem than the human accompanying the client.

As they stood in the street, Marsland clutching his briefcase, they looked at each other, both nervous, but for very different reasons. Marsland was about to embark on an acting performance, while his director was hoping that his star turn wouldn't deviate too far from the script.

"Ready?" asked Withers tremulously.

"Ready," Marsland confirmed with steel in his voice.

"Then good luck." To both of us, Withers didn't need to add.

* * * * *

With its registration number and description circulated, it didn't take long for a patrol car to track down the SUV. Two officers, guns drawn, approached the vehicle cautiously, aware that it had been involved in an incident reportedly involving Sheriff Withers. They therefore trod carefully, expecting some kind of confrontation.

The tall one, name of White, took the driver's side, while his partner, Porter, kept the other side, a couple of steps back.

"See anything, Dan?" Porter asked, his eyes sweeping the immediate area.

"All quiet, Wes," White responded. He had reached the front of the vehicle and peered through the windscreen. "Nothing here."

Porter came up opposite, so that they could look at each other through the side windows. Nothing. In tandem, they moved towards the back of the car and looked at the passenger seats. "Looks like the remains of a sandwich my side," Porter said.

"I see it," said White. "Newspaper my side."

"Looks like whoever was in here left in a hurry," said Porter.

"They must have known we were on to them."

Porter looked over the roof of the car. "Throw the lever on the boot, Dan. Let's see if they've left us anything in the back."

White opened the driver's door and located the switch. "Be my guest, Wes," he said drily, knowing it would draw a blank. It always did in these circumstances. Both he and his partner were used to abandoned vehicles. He was just surprised that it hadn't been torched, like so many others he had come across while out on patrol.

Officer Wes Porter strolled to the back of the car, where the boot was slightly up, bouncing gently from the releasing of the locking mechanism. It didn't take any effort to lift it to its full height. "Holy shit!"

Porter was beside him immediately, both of them looking down into the pit of the boot, where the body of Gil was curled up, a large amount of blood running into a pool from a bullet hole in the side of his head.

* * * * *

Marsland walked into the foyer of the hotel and made his way to the small, intimate café which looked out onto the street. He saw Arusi immediately, seated in a corner, sipping coffee out of a porcelain cup. Marsland gave a small gulp as he also took in the suited substitute bodyguard standing close by, a hand almost casually tucked into his belt. Everyone in the place knew he was armed, but they went about their lives without concern. *Nothing unusual here, folks. Move along.*

"Mr Marsland?" said Arusi, eyeing the visitor almost with disdain. "Please, take a seat."

"Thank you," said Marsland nervously.

Arusi looked at his bodyguard, who edged a little closer, and then back at Marsland. "Your secretary said you wished to discuss something important."

While Marsland knew that the 'secretary' must have been Withers, he nodded. "Yes, indeed. Now, may I talk frankly?" He inclined his head towards the bodyguard.

"Of course, Mr Marsland. My colleague here has large ears, but no tongue. He will listen, but cannot pass comment." Arusi gave a little laugh, and Marsland wasn't sure how much of that had been a joke. He preferred not to know.

"Very well. It concerns your son Dume."

Arusi was immediately on edge. He was surprised that Dume should be a topic of discussion, considering his entry into the country had not been common knowledge.

Naturally, Arusi had checked out the man sitting opposite him, and had confirmed he was a solicitor working for a company in Thurlow. But how did any of that connect with his son? "In what way, Mr Marsland? What has my son to do with you?"

"Oh," grinned Marsland, beginning to enjoy himself, "not me, Mr Akintola. My client."

"Who is?" Arusi had no idea what this man was getting at.

"Mr Okele, sir. Kashim Okele. I believe you know him." Marsland had been tutored extremely well in the few minutes Withers had with him. And he was a good pupil.

"Kashim, yes, I know him," Arusi said, bewildered.

"Mr Okele would have sent his greetings, but for one thing." At that moment it was clear to Marsland that Arusi had no idea what he was talking about.

"I don't understand. Kashim is one of my son's friends."

Marsland felt it was the right time to give a little chuckle. "Oh, I don't think so!" Before Arusi could say anything, Marsland continued, "Your son has been a very naughty boy, sir. Mr Okele is not happy."

The bodyguard had stepped even closer now, sensing danger. Arusi put up one finger, which stopped him in his tracks. "I think you need to explain yourself, Mr Marsland. You are talking in riddles."

"I have a message from Mr Okele, sir. You will need to put it to your son."

It was all rubbish, of course, but Arusi was never going to know that. He was flustered, unsure of how to proceed. He knew what his son was capable of, but this sounded worse than anything that had gone before. Perhaps now he was going to find out why his son had slipped into the country. "Please, tell me what you want. Otherwise my silent friend will…"

Marsland did not let him finish. "Your son has kidnapped Mr Okele's son."

Arusi's mouth tightened, but he squeezed out the word, "Sani?"

"Yes, Mr Akintola. We are fearful as to what Dume intends. Kashim needs you to talk to your son."

Arusi stood, his chair sliding back across the polished floor. "I don't believe…" he began, but the words wouldn't cross his lips, because he *did* believe. He suddenly knew how evil his son really was, and it cut him to the quick, ripping out his heart and tossing it aside like offal. A tear crossed his eye and he swept it away angrily. "Stay there!" he ordered, as he pulled out his phone and took a few steps away.

Dume replied almost immediately, and the discussion, at least from Arusi's side, was raucous. When he finally put his phone back in his pocket, Arusi was clearly fuming, and his self-control was barely contained. Not only did he want to strangle his own boy, but also the man sitting at the table, the messenger of doom who had the audacity to open a Pandora's box of past doings and present evil. He clenched his fists.

That was when Withers came in. "Mr Akintola," he said breezily, "how pleasant to see you again."

Arusi gave Withers a look of distain as the sheriff sat at the table. "What do you want now?" he asked. The body-guard flexed, fingers hovering over his jacket, feeling for the gun concealed beneath.

Withers shook his head and tutted, and the bodyguard pulled back ever so slightly, unsure. He was a big guy, but it looked more like fat than muscle, and Withers wasn't too alarmed. He had already dealt with Mr Sumo – so this Fat One shouldn't prove too much of an obstacle.

"I have some good news and some bad, Arusi. You don't mind me calling you Arusi, I hope. I like to keep things nice and friendly. Don't you agree?"

Arusi wasn't in the mood. "Get to the point."

"I have a hospital report on your man Benjamin…"

"He's alive?" Arusi exclaimed in shock and delight.

"Barely," said Withers. "But he's hanging in there. A close call, though. Your son cut it very fine – or perhaps he really didn't want Benjamin dead. Perhaps he's not really wicked," Withers said, his voice clearly indicating that he felt Dume *was* really wicked.

Arusi took his time to respond. "So, what's the bad news?"

"I'm going to get your son," Withers stated calmly. "And you've just helped me."

Arusi's veins throbbed even more, his bile rising along with his pulse rate, and he stared at the sheriff, eyes piercing. "I'll never help you," he snarled.

"Oh, but you already have. Now, I'll take your phone if you don't mind."

Arusi chortled, the sound echoed by the bodyguard, whose stomach moved in sync. So out of condition, thought Withers, knowing he could take the man on if it became necessary. Hopefully, it wouldn't come to that.

"What makes you think I'm going to hand it over, sheriff?" Arusi said, the chortling at an end.

"It's not a request, Mr Akintola."

"Is that so?" said Arusi, smiling at his bodyguard. The Fat One returned a toothy grin. Arusi looked back at Withers, his eyes narrowed, jaw set. "You are ordering me, then?"

Withers smiled sweetly. "Let's call it a deal, Mr Akintola. You do this for me and…" He stopped, waiting for Arusi to fill in the missing words. He wasn't disappointed.

"And you will do something for me."

Withers gave the slightest of nods.

Arusi offered a crooked smile. "And what on earth could you possibly give me, sheriff? There is nothing that would be of the slightest interest to me. You are sadly mistaken if you think I am open to offers."

Withers leant forward, invading Arusi's personal space. He breathed on the other man as he said, "I will keep your son alive."

Arusi's eyes flashed. "What do you mean?"

"Just that," said Withers. "It's a wicked world out there, Mr Akintola. Anything could happen."

Arusi was seething. "You dare to threaten me?" he asked, voice rising.

"I'm just saying, that's all. Who knows what sad event may befall your son. A stray bullet, perhaps. In the heat of the moment, of course." Withers gave him a grin of resignation, as if it was all out of his hands and in the lap of the gods.

"You would do that?" Arusi asked, stunned.

Withers did not answer him, but tilted his head slightly. The bodyguard made a movement, but Arusi settled him with a wave.

"I was under the impression that this is a civilised country, Mr Withers," Arusi sneered, still not sure how serious the sheriff was.

"I am speaking for myself," said Withers, "not my country." He paused. "Your son is a killer. He stinks!"

Arusi jumped to his feet, and the Fat One reached for his gun. Withers was too fast for both. He pushed Arusi back, making him fall into the bodyguard, who went sprawling, the gun rattling to the floor and skidding under a nearby table. Arusi just held on to his balance by gripping a table, but as he turned he came face to muzzle with Withers's pistol. The Fat One stood back up, preparing to pounce.

"Sit down, Mr Akintola," Withers hissed, thoroughly pissed off. He'd had enough. "Call off your thug, or I will not be responsible for the consequences."

However, in the few seconds all this had taken place, Marsland had seen the threat and jumped to his feet. Using his briefcase as a swinging club, he dealt the bodyguard a crushing blow across his cheek, throwing him backwards so that his head hit the wall with a dull thud. Marsland then casually handed the Fat One's gun to Withers, before sitting back down and adjusting his tie.

Withers grinned at him and gave him a thumbs-up. Bloody hell, he thought, this solicitor must be a caped crusader in his spare time.

The hotel manager had been standing by from a safe distance, face contorted in anguish, fingers nervously stroking the creases in his trousers, wondering how on earth he was going to explain this destruction to the hotel's executives.

Arusi sat on the chair Marsland had pushed his way.

"You are extremely quick, sheriff," he said, "for your age."

Withers ignored him. "Now, let's talk business, shall we?"

"It would appear you have the upper hand."

Withers smiled. "I'd call it a full house, Mr Akintola. And you've been dealt a crap hand." He looked at the Fat One with disdain, still splattered against the wall, then back to Akintola. "Not only is your bodyguard a busted flush, but your son is wanted for murder. Time to cash in your chips."

Arusi was not a stupid man. He sat upright in his chair, sighed heavily and looked hard at Withers. "You know that if anything happens to Dume, I will kill you."

"I do," said Withers. "But your son will still be dead." He pulled his chair closer, the scraping sound echoing ominously through the now-empty café. "I don't like perverts, I hate killers, and I detest people who soil my towns. Your son has managed all three, Mr Akintola, and now it's time he paid."

Arusi slumped in his chair. "You will protect my boy?"

"To the best of my ability."

Arusi slowly took out his phone and handed it over. Withers gave his gun to Marsland. "Eric, keep an eye on these two, will you?"

Marsland smiled. "Yes indeed, sheriff." He was enjoying himself immensely.

Withers checked on the last number Arusi had called, and saw it was under the name of 'Ayo'. If he hadn't known, it would have taken some time to work out this was Dume. "What's in the name Ayo?" he asked.

Arusi sat stony-faced, his eyes fixed on the sheriff. "When he was born, I called him Ayòwolé, which means 'Joy has come in' in our language. He brought me much joy…"

Withers sneered and then quickly tapped in a message, and waited.

Dume looked at the boy. It had not been personal, or even sexual – just a means to an end. He had no interest whatsoever in Sani Okele; it was Sani's father that ate away at Dume's insides, filling him with such a deep hatred that it felt like a cancer gripping him.

Sani's eyes were wide. He had stopped shaking, the fear subsiding a little, but he was still in shock. He had come across many men like Dume in his short life, and he was stoic enough to know that there was nothing to be done about his current position. There was no doubt in his mind how serious this was, because he knew that Peter the chauffeur was dead, along with the man driving the other car, both shot by Dume's men, and he had been forced to leave Bryn in that cellar. It was a fact of life. Live with it.

He knew better than to open his mouth, so he just watched as Dume paced the room. It had come as a surprise when the two men had dragged him away from Bryn and bundled him into the boot of that car, a plastic bag over his head. That had been the worst part – the clinging smell and terrifying confines of the bag. He had been desperate for the journey to be over, his breath catching and his nerves jangling as the car raced round roads that he could not see. On top of that, he had been transferred to the second car for another trip, and now he was tied to a chair, a piece of rag round his neck where Dume had loosened it from his mouth, and at the mercy of a man his father had told him about many times. Once, they had been comrades; now they were sworn enemies, and Sani was the helpless link between the two.

He watched intently. Dume was expecting something.

When the mobile rang, it surprised both of them. Dume took the phone from the table and looked at it, wondering why his father should be texting him so soon after their bilious conversation only minutes ago. Dume had been shocked that Arusi knew what he had done, and he felt a small tremor through his body. It was true that he hated what his father had become, but he was still his flesh and blood. There was no respect, but there was love.

We need to talk.

This was clearly not what Dume was expecting. He tapped in: *What is the problem now?*

There were a few seconds before a reply pinged back. *Meet me.*

Dume looked at the boy, and back at his phone. He thought about it, then typed: *Why?*

More seconds elapsed, as Dume waited. He was confused, wondering what this was all about. He had the boy, so why should he worry about anything else? All he was waiting for was Kashim's call so they could negotiate.

They will destroy you, Ayo.

Then there was nothing.

Arusi Akintola's phone had fulfilled its role. Withers put it in his pocket and signalled for Marsland to get up. He had thought of saying something pithy and deep, but instead he just let out a long sigh and led Marsland out of the café. Arusi was still shaking. Withers couldn't be sure whether it was shaking from fear or anger, but he didn't much care. It was time to prepare, and he sure as hell didn't want to think of the father when the son was in his sights.

They passed the shattered manager with nods and stepped out into air that was fresher and more agreeable than the kind they had just left.

Two agents were waiting. "He's all yours," Withers said, before walking down the road and taking out Arnie's mobile. He pressed some buttons.

"Arnie?" The voice on the other end sounded plaintive, almost broken.

"Not this time, chum," Withers said. "But I'll do a swap."

"What do you mean? Who are you?"

Withers waited, ratcheting up the tension. "Listen, Ayo, there's been a change of plan."

"What?" Dume was shocked at the use of his childhood name by a stranger.

"Those texts from your father – well, they weren't. You're coming to see me."

"Who are you?" spluttered Dume again.

"If this was a movie, I'd say, 'Your worst nightmare'. But it's even worse than that." Withers was pleased with that line. If circumstances allowed in the future, he might use it again. "I want the boy, you want your father." The bargain was a bit of a moot point, seeing as Withers didn't have Dume's father: at this moment he was being escorted to a cell by two burly agents. But what the hell? What Dume didn't know wouldn't hurt him, even though Withers knew that it would do in the end.

Dume remained silent as Withers explained what was required of him, finally grunting a reluctant acceptance before Withers cut the line and placed the phone back into an evidence bag. Sure, the phone would have his prints on it, but it would also have Arnie's, and they supplied a direct link to Dume. Just one more piece of evidence to help nail him.

"You know, sheriff," said Marsland, puffing out his cheeks, "that was a whole lot of fun."

"You did well," Withers complimented him. And he meant it.

"Thank you," said Marsland with deep humility. "I think the adrenaline is still pumping round inside me." He stopped walking and looked straight at the sheriff. "I've been a bloody fool, haven't I?"

Withers wasn't sure what he meant, so he said nothing.

"All that booze. It almost destroyed me."

Withers couldn't argue. "It's a slippery slope, if you're not careful." He thought of himself, the days and weeks after the death of his wife. How he had spiralled out of control: drinking, not sleeping, his life a void created by wickedness and filled with regret and anger – so much anger.

He put his hands on Marsland's shoulders. "Listen, Eric, the future is yours. How you deal with it is up to you. If you're anything like me – and I think you are – you'll come out the other end." He grinned, thinking of his new beginning with Judith. "Who knows, perhaps even Maureen will see the new you."

"Ah," chuckled Marsland, "now wouldn't that be something, eh?"

Without thinking, they fell into a man-hug, thumping each other enthusiastically on the back, before sauntering down to the underground car park together. Despite his new-found bonhomie, though, Withers wasn't in the mood for tipping the valet this time.

Chapter Twenty

He didn't know what to think, what to do. The phone call had thrown him completely. He was normally so calm and collected, some might say driven and focused, but now he sat in the chair, rubbing his mouth with the back of his hand, mind beginning to coagulate horribly. He knew the boy was watching, and that didn't help his thought control. He shook his head to clear it.

Dume stood and began to pace the room, feeling the perspiration on his brow, and he wiped it away with an angry swish of his hand.

Who was this man taunting him? Not Nigerian, clearly. He sounded white and strong, perhaps too strong even for him. So, did he work for Kashim? Or was he independent, someone who knew Dume's story and had some inside information on the kidnapping. A cop? No, stupid thought. The police didn't threaten people like that. They didn't offer to exchange one hostage for another, no matter what the situation. They had a strict code of rules to abide by. And that always helped people like Dume.

So, not a policeman, then. But who? Why would Kashim employ a local? And how many more of them were there? An unknown quantity.

Dume did his own sums. Arnie had given up his phone, which meant that he was probably dead. Mr Sumo, too, bearing in mind that they had been working together. Dume had lost two others at the house after he had spirited the boy away, also leaving Gil behind with a bullet in the head for company. That left Dume with four men, none of whom filled him with confidence. There might be some brawn there, but zero brain cells. How he could do with Mr Sumo and Arnie now.

The boy stirred in his chair, causing Dume to look at him. His hatred of Sani's father came back to the surface and he walked over to the boy, stood above him, and brought his hand down with a sickening slap which left a red weal on the youngster's cheek. Sani whimpered softly, aware that any show of bravado now would encourage more violence.

"You for my father," Dume hissed. "I will make the exchange, but at the end of it, only he will be alive."

* * * * *

Withers was amazed to see Dawg already there. He was even more shocked to see Ty Cobden standing beside him.

"He wanted to come along," explained Dawg. "After all, you did say he was a deputy."

"So I did," said Withers. "Whatever was I thinking?"

Ty smiled. "I wanted to see this through before you lock me up and throw away the key. We need to finish what we started."

Withers nodded. For some reason he couldn't explain, he trusted Ty, and knew he would be an asset.

They were in the place where this sorry mess had begun – the railway sidings in Thurlow Junction. Where the body of Jet Carmichael had been found only days ago, strangled by the mad Richard Towers, aka Mr Sumo, and discarded like a rag doll.

The two footballers had sacrificed themselves in the false belief that Dume was about to molest one or more of the youngsters at the club.

Jet was dead, and Bryn was in hospital, his leg hopefully being saved by dedicated surgeons, but his career over. Although sedated, he had spoken to Withers, who had sat by the bed, his hand on the young man's shoulder, offering silent sympathy and support.

"Mrs Chivers told me he was back," he had said through gritted teeth. "Dume Akintola. I had to warn Jet. We didn't want it to happen again."

Withers had nodded. "Jet was abused by him."

"Yes," confirmed Bryn with a deep sigh. "We were close." He had shut his eyes for a few seconds, remembering.

Withers had let him, before asking, "Jet wanted to come back to Altona?"

"No, sheriff, he *needed* to come back. He had to save those lads. He'd been through it… he knew what it was like. He had to stop Akintola."

It was just as Withers had thought: Jet Carmichael pulled every string to get back to Altona. Then he and Bryn had tackled Akintola in the belief that he was getting back to his old ways. How wrong they were! It was much more complicated than that. But suddenly they were a threat to his plans, so he had to secure them. He might, possibly, have let them go after his plan had succeeded and he'd gone back to Nigeria, but when they made an escape bid, Dume had no compunction in ordering a death warrant on Jet. The big man, Mr Sumo, had duly obliged…

There was an eerie silence, as if the spirit of Jet had sucked out all the life from the place, almost creating its own atmosphere of mourning, keeping its peace for the dear departed. Withers shivered, and stamped his foot to mask his emotions. He looked around, taking in the sad sight of disused carriages with their fading livery, expanding rust spots and glassless windows, sprouting greenery and shrubs, as if the whole world had abandoned them to the elements without a thought.

Withers turned away. "Dawg, is everyone in position?"

"Yes, boss."

"Then we wait."

"The priority is my Papa," Dume said. "Everyone else can go to hell!"

The driver offered a nod, while the three men squeezed into the back of the car sat like statues, each wondering whether their lives were about to end.

"Understand?" boomed Dume.

"Yes, boss," they sang in unison, like a thuggish version of the Temptations.

"Good," Dume concluded softly, almost to himself. He was still trying to work it all out. Was it even possible that Kashim had secured the services of somebody so quickly? And a white man at that. It was unheard of. It was like the

Mafia using someone with no Sicilian blood. Impossible! So who is this guy?

The car was making good progress. He had been told – no, *ordered* – to be at the railway sidings at a certain time, and that time was fast approaching. It went against the grain, but he had to comply. His Papa's life might depend on it.

Dume's mind went back to the day, twelve years ago, when his father first learned of what had occurred with Jet. His face had thundered, and his body shook. Dume had never seen such a sight, not from anybody, let alone his father. Arusi had turned a blind eye to the fact that Dume liked men, even though it was an abomination to him. But this was different. Jet was a child.

Arusi had taken his belt to his son, despite his age, and Dume had accepted the punishment because it was being carried out by his father. Those were the days when respect was closely bound up with familial love.

The next day, Arusi had told the football club that he was returning home immediately, and Dume was put on the next flight, a cock and bull story quickly fabricated to give to those at home so that the truth never emerged. Until now.

Dume pressed a button and the window glided down silently, sending in a rush of cool air, which played round his face and through his hair.

With a feeling of helplessness mixed with anger, he spat out a mouthful of phlegm and banged his fist on the car door. "Bastard!" he screamed, causing the other men to sit back in deference and fear. The driver gripped the wheel a little tighter.

Withers could feel the air cooling. It was that time of the afternoon, when the sun seemed to slink away and greying clouds came to the fore. It was a similar sort of day the last time, when he and Dawg faced the General… and poor Phil Lenier had lost his life.

He couldn't help himself: his mind replayed the scene – the shouting, the confusion, and, finally, the sightless eyes of the General as Withers lay beside him in the dirt. It was that last vision which had etched itself into his brain, and he felt guilty for that, because he knew that it should have been the sight of Phil's body lying in the undergrowth seared into his psyche, not that of the cold-blooded killer.

He looked at Dawg and was grateful that he, at least, had come through it relatively unscathed. But now Withers was endangering him again, and he prayed that there would be a more positive outcome this time.

His radio crackled. "Car approaching, boss," a voice said. "Looks like our subject."

"Good," replied Withers. "Can you see the boy?"

"Negative. Five IC3 males. No juvenile."

Withers thought about it. This might be a complication. "Okay, let me know when they are on foot," he said.

"Yes, boss."

Dawg, too, had been thinking of Phil Lenier. They had been colleagues for two years, close friends for slightly less than that. They had shared a passion for football, albeit at opposite ends of the spectrum. Phil had occasionally turned out for Thurlow Town in the Minor League, but also supported Bakerton. Neither club was at the level of Dawg's team,

Altona City, of course, but that encouraged the friendly banter between the two young policemen. Yes, Dawg missed his friend.

He looked across the siding. He could see Withers, but only because he knew he was there. He looked for the others: Keene, young Morgan on his first serious outing, Wilson… and then he spotted Ty Cobden moving between some bushes. He had thought it mighty strange that his sheriff had deputised a wanted killer, and he treated the man with suspicion. True, he had waited at the lake for Dawg and the ambulance to arrive to clear up the body of the big man, and had answered all the questions asked of him, in a courteous and impressive way. Still, one could never be sure…

Dawg's mind wandered further, this time to Kitty and their son. He had been in love with her since his eleventh birthday, when their eyes met across a crowded playground. Young love it certainly was, on both sides, and it was rock solid, surviving hectic teenage years and separation while Dawg was at police college. The arrival of little Matthew had brought the final joy, although life had been a strain for the first year, as Dawg settled into his position as lead deputy to the enigmatic and at times annoying Sheriff Withers.

Ty Cobden was moving faster now, heading away from Dawg and the others. He looked furtive to Dawg, and the deputy was ready to follow him, convinced that he was up to no good. Killers don't change their spots.

The entrance to the sidings was eerily silent as Dume opened the door and got out of the car. He clutched his pistol a little tighter, his fingers wrapping around the grip and the trigger almost lovingly, a caress of imminent death. He didn't like this one bit. "Anil, stay here. The rest of you, spread out."

There was a grunt of acknowledgement from the others as they emerged from the car, adjusting their jackets and removing various firearms. They looked ready for action, even if they did not fill Dume with total confidence.

Two of them peeled to the left, skirting one of the carriages which lay at an unusual angle, partly submerged in a crater obviously formed when the soil had fallen away during the rains. The men crouched and moved as stealthily as they could, neither of them confident or relishing the prospect of an uncertain or painfully short future. They edged carefully round the carriage, leaning on it at times to avoid falling into the shallow water a metre below, knowing that to do so would not only infuriate their leader, but would also mean being left behind. Not an outcome either of them would want. They needed to stay together.

Dume sent the other one off to the right, believing in the value of the famed 'two-horn' attacks carried out by the Zulu impis in the nineteenth century when they caused such destruction and death to the British Empire. If not exactly a devout military tactician, Dume knew well enough the value of learning from history.

He waited for a minute, listening. He could hear his men, wheezing and struggling, and knew that whoever was out there would also be alert to the sounds. It was a sobering thought.

Withers spotted Ty just as he broke cover and edged towards him, waving. Withers crawled over and they sat in the long grass, shoulder to shoulder, breathing muted.

"I can tell you, Dume won't set foot in here, sheriff," said Ty. "If he's had any guerilla training – and my guess is he's had plenty – then he'll hang back and wait for us to make a move."

Withers nodded. "I agree."

"So I suggest we go after him."

Withers smiled wickedly. "Sounds good. Follow me."

Ty hesitated, a strange look on his face. "What?" asked Withers, studying the other man. He hadn't expected him to baulk at the prospect of confrontation. "Don't tell me you're scared!"

Ty gripped the sheriff's arm as his features darkened. "That's not even remotely funny." Then, as his grip slackened, he grinned, the dark moment past. "It's just that I'd prefer to be armed."

Withers chuckled silently. "Of course! Sorry."

Without thought, the sheriff scurried back to one of his deputies and relieved him of his firearm, placing it firmly in Ty's hand when he returned.

"Thanks, John," whispered Ty with feeling.

Withers was surprised at how agile Ty was as he crawled through the grass that had been free for forty years to engulf the old sidings. They stopped only once, both of them listening intently for any sign of Dume or his men. There was nothing, so they moved on, each on full alert, but strangely relaxed in the knowledge that they had each other's backs. Once again, Withers found himself thinking how Ty might have been a formidable deputy – or perhaps even a sheriff in his own right. The military training helped, of course, but Withers knew there was something else driving Ty forward, as if making amends in some small way might erase the pain and humiliation gnawing away inside his head, mixing a lethal cocktail with the memories of war which still might cloud his judgement at the final hurdle. Withers put such thoughts out of his mind as he came up next to Ty.

"I can see their car," the sheriff whispered from the corner of his mouth.

Ty nodded. "And two men."

Withers lifted his head a fraction, his eyes scanning the view in front of them. "No sign of the boy," he said.

"Would he have brought him?" asked Ty.

"I reckon," said Withers. "He thinks we're working with Kashim, and he desperately wants his father back."

Ty grinned. "Pity he's locked up in a cell, then."

"Luckily, Dume doesn't know that," breathed Withers, eyes scanning the view in front of him. He could just make out the car, part-hidden in the undergrowth, and could see two pairs of legs, one in blue and the other in grey.

Ty voiced his own thought. "Which one is Dume?"

Withers shook his head. "Not sure. We need to get closer."

Without waiting for a response, Withers edged forward, belly flat, and his wound beginning to throb both with the exertion and the adrenaline.

Dume didn't like silence. He had grown up in a raucous environment, full of arguing men and bickering women. His whole life had involved a deep mistrust of his family (apart from his beloved father) and a hatred of non-family affiliations, of veneer-thin friendships and unholy covenants with people he wouldn't trust to look after the family pet. He had long ago become bitter and twisted, but the magical moments he spent with his young 'friends' seemed somehow to keep him sane. He thought now of young Learie, in the days before he became Jet and scaled the heights; and Dume even felt the smallest pang of guilt… But it didn't last long.

There was a rustle in the undergrowth, and Dume instinctively fell to the ground, eyes primed, gun at the ready. He didn't like this one little bit.

"Anil, get in the car. Now!" he hissed, his voice carrying further than perhaps he had intended. There was something wrong. The birds had flown and the silence was beginning to stifle him. His narrow eyes darted from side to side, searching for an answer. Danger had crept up on him, and he cursed his lack of concentration in allowing such a thing to happen. Momentarily, he had thought of his father, but then self-preservation had taken over. It was every man for himself, and Dume was still the top man.

His driver hesitated, unsure of the order he had received. Surely they weren't going to leave behind their friends? "But…," he began.

The noise had been caused by Withers, who had stretched forward, intent on seeing more. Grey Trousers was making for the car door, although from his angle the sheriff couldn't be sure whether it was the driver's side. He craned his neck further, seeing Blue Trousers moving to the other side of the car. Withers was confused. What was going on here?

Suddenly, he heard distant gunfire, lasting only a moment, but the sound seemingly hanging in the air for many seconds. He thought of Dawg and the others, of death, of Phil Lenier and his beloved Heather. Then he felt Ty gripping his arm strongly, and they were up and running, guns raised, heading for the clearing, both shouting at the top of their voices for Dume to surrender.

There was no chance of that. Dume slipped onto one knee and fired at the advancing lawmen, but his shot was wayward, and he realised that there was only one chance of escape. He stood, swivelled and fired again, before charging into the undergrowth on the far side of the car.

Withers and Ty made their way onto the roadway. Dume's man was slumped against the driver's door, a dark red patch staining his once-white shirt, the short sleeves flapping gently in the breeze, the only motion in the silence. The blood was already dripping onto his grey trousers.

"He shot his own man," said Ty in disgust.

Withers noted the irony in Ty's comment, but said nothing. He bent down and felt for a pulse, although he knew that there was no possibility. "Stay here, Ty!" he ordered, before moving off at speed in pursuit of Dume. "Check for the boy!" he shouted over his shoulder as he disappeared into the undergrowth.

It had all happened so quickly. Dume had become flustered, something that had never happened before. He felt the sweat running down his back and the faster beating of his heart, and it was all alien to him. He always had a measured approach to everything he did, but this was different. He still wasn't sure why he had turned his gun on Anil, but somehow it had seemed the only thing to do. He needed to preserve his own life, to secure his freedom, and he hoped that sacrificing Anil would gain him valuable time. Yes, it had to be done. It was a very small price to pay.

He was running at breakneck speed now, his legs pumping, the adrenaline forcing him on, propelling him further into the countryside and safety. He dare not stop or look back, because this time he was the hunted, and he knew that flight was his only option. He gripped his pistol tighter, as his arms pushed aside branches and bushes, sensing the bruises and scratches without really feeling them.

Withers tried desperately to keep up. The African was younger and fitter, but at least the terrain appeared to be in the sheriff's favour. All he had to do was follow the path created by Dume as he stumbled through the undergrowth.

They had left the sidings far behind, and were now in dense woodland to the east of Thurlow, somewhere Withers had never been – and he was damn sure Dume was in unchartered territory as well.

He could hear Dume crashing through the trees, and followed the sounds, still unable to see him. If only he could just get one decent shot away.

Then there was silence. A frightening silence. Withers stopped, listening, breath shallow from the exertion. He was grateful for this respite, but knew there was danger lurking. He edged forward slowly, gun extended, as per the text book. Bloody text book, he thought. *This* is real life!

He knew that Dume was out there, lying in wait, armed and dangerous. It was a sobering thought, but not one which filled him with dread. As long as he took things slowly, he knew he could come out on top. The priorities were stealth and using your ears – just like a hunter. Easy!

Withers stopped again and crouched. Waited. There was no sound of cracking twigs or crunching leaves. He knew he was unlikely to be close enough to hear breathing, but that didn't stop him worrying that his own was loud enough for Dume to pinpoint his location exactly. Then came the sobering thought that there was no reason for Dume to move at all; all he had to do was sit and wait for Withers to come into view and…

He banished the thought before it had time to solidify in his brain. Think of something else, man. Like, how do I draw him out?

When it came to him, the answer was so ridiculously easy that Withers assumed it couldn't possibly work. It depended on him being agile enough to move a reasonable distance in a matter of seconds – silently, of course; but, most importantly, everything would hinge on one person doing the right thing – Dawg.

Withers carefully took out his mobile and tapped in Dawg's number, at the same time readying himself for the next phase. Just as Dawg answered, Withers clicked off and put down the phone, scampering away as best he could, allowing for his prone position and his wound.

He stopped about ten metres away and looked round, taking in everything before him. Dume was out there, watching, but Withers had been remarkably quiet in his movements, and the *status quo* had been maintained. It was all down to Dawg now.

Withers waited, eyes peeled. The seconds ticked by.

What if Dawg hadn't registered the number? What if he was in a fierce fire-fight of his own? What if he was de…? No, not that! Anything but that.

Involuntarily, Withers's glance shifted to his phone, almost willing it to ring, before he regained his senses and averted his eyes. Out front was where he needed to concentrate.

When his phone rang, he was almost caught out. He took a deep gulp and watched. Sure enough, Dume had reacted to the sound, shifting his position, probably to get a better view and perhaps a telling shot. It was enough. Withers aimed and fired, to be rewarded with a howl of pain and a growl of anger, before Dume staggered forward, holding his left thigh, where the blood was seeping from his wound.

"Drop the gun," Withers said, not moving.

Dume picked up on his location and swung round, firing his pistol as he did so.

"It's over, Dume," Withers announced.

"Only when I say so, *matapuko*!" Dume answered, letting off another burst even as he tumbled forward, his leg finally giving way.

"It's over," Withers repeated. And this time it really was.

* * * * *

Ty had thought about following the sheriff, but he had been trained to take orders, and Withers certainly barked out a mean order. So Ty carefully moved the dead man away and peered inside the car, in the hope that the boy was bundled behind the front seats. Nothing.

He went through the pockets of the dead man until he found the car keys, using the man's shirt to wipe off the spots of blood. He went to the boot and unlocked it, holding his gun in anticipation.

As Ty lifted the boot, Sani blinked at the sudden burst of light, and his large eyes studied Ty as he looked down. Ty gently pulled away the tape over the boy's mouth, and Sani licked his dry lips. It felt as if he had been in there for hours. He leaned back against the spare tyre, and suddenly he had that air of cockiness which sets the vicious criminal apart from the rest of the world. He looked directly at Ty. "I knew my father would send his boys to get me."

* * * * *

The clearing was awash with police and forensics, the body had been removed and Dawg was accompanying Dume's men to Bakerton police station. They had surrendered in a matter of moments, not having the backbone for a fight. Dawg felt nothing but contempt for all of them.

Sani Okele was about to be returned to the bosom of his crooked family, and all was pretty near right with the world. Ty and Withers sat on a grassy bank, surveying the scene in silence. After everything, the end had come so quickly, and Withers was grateful for that.

Ty stirred. "You did well getting Dume."

Withers looked at him. "Elementary, my dear Ty." Both men grinned. "We all knew it was only a matter of time," Withers added.

"Mm," said Ty, "and that's something I don't have."

"Meaning?"

Ty gave a watery grin. "It's all over, sheriff. At least for me."

Withers knew what he meant. Both men had understood long ago that this moment would arrive, but neither of them were prepared. There were too many strands to the thread linking them together. It was impossible for Withers to think clearly.

"Listen, Ty…," he began, but faltered.

"Yeah," said Ty, trying to ease the burden, "I know. A lot of water under the bridge."

"A bloody torrent!" Withers smiled. "You've caused me untold grief, man… and yet you've come out the other side. I don't know whether to kick your ass or kiss your cheek!"

"Steady on, old man!" said Ty, pushing Withers's shoulder playfully. "This could get serious."

The silence returned, and they just sat there, comfortable in each other's company, watching the officers of the law carry out their crime-scene duties around them.

Eventually, Ty turned to the sheriff. "Look, John, I know you are finding this difficult."

"Yes."

"So can I make a suggestion?"

Withers looked into his eyes. "What, exactly?"

Ty hesitated. He wasn't sure of the reaction he would get. "Give me an hour."

"An hour," Withers stated flatly.

"That's all I need. Then all your problems will be over."

Withers thought about it and understood. He got up and walked towards a patrol car. Ty followed. They looked at each other and shook hands brusquely, as if embarrassed, although there was much warmth in the gesture. Withers leant into the car and, satisfied the key was in the ignition, he looked back at Ty. "Just don't damage the car."

"Thanks," was all Ty could say.

"It's been a pleasure, Ty," said Withers, voice breaking just a little.

"Likewise, John," said Ty.

Withers grinned. "Be seeing you around, partner."

"One day, that's for sure." Then Ty Cobden slipped into the car and drove away.

Chapter Twenty-One

Pat Rafferty was busy. He was also very happy. Word had come through that he would be returning immediately to his former duties, so his spell as temporary sheriff of Bakerton was officially over. He was whistling some obscure tune as he packed his cardboard box with his worldly goods and prepared to say goodbye to this place forever.

Although he did have one or two misgivings. He would be sorry to leave John Withers, whom he'd got to know pretty well over the weeks and who, despite himself, had warmed to the Irishman as well. Then there was Doug – or *Dawg*, as the sheriff was wont to call him. Poor old Dawg: he didn't have a clue about the nickname – far too young. Never mind, he was a fine deputy, and Rafferty knew he would go places one day.

Scotty's Diner had been a sinful pleasure, too. He'd never tasted better omelettes, and the take-away cakes had been to-die-for. His stomach groaned at the thought, and he realised that it was almost 3pm, time for afternoon tea. Yes, he would take his last meal at the Diner, before heading back up to Altona and settling into the office chair he had vacated weeks ago. Or, then again, he might just treat himself to a sticky toffee muffin and sit out by the Western Lake, drinking in the beauty of it all. His boss would be understanding, he thought, so why rush back? He might even stay another night and paint Bakerton red, perhaps with Withers and Dawg in tow. Now, that really would be something…

The door opened and a fresh-faced youth appeared.

"Yes?" snapped Rafferty. He thought the lad was far too callow to be a policeman. Whatever was the force coming to?

"Er, sorry, sir, but there is someone asking to see you," the young man spluttered, knowing his station in life.

"I'm not in!" Rafferty bellowed, his lilt more pronounced than ever.

"He said it was important, sir," persevered the young man.

Rafferty sighed melodramatically, rather like an ageing thespian. "Now look here, Muldoon…"

"Mulligan, sir."

"Whatever! As you know full well, Muldoon, I am leaving today." He looked at his watch. "In five minutes, to be exact."

"But, sir…"

"Are you deaf, Muldoon?" Rafferty blasted.

"If he wasn't, he is now," said a disembodied voice from the outer office, and Rafferty came to the door, brushing the deputy aside.

"I am sorry, sir, but you will have to see Sheriff Withers when he returns," he said sharply to the figure in the outer office with his back to the agent.

Ty spun round and smiled sweetly. "I've just left him. Can I come in?" He breezed past Rafferty and sat at the visitor's chair in front of the desk. "Thank you, Deputy Mulligan, that will be all."

"Yes, er, sir," mumbled the youngster, beating a hasty retreat, Rafferty's eyes drilling into his back.

Rafferty returned to his desk and sat down. "I don't understand?"

"It's simple, Mr Rafferty. I am Ty Cobden, aka Lucas Black, and I am giving myself up."

Rafferty winced. "I know who you are, but why are you here? If you were with Sheriff Withers…"

Ty leaned in. "There may be conflicting interests, sir. I didn't want the sheriff to feel at all uncomfortable, so I thought I would surrender to you instead. That way, I will become a federal case, rather than a local police matter. Easier for all concerned."

Rafferty thought of all the extra paperwork involved. "Easier for some, perhaps," he said wistfully.

As it turned out, Ty hadn't needed the full hour. He had stopped off at Grace Templeman's place, making sure she was okay and telling her that, at last, he was about to give himself up. They had one last cup of tea together out of her fine bone china cups, and she had given him a motherly hug, which he accepted gratefully. There was nothing they could say to each other because of his history, but he felt that she had moved towards offering him some semblance of forgiveness, and that was something he would cherish. It was now time to pay for the murder of Ralph Baxter.

* * * * *

They sat on a bench, gazing out at the lake, both munching on a cake and sipping from their polystyrene coffee cups.

"I'm glad you stayed on for a bit, Pat."

"Yeah, well, I couldn't leave without seeing you one last time, John."

"Are you sure it was me you stayed for?"

Rafferty feigned a pained expression. "Oh, John, whatever do you mean?"

"There is also the charming Mrs Rawlings…"

"I cannot disagree, my friend. Ursula is certainly worth a second look, and a third, and…"

"Yes," grinned Withers, "I get the point."

Rafferty turned serious. "Thanks for your help in that department, John. I was a little rusty when it comes to matters of the heart. Love may conqueror all, but a helping hand is always welcome."

"I didn't do anything, Pat. I just passed on Ursula's message… although I might have nudged you in the right direction a few times as well. You definitely needed nudging!" Withers raised his cup in salutation, and Rafferty clinked it.

"Cheers," said Rafferty, gazing out across the water. After a moment, he said, "I'm going to miss this."

"Yeah, can't beat it." Withers went quiet, before earnestly saying, "Thanks for sorting out Ty."

"No problem."

"I hope he gets leniency."

Rafferty took a gulp of his coffee. "Don't see why not. Good military record, mental damage sustained while in the service of his country. A good lawyer should do something with that lot."

Withers looked at him. "You sound like you don't approve, Pat."

"Well, he did kill a man."

Withers fell silent. He couldn't argue with that, the same as he couldn't forget the fact that if Ty hadn't been around, Mr Sumo would have finished the sheriff off. Withers owed him.

Rafferty finished his muffin and wiped his mouth with the paper napkin. "I know what you're thinking, John. Ty Cobden saved your bacon. I understand that, and so did he; and that's why he came to me. He wanted to save you having to make the decision of whether to arrest him or...." He paused, shaping the next question. "But tell me, why did you let him go? He could have been miles away by now."

Withers grinned. "Because I know him better than you do, Pat."

TWO MONTHS LATER

From: <u>p.rafferty@federaloffice.com</u>
To: <u>sheriff@bakertonpolice.com</u>
Subject: Surprise, surprise

Hi John,

My boss just told me that the Nigerian government are looking to extradite the Akintolas. Wouldn't surprise me if they succeeded. Politics, eh?

Keep smiling, pal.

FIVE MONTHS LATER

Allen Avenue
Lagos
Nigeria

My dear Mr Withers,

Greetings, and my sincere thanks once more for the part you played in the rescue of my beloved son Sani.

I know I showed my appreciation at the time (I do hope you enjoyed the meal at the five-star restaurant?), but I thought it only polite to let you know how the story has ended, as it were.

As you know, my government and yours secured a complex extradition agreement and a few days ago the Akintolas were repatriated to my country.

Arusi is now serving time in our largest prison for his part in the wicked crimes the family committed both here and in your country.

For your interest, I enclose a photograph of the foundations for our new orphanage, of which I am the patron.

You will be pleased to know that Dume Akintola has been integral to these foundations and will be supporting the enterprise from now on.

Good luck in the future, my friend.

With sincerity
Kashim Okele

Postscript

It was the first time Withers had been in Thurlow church since the funeral of Deputy Phil Lenier. He looked around at the assembled masses, all dressed in their finery and smiling – so different to that other day.

Pat Rafferty was beside him, fussing over buttonholes, while Dawg and Kitty Janowski, him in crisp uniform, her in the most stunning purple trouser suit, were behind, Dawg holding the hand of two-year-old Matthew, their son.

Withers saw, too, his chief of police, who winked and smiled, despite the travails Withers had put him through. The chief often despaired of his sheriff, but he wouldn't have any other. Unorthodox he might be, but he always got the job done. Dume Akintola was dead, his father in prison, and the town was slowly returning to normal. No wonder the chief could offer Withers a smile.

Nona Carmichael sat a few rows back, dressed in dark green, the claret and blue brooch proudly displayed. She was still mourning the passing of her dear son, but she had to be here today.

Withers looked anxiously around, his eyes searching. Rafferty nudged him, trying to offer calmness in a sea of nerves. "It will be fine," he whispered.

"Course it will," Withers replied.

Then, the organist burst into life, offering a passable rendition of Pachelbel's 'Canon in D', and all eyes turned to the back of the church.

Withers watched, spellbound, as Judith walked serenely down the aisle, her billowing dress offering a tantalising dance in the slight breeze coming through the open church door. His breath caught in his throat. God, she was amazing!

"Beautiful," offered Rafferty, understanding what was in Withers's head. "And the bride is stunning, too."

"What? Oh, yes, of course," mumbled Withers. It was true, Maureen Pelham looked a million dollars as she made her way to the altar, to the man of her dreams, Eric Marsland.

It had been a bumpy road for them both, but true love had paved the way to this moment, and all those present would remember this day forever.

Especially Withers, who, he had to confess, had fallen deeply in love with the bridesmaid.

AUTHOR'S NOTE

While the detectives among you may have deduced that Thurlow Junction, Bakerton and Copper Ridge, as well as the many characters gracing these towns, are figments of my very fertile imagination, I have to point out that three people in this work are, in fact, very much alive and are dear friends. I refer to the "Three Women" from the "book" of the same name, all of whom wanted to be included and who did actually come up with the idea for the roles they play.

I should point out, however, that Jannette, to the best of our knowledge, has never poisoned a husband with digitalis… or any other kind of toxin, for that matter.